JUSTICE CALLS

An Ari Adams Mystery

Ann Roberts

BELLA
BOOKS
2018

Bella Books, Inc.
P.O. Box 10543
Tallahassee, FL 32302

Printed in the United States of America on acid-free paper.

First Bella Books Edition 2018

Editor: Katherine V. Forrest
Cover Designer: Judith Fellows

ISBN: 978-1-59493-617-3

Acknowledgments

I'm indebted to Karin Hansen for her knowledge of autistic individuals and appropriate group home settings. She ensured I got it right. As always, my wife was my first and most critical reader. The pages would be blank without her support. She's come to love Ari and Molly as much as I do. Bella Books continues to guide and promote my writing, and I am honored to collaborate with them. Special shoutout to Linda and Jessica Hill for always answering my emails and incorporating my suggestions. It is always a privilege to work with my editor, the legendary Katherine V. Forrest. After each journey through a manuscript, I am confident the story is ready to be shared with readers thanks to Katherine's sage advice. I cannot thank you enough, Katherine, for all that you have taught me. And finally, to all of the readers joining Ari and Molly on their adventures, I am so grateful to have you along for the ride.

About the Author

Ann Roberts is the author of nineteen novels, including the Goldie winner, *Point of Betrayal*. A winner of the Alice B. Medal, Ann also edited *Conference Call*, an anthology to benefit the Golden Crown Literary Society (GCLS). Ann currently serves on the GCLS Board of Directors as the Director of Organization. When Ann isn't writing or editing, she can be found wine tasting in the Willamette Valley or, along with her wife of nearly twenty-four years, chasing after their tiny kitten, Simon, who has more energy than both of them put together. You can learn more about Ann at her website, annroberts.net.

"The dead cannot cry out for justice.
It is the duty of the living to do so for them."
-*Lois McMaster Bujold*

CHAPTER ONE

This is Richie's blood.

Ari Adams turned over the large plastic bag, the word EVIDENCE written in bold script across a label slapped haphazardly to one side. The bag contained a portion of her dead brother Richie's baseball card collection, his 1992 Dodger stack, made crimson when he dropped to the floor after being shot. Most of the cards had congealed, but she could still read the name on the top card. Darryl Strawberry, Richie's favorite player.

He would routinely lay the trading cards across the kitchen table, like a version of solitaire only he understood, his somber expression conveying the importance of his work. She'd imagined he was memorizing his baseball statistics. While he collected cards for all the teams, his favorite was the L.A. Dodgers. He'd coveted the Strawberry card and always kept it on top of his Dodger stack. He had the entire 1992 Dodger team—except for Eric Karros, the first baseman. Richie had died searching for that last card. Her hands shook as she set the bag on the floor. His beloved cards defaced by his own blood…

She raced downstairs to the bathroom. A strong whiff of pine suggested her father's cleaning lady had visited recently. She leaned over the toilet but the sick feeling passed. It was time for a break. She headed for the kitchen and a glass of water, mulling over her actions. *Have I committed burglary?*

She had a key to her father's house, and she had a specific reason for her visit today: to water his two ferns, Lucy and Ethel. He was vacationing with his new girlfriend, Dylan Phillips, Phoenix's Chief of Police. It was a test to see if they could travel together. Ari liked Dylan and had come to terms with her father's romantic involvement with someone who wasn't her mother. After Lucia died from cancer, Jack Adams had closed off his heart—until he met the new chief.

But Ari had an ulterior motive for her visit. She was here for answers, ones her cop father wouldn't provide. As she passed a mirror in the hallway, she glanced at her reflection—and saw her mother. Her short, black hair framed her Mediterranean features, olive skin, chestnut brown eyes, aquiline nose. She'd always considered Lucia beautiful, but it wasn't a quality she'd ever associate with herself. She hated wearing makeup or formal clothes, anything that required much attention to herself. Fortunately, her girlfriend Molly didn't care.

She headed back upstairs to Jack's office and opened a window, welcoming the fresh scents of spring and allowing the cool April morning breeze to circulate throughout the room. It provided a counterbalance to the tableau on the floor: the evidence bag of bloody baseball cards, Richie's Dodger hat, a scrapbook, and his case file. She'd found it all underneath a false bottom of a drawer in her father's desk, a desk he'd built himself.

She sifted through the contents of his in-basket—electric bill, storage unit bill, and weekly ads. At the bottom was a greeting card with a sexy message on the front. She groaned, imagining it was from Dylan, celebrating something like their three-month anniversary. She returned everything as she'd found it, but something nagged at her. She pulled the bill from

Quick and Safe Storage. When her father had relocated from Oregon, he'd brought little with him. *Why does he need a storage unit now?*

She dropped into the comfy desk chair he'd owned since she was a little girl. The smell of quality leather still lingered decades later, and when she inched the chair forward, it squeaked. She'd often interrupted his work and climbed onto his lap while he made notes on a case, but whenever she ran through the door, he would quickly flip over the crime scene photos before she could see the gruesomeness of his world. When she grew older and the curiosity she'd inherited from him blossomed, she once snuck into his office after he'd gone to bed and peeked at a file. She wanted to see the front side of those pictures. But the black and white images of a man and woman with slashed throats extinguished her curiosity. Until the night Richie died.

Sometimes Jack locked the office door, but she knew the key's hiding place. She wondered if he'd wanted her to find it, recognizing that the only thing that would slake her natural curiosity were answers.

A month after Richie's death, she'd again snuck inside the office and found a headshot of her eight-year-old brother, lying sideways on the linoleum floor of the convenience store where he'd been shot. His expression, eyes wide open and mouth agape conveyed his shock, as if he couldn't believe what had occurred. She'd stared in disbelief before she burst into tears and ran out of the room, not bothering to close the door or replace the key. She'd stewed for hours, thinking her father would yell at her. But he never mentioned it. And she never sneaked into his office again. That image of her brother lingered as the official photo of his death.

She took a deep breath and slid off the chair. She set aside the evidence bag of cards. *Why is this here?* Richie's murder was an open case, a cold case definitely, but no one had been convicted—even accused—of his murder. Ari had suspected Jack was secretly investigating the case. This was her proof.

She picked up the Dodger hat, the one he wore every day, even to bed. She brought it to her cheek and the tears flowed as she remembered. He'd gone to the 7-Eleven around nine p.m., his allowance burning a hole in his pocket. It was summer and he'd been sure he'd find the Eric Karros card. He begged her to go with him, knowing that Jack and Lucia would probably agree to the trip if his twelve-year-old big sister went with him. He'd wanted to go to a 7-Eleven that was an extra ten blocks away, almost to the northern edge of Glendale. But she'd said no, so for the first time in his life, he'd defied their parents and left through his bedroom window.

If only I'd gone with him.

She cried until her tears turned to ragged breaths. She inhaled a sharp musty odor from the cap. *If only I'd been a good sister. He would be here.*

She placed the cap on top of the cards and opened the scrapbook—to Richie's second grade school picture and his obituary. She loved that picture. His smile was natural, despite two missing teeth. It would've been unnecessary for the photographer to coax a grin from him. He lived in a constant state of happiness. He was eight and innocent. He wore his dark brown hair longer than most boys, and curly locks covered his ears.

The obituary was only a paragraph. By then so much had been written about him in the Glendale and Phoenix newspapers, there wasn't anything left for Jack or Lucia to print except what they had included. "Our beloved son Richard went to heaven on August 25, 1992. He was a wonderful brother to Ari and a friend to all." That was true. Richie rarely met a person he didn't like or couldn't persuade to like him.

She closed the scrapbook and picked up the case file. As a former police officer, she knew what she'd find there, including the grisly photos of the night he died. She guessed the file weighed a few pounds and imagined it was complete. Although Jack had worked for Phoenix PD, he had many friends amidst the various law enforcement agencies in the metropolitan area, including their home city of Glendale, where Richie died. She imagined a sympathetic brother in blue had copied the file for Jack.

It would take hours to digest all of the interviews, reports, and Jack's notes that littered each page. She skimmed the initial report from the first officer who arrived on the scene, Grady Quigley. She'd actually met him a few weeks prior. He'd been young and green in 1992, but he'd been genuinely affected by what he'd observed that hot August night. She knew the story by heart, particularly the clerk's eyewitness statement. Richie had been in the candy aisle choosing trading card packets when a man in a plaid shirt entered and demanded the money from the register. Richie came around the corner and surprised the gunman, who shot him and ran off with two hundred dollars from the register. Glendale PD conducted an exhaustive search for the killer, but he never surfaced.

She shuffled through the top pages of the file and found the composite sketch provided by the clerk, one she'd seen several times on the news during the first month of the investigation. There was nothing memorable about the killer's face, but she'd forgotten about the baseball cap. Covering his close-cropped brown hair was a green ball cap with a John Deere logo.

The sketch was only mildly accurate. After twenty-five years without a real lead to the killer's identity, Ari had found one—film footage that provided a split-second look at the man in the plaid shirt entering the 7-Eleven. She pulled a computer printout from her back pocket. She'd taken a picture of the exact moment he faced the camera. It was grainy and slightly out of focus, but when she placed it next to the sketch artist's rendering, she grimaced.

While there were some similarities, she didn't think they looked anything alike. It wasn't surprising. Eyewitnesses often were not reliable, especially ones held at gunpoint. "And he put on his hat," she muttered. She shook her head. No wonder the police hadn't found him.

In the back of the file were the crime scene photos. She knew there would be several of Richie lying in his own blood, including the one she'd seen when she was twelve. She wasn't sure she could—or should—look. It had been so long ago. She'd catalogued a series of memories, each one serving a different purpose, whether it was to cheer herself up, build her self-esteem, or motivate her to finish a task. Ironically her dead brother had become her life coach. She worried the crime scene photos would forever taint her perfect pictures.

What about justice?

She pulled out the thick stack of photos. Several showed the 7-Eleven's interior. The harsh fluorescent lighting obscured the finer details, but enough was visible to jog her memory. She'd been in the store frequently until Richie's death. Now it all came back. The ice cream case, the Slurpee machine, and the candy aisle. How many times had she stood with Richie in front of the baseball trading cards?

She flipped to the next photo. There he was, face down. Wisps of curly brown hair rested on the collar of his striped polo shirt. His hands outstretched, the baseball cards around him. In the corner of the photo were three trading card packets still in their wrappers—the ones he intended to purchase.

She frowned and grabbed the evidence bag. She couldn't see any cards in a wrapper. *Where are they?*

She moved through the next several photos, her emotions detaching as she theorized what might have become of the missing packets. When she came upon the familiar photo of his face, her lips parted and a wail burst forth. She slapped the photo over, face down. No clues would come from staring into his soft brown eyes.

The final set of pictures were of the 7-Eleven's exterior. There was little to see except the empty parking lot, the back dumpster and the side lot, which contained an old sedan that Ari surmised belonged to the store clerk. A shot of the storefront showed Richie's abandoned Schwinn just to the right of the front door. He hadn't planned to be there very long, and he'd already broken curfew, so it wasn't surprising that he'd neglected to park the bike in a rack and lock it.

She scanned the front parking lot photo again. The light pole that illuminated it sat at the edge of the property. In the movie she'd found, Richie and their friend Glenn had met under that pole before Richie went into the store. Glenn had stayed back filming, just long enough to catch the image of Richie's killer before his camera ran out of film.

The crime scene photographer had deliberately taken several shots of the crowd that had assembled, thinking perhaps the killer might have stayed and watched the police work. She thought she recognized the faces of several neighbors lured outside by the wail of the sirens, but the man in plaid was not among them. Some wore bathrobes and slippers since the police had not arrived until after ten p.m.

The beginning of a headache tweaked her skull. She scooped up the reports and pictures and shoved everything back in the file. She debated whether to take it with her. Would her father miss it? She guessed he didn't review Richie's case on a regular basis. He'd often told her the best way to catch a break on a cold case was to periodically reread the file. "Eventually," he said, "a lead will jump out at you."

And I found one. But she hadn't shown the movie to anyone— yet. Jack was out of town for three more days. Molly was also away, providing security detail for a millionaire tech guru, but she would return Saturday night. She hadn't phoned Glenn and asked him more questions about the film because she had no idea how to contact him, and she wouldn't know how to approach the conversation over the phone since Glenn was autistic. He'd rarely spoken to anyone that summer, and he'd left Arizona immediately following Richie's funeral.

Ari decided to take the file and the scrapbook to see if anything jumped out at her. Then she'd return it all before her father got home. She picked up the cards and hat. She'd take the cards as they might provide clues, but she couldn't decide whether or not to take the hat. Sentimentality won out and she set it on top of the file. She resituated the bottom of the drawer and saw a folded paper that had fallen out with everything else.

It was a handwritten note in Jack's chicken scratch. *Ari, if you're reading this, it's time to talk.*

CHAPTER TWO

After six hours of studying Richie's case file, Ari realized her parents had kept an important fact from her. Parts of the file were now splayed across her dining room table, and she'd taped several crime scene photos to the wall, excluding the one of Richie's face. That one she kept inside the file folder, determined never to look at it again. She couldn't gaze into his sweet eyes, knowing there was nothing she could do to bring him back. Instead she retrieved her favorite picture from her bedroom. It showed the two of them on the swings at Encanto Park. Lucia had taken it as they each swung to go higher than the other. It was just like Richie. Always so competitive. Always wanting to keep up with Ari.

"And he usually could," she murmured. The picture brought her joy and strength—and the resolve to find his murderer even if the memories brought her pain.

She returned to the crime scene photos and the fact she'd unearthed. She was twelve when Richie died, old enough to ask questions about his death once the initial shock passed. Jack and

Lucia were always candid with their children, and up to this point, Ari assumed she knew the entire truth. Jack maintained Richie was only in the candy aisle, and when he came around the corner, headed for the cashier, he surprised the robber, who, according to the clerk, turned suddenly and fired.

She now had proof Richie had ventured to another aisle— to get a treat for her. One photo captured everything he'd held when he was shot, including a box of animal crackers, her favorite childhood snack. And the photos of the store's interior confirmed what she remembered: crackers and cookies were in a different aisle. *He was buying those for me, even though I refused to go with him.* The realization started the tears again.

She understood why Jack and Lucia hadn't told her about the cookies. They knew she would have blamed herself. What they didn't know was that she already did since she refused to go with him. And he'd returned her insensitivity with kindness. To know that would have destroyed her young heart.

Yet it remained an important clue. Whereas the candy aisle was past the cash register, the cookie and cracker aisle was directly in the clerk's line of sight. He would have seen Richie in that aisle, but he hadn't mentioned it during any of his interviews with the police or Jack.

The clerk was Elijah Cruz. She found his original statement from that night. *The kid headed straight for the candy. By the time the guy came in and hurried up to the register, I forgot the kid was even in the store. The guy's gun was already out. He was nervous, shaking. And his voice cracked. I couldn't understand what he said, but I opened the drawer, figuring that's what he wanted me to do. I handed him the money as the kid came around the corner. I musta looked over at him, and the guy whirled around and pulled the trigger. It seemed like an accident. He made this gasping sound and ran out. Then I called the cops.*

She read through two subsequent interviews with Cruz, all conducted by the lead detective, Floyd Hubbard. Cruz's story changed during his second interview, as he remembered more. He acknowledged other customers had entered between the time Richie walked into the store and the appearance of the gunman. She found Cruz's background attached to the second interview. Nineteen years old. No priors. Attending Glendale Community College to start an electrical engineering program.

She lined up Hubbard's interview transcripts side-by-side and read them again. Never did Cruz mention Richie in a different part of the store. The third interview, conducted two weeks after Richie's death, was the longest. Hubbard asked Cruz to recount the events as he remembered them, and he told the same story. But then Hubbard asked him to describe the last customer before Richie was shot and the purchase. Cruz struggled to remember. Ari frowned. One of the most confounding facts of Richie's case was the lack of video footage. The franchise had not yet invested in video cameras.

She went back to Cruz's last interview. He said he thought the last customer before Richie's murder was a woman buying beer, but he couldn't be certain. He mentioned "the kid with the camera" came in earlier that day, the one who'd come in several times before with other kids that summer—Glenn, the autistic cousin of one of Ari and Richie's best friends, Scott Long. Glenn's mother had dropped him off in Arizona at the beginning of that summer with his aunt Henrietta, Scott's mother, claiming she couldn't handle him. Glenn was indeed quirky, and he instantly took to Richie. He spent the summer with a movie camera to his eye. *And his love of film might be the reason we find the killer.*

Ari highlighted the part of Cruz's statement about Glenn. *The kid came in around four thirty and walked through the aisles a few times. Just up and down. Didn't bother to stop and look at anything or buy anything. He started bothering people and I asked him to leave.*

But that was nearly five hours before Richie died.

Behind Hubbard's transcripts were Jack's notes. He'd interviewed Cruz three times on his own, the first interview a year after Richie's murder. By then Cruz had abandoned his engineering degree and was working at the Palo Verde Nuclear Power Plant as a Nuclear Operator. "He must be competent if he's babysitting nuclear reactors," she muttered.

Jack had included a newspaper clipping of Cruz's wedding announcement to Isolde Tovar in 1995. However, two children who looked a lot like Elijah and Isolde were included in the picture. They had obviously been conceived before the marriage.

Jack had interviewed Cruz again in 1999. By then Cruz was serving on one of the Glendale mayor's ad hoc citizen committees, was a deacon at his Catholic parish, Little League coach, and never had been in trouble with the law.

"He made a good life for himself," she murmured.

At the end of Cruz's biography was another newspaper article dated August 19, 2015. A short message was scrawled across the top. *Jack, I thought you'd want to see this. G.* It was a human-interest piece on Elijah Cruz, now in his mid-forties, celebrating his twenty years of volunteerism with Habitat for Humanity.

She plugged in the movie projector and started Glenn's last reel of film. It opened outside the 7-Eleven. His vantage point appeared to be the edge of the parking lot. Ari glanced at one of the crime scene photos and confirmed his exact location. *Facing north, east of the light pole.* Richie approached on his bicycle and stopped beside Glenn. Richie waved and held up his stack of trading cards. There was no audio, so she couldn't understand what he said, but his excited gestures suggested he was eager to spend his allowance. He seemed relieved to see Glenn, who, unlike Richie, regularly snuck out. *Oh, Richie.* He waved goodbye and headed for the front of the store.

A few seconds later, the man in the plaid shirt came into the light from the west, looked over his shoulder and flung open the closest door. Glenn's zoom lens caught him in that moment. She guessed he was in his early twenties. His blond hair was close-cropped over his ears but longer on the top and parted on the side. Stubble surrounded his mouth and his eyes were close set. He was thin, gaunt. It was the face of a user.

Ari yearned for a few more seconds of the movie, but the screen went white and the reel's tail flapped. She rewound the scene again. She'd seen the movie so many times that she could perfectly judge how much celluloid was needed to fill the empty reel for Richie to immediately pop up on the screen.

This time she stopped the second the killer entered the frame, his profile still visible. She recognized the outline of something in his back pocket—his John Deere cap. She started the film again, saw his profile, and noticed that as he pushed the glass door open with his left hand, his right hand grabbed the cap and the screen went white.

She rubbed her temples. She'd watched the film at least thirty times. Half a day couldn't pass without her threading the old projector and watching Richie come alive once more. She loved the part when he pointed to the stack of cards. She knew he was telling Glenn that he was sure he'd find the one card he needed to complete his 1992 Dodger team.

Richie was that kid. Always the optimist. Always the believer in the underdog. Glenn was routinely shunned for being different, but Richie would have none of it. He looked at Glenn and saw a friend. Richie's only struggle was his black and white view of the world, a typical quality for an eight-year-old. Still, Ari imagined he would've been student body president of his school. Homecoming king. Head of a community service project. Editor of the Law Review at a university. His life would've shone.

She sobbed again and found herself standing in front of her liquor cabinet. She debated whether to pour herself a scotch. While Molly was the acknowledged alcoholic, Ari knew from past experience that she sometimes relied too heavily on the mind-numbing effects of a few scotches. She raised her hands in surrender to her better angels and backed away.

She vowed to watch the film just once more before she went to work. This time she'd focus on other angles. She'd already missed a late morning meeting with her business partner, but would spend the early evening researching prospective houses for her new buyers.

She prepared the footage and the all too-familiar front of the 7-Eleven appeared. She stared above Richie's head. Perhaps someone else entered the frame? It was common in the early nineties for kids to ride their bikes throughout the neighborhoods after dark. Although Richie had broken curfew, had he arrived home safely, the punishment would've been mild. Neighbors knew each other and looked out for every child, which made Richie's murder all that more shocking to the community.

She could see the silhouette of the trees lining the street along the east side of the 7-Eleven. One was especially memorable because of a low-hanging branch that had smacked her on the side of the face one day as she rode her bike down the sidewalk. Fortunately, it had missed her eye by a few centimeters, but she still had a tiny scar on her temple that Molly routinely traced with her finger. Ari stared at the limb—and then it vanished. Just at the moment when Richie's assailant appeared on the screen.

What?

She stopped the projector and found the rewind switch that pulled the delicate celluloid back a few frames, to the point where Richie waved goodbye to Glenn. The nasty tree branch was just over his shoulder. She was certain of it. Richie rode away and her hand remained poised on the dial, ready to stop the projector if in fact the branch disappeared again.

Now.

She held up a crime scene photo that closely matched the angle of Glenn's lens—and saw the difference. Not only was the low-hanging tree branch missing, but more of the 7-Eleven's east wall was visible, including the graffiti tag "WHB," Westside Homeboys, the gang whose territory included the 7-Eleven. She rewound the film again and focused on the exterior wall. It was difficult to see, since the glare from the light pole bounced off the tan paint, but at the moment the tree branch disappeared, the "B" of the graffiti tag appeared.

"He paused it."

She looked around, as if there were someone to share her epiphany. She recalled the hours and hours of footage she'd watched of Glenn's tapes when she helped her friend Scott solve the mystery of his mother's murder. Glenn would randomly pause the camera, but his eye remained glued to the viewfinder, so no one really knew when he was filming. It was a safe way for him to see the world. Whereas most of his films jerked from breakfast to afternoon car rides to games of horseshoes in the evening, this transition was nearly undetectable. Although he was standing in practically the same place, it was two different moments in time made imperceptible by the shadows of the night and the intermittent glare of the light poles. But it could be highly significant. There was missing time between Richie entering the store and the killer arriving.

"What the hell happened in that store?"

Unable to sit still, she paced. In less than a week, she'd found two important clues. She needed to tell someone, and the only person she could think of was her best friend Jane Frank. As she picked up her phone, mariachi music played and Lorraine Gonzalez's name appeared on her screen. She cleared her throat and prepared to be reprimanded by her business partner.

"Hi," she said tentatively.

"Where are you, Ari?"

She winced. Lorraine hadn't offered her customary greeting. She was pissed. "I'm so sorry for missing our meeting. It's just—"

"That's not why I'm upset. How about a phone call or a text, huh?"

"I'm sorry."

"What's up with you? You never miss our strategy sessions."

She heard her genuine concern. Lorraine wasn't one to dwell on negative emotions. Ari owed her the truth, and although she was dying to tell someone about the film and what could be breakthroughs in Richie's case, she couldn't fathom sharing the information with anyone but Molly or her father first.

"Ari?"

She could at least be vague and honest since Lorraine was quite familiar with her tragic and complicated past. "I'm in the middle of something personal right now. It's taking over my mind, but I apologize for being rude and not calling. I should've at least done that."

"No worries, Chica. Is there anything I can help you with?"

"Not right now, but I'll let you know if that changes."

"Please do. You know I have many connections," she added seriously, referring to her family's network of shady characters throughout the metro Phoenix area. There wasn't any service or product—legal or illegal—that Lorraine didn't have at her disposal.

"I know."

"Are you good to meet the Carpenters tomorrow or should I go in your place? You know how nervous they are about buying their first home."

"No, I'm fine. I'll be there. I've already got four great listings to show them." She hoped she sounded convincing. By tomorrow, she would have four listings—at least.

"Okay. Call me afterward, Chica. I'm here for you."

"I will. Thanks. And again, I'm sorry."

"No worries."

She hung up and smiled, grateful to have Lorraine as a co-broker in their realty firm. She looked down—at a highball glass filled with scotch. She closed her eyes and groaned. She'd gone on autopilot.

"No sense in good liquor going to waste." She picked up the glass and stared at Richie's broad grin that filled the small screen. "Here's to you, little brother. We're gonna figure this out."

CHAPTER THREE

House-hunting with the Carpenters had not gone well. They were unrealistic nitpickers, the type of client who most frustrated real estate agents. Their expectations and what they would pay for a home were unaligned. By the end of their three-hour hunt, they were completely frustrated. They'd left with a curt goodbye, and Ari berated herself as they drove away. She'd done nothing to ease their anxiety, and she was certain they'd caught her rolling her eyes at least once.

"I should've given them to Lorraine."

Lorraine would be upset. The Carpenters were friends of former clients. Ari's behavior probably had cost Southwest Realty a commission. Her phone rang and she groaned as she fished it from her purse. She exhaled when she realized it was her best friend Jane, who she'd been trying to reach for three days.

"Where are you?" she barked. "Why aren't you returning my calls?"

"Simmer down," Jane replied. "So much for hi and hello."

Ari ran a hand through her hair. "Sorry. Bad morning. I blew it with some clients."

"I doubt that. You're the master of cool, calm and collected. You could be your own deodorant commercial."

Ari cracked a smile.

"And to answer your question, I'm currently on the deck of... Hell, I can't see the name of this thing. I'm on a ship, sipping a cosmo."

"You're on a cruise ship?"

"I am...with Rory. She called me as I was pulling away from your house last week. She begged me to forgive her dalliance with the young bar girl, and of course I had to since I'd had my own indiscretion...or indiscretions. But who's counting? She told me to go home and pack and catch the first plane to LAX, which I did. We're cruising from L.A. to Seattle. We just finished throwing confetti and flashing *Love Boat*-worthy smiles at the landlubbers stuck on the dock."

"That's great."

Jane was a chronic womanizer, and the only woman who'd ever tamed her was Rory, a long-distance love in California. Jane and Ari had met Rory a few years before during a visit to Newport Beach. Since then Jane and Rory had been an on-again, off-again couple. Ari foresaw a permanent commitment at some point in the future.

"So, other than being a less-than-perfect real estate agent, what else is going on?" Jane asked.

Ari was about to spew all the details, but she stopped herself. Jane was one of the few people who knew her *complete* bio. She was the most inner of the inner circle, and the only other person with as much dirt on Ari was Molly. If she told Jane what she'd found—on Glenn's movie and in her dad's house—Jane would most likely commandeer the ship and demand to be let off at Santa Barbara.

"Not much else, really," she said as convincingly as she could. "Molly's still gone."

"Ah, that's it. I detected some melancholy in your voice."

"Melancholy? Is that the word of the day?" Jane loved vocabulary, and one of her passions was Scrabble. The only person who could beat her was Rory. A game of strip Scrabble was probably on their cruise itinerary.

"No, the word of the day is trypophobia, a fear of holes, obviously something I've never suffered from."

Ari laughed and it felt good. She wished Jane could be in two places at once. She was ecstatic to learn Jane and Rory were back together, but she desperately needed her friend. "Well, have a great trip and send Rory my love. Don't get in any fights on the ship. Just have fun."

"Aye, aye."

She hung up and stood motionless in her dining room. She closed her eyes and immersed herself in the silence. A memory of Richie pushed forward—a family vacation to California, and a visit to the Queen Mary, which was permanently docked in Long Beach harbor. Richie, who was six at the time, had been excited to be on the ship. He was always excited about anything new. Their mother had taken them to the public library a few weeks before they left, and Richie had checked out five children's books on the Queen Mary and cruise ships. He'd pored over them, so when they actually walked up the gangplank, he spouted a litany of facts and impressed the tour guide.

She smiled broadly and her tears touched the edges of her lips. She quickly dried her eyes and took a deep breath. What to do now? She should call the Carpenters and apologize, but she couldn't find enough cheerleader-like energy necessary to convince them everything would work out. She wasn't enthusiastic about anything. Jane was right. She was melancholy.

Needing to poke at her concerns, she faced the gallery of photos taped to the wall. She'd start with the clerk, Elijah Cruz. The only eyewitness, his testimony framed the entire case.

According to the Internet, he and Isolde still lived at the address where he'd met Jack years before. She grabbed a notepad and a few of the crime scene photos and drove to Buckeye, Arizona, a Phoenix suburb that boasted as many ranches as residential communities. The original settlers of Buckeye were stubborn cowboy holdouts, unwilling to sell to the developers once Phoenix's urban sprawl crept to the extreme west valley, which was regarded as the end of civilization for people traveling on I-10 to California.

She reviewed what she knew about Cruz, his career at the power plant, and his humanitarian efforts. A family man with kids and grandkids, he'd understand now, perhaps more than she did, what it would mean to lose a child. It was always helpful to have a standup guy in the middle of the investigation. He'd been extremely cooperative, talking with her father on multiple occasions. Jack had added notes like "honest and sincere" to the case file. If there was anything left to learn, he'd tell her.

She found the modest stucco house with dusty rose roof tiles amid a few hundred homes that looked exactly like it— approximately fifteen hundred square feet with a small backyard. The Cruzes lived on a quiet cul-de-sac, and as Ari swung her SUV around the curve, it appeared everyone on the block was at work. Each house was buttoned up for the day, shades drawn and garages closed.

The Cruzes' house sat on the corner. A winding concrete walkway twisted and turned through the predictable desert landscape of cacti, palo verde trees, and hardy shrubs. She smiled when she saw a set of ceramic, multi-colored mushrooms sitting in an oak planter on the porch. They were out of place but added a touch of color to the muted desert tones. A simple sign hung above the doorbell. *Peace to all who enter here.*

She rang the bell once and heard a voice say, "Coming!" She leaned toward the security screen door so she could see past the twisted metal.

The woman who appeared had a youthful face and only a few gray strands in her long ponytail. She bounced up and down, and Ari realized a swaddled baby lay against her chest. "May I help you?"

"Hi. I'm looking for Elijah Cruz. My name is Ari Adams. My father is Jack Adams with the Phoenix PD." She paused, wondering if the woman recognized her family name. When she continued to stare, Ari added, "My brother, Richie, was killed in a 7-Eleven and Elijah Cruz was the clerk."

The woman bowed her head in reverence. When she looked up, she wore the tragic smile Ari routinely saw any time she mentioned her brother's death. "I know who you are. I saw you at the funeral, but you were a child. I'm Isolde, Elijah's wife." She worked the doorknob and motioned for Ari to enter.

The Cruzes' great room was spacious and included a dining room and kitchen. Isolde disappeared down a hallway in search of Elijah, while Ari studied the walls that paid homage to Catholicism. Pictures of Christ, crucifixes, candles, and wooden artwork with biblical sayings surrounded the family photos. The fireplace mantle supported a shrine. A series of candles surrounded the framed photo of a young woman. The inscription at the bottom read, *Our beloved CeCe, Always in our Hearts.* She remembered reading that Cruz's sister had died from cervical cancer, not long after Richie's death. She stepped toward an eleven by fourteen group photo. Elijah and Isolde were surrounded by their six adult children, the children's spouses and the grandchildren. Everyone wore smiles or had been caught in a laugh when the shutter was pressed. A pang of jealousy struck her and she bit her lip. *That could've been my family. The picture wouldn't have included as many people, but it would have radiated just as much happiness.*

"That's my favorite."

Ari jumped and turned to meet Elijah's outstretched hand. He looked exactly as he did in the photo—bald pate, a well-trimmed salt and pepper goatee and kind brown eyes. *Like Richie's.* She surmised from his attire of cargo shorts and a gray T-shirt with bits of leaves spattered around his belly that she'd interrupted yardwork. She wondered how long he'd been standing there, watching her gaze at the photo.

"I'm sorry I scared you, but you looked like you needed a moment." His voice was quiet and his face solemn. He gestured to the sofa. "How is your father? I spoke with him about a decade ago. He was planning on retiring and moving to Oregon."

"He's fine. He did retire and he moved to Oregon, but he was bored. So now he's back in Phoenix."

"Oh, really? Is he still retired?"

"Yes and no. He's a consultant for Phoenix PD. He gets to do police work without too much of the red tape."

Cruz's eyes narrowed. "Does that make him happy?"

"Oh, yes."

He rubbed his palms together, thinking. "I'm retiring soon. I'm worried I'll become restless. Isolde is begging me to make some plans to fill my schedule."

"Are you still building homes for Habitat for Humanity?"

"Yes, and I work at the food bank, and I serve as a deacon at our church."

"I don't mean to sound disrespectful, but when would you find time to do anything else?"

They both laughed and he said, "That's what I keep telling Isolde." He raised his chin and quieted his hands. "You're not here to talk about me. Ask me what you want to know. Years ago I told your father that I was willing to speak with him at any time. If talking with me helped him learn more information or deal with his grief, then I was available. I extend the same courtesy to you."

Ari could see the sincerity in his eyes. She blinked to hold back the tears. She gathered her thoughts, reminding herself that he was a witness, not a counselor. She wasn't here to share her grief, although he seemed completely willing and able to shoulder her tears if she broke down.

"I've read the statements you gave to Glendale PD and my father, but I'd like to hear the story from you."

"Of course." He waited until she opened her notepad and pen before he began. "It was like any other night. I took over at three p.m. from the day person, a guy everyone called Mellow. I can't remember his real name, but he was a low-level marijuana dealer. Anyway, I remember it was a really hot day, and I had a lot of traffic in the late afternoon. Sold lots of Slurpees and fountain drinks. But by nightfall it was quiet. We didn't get a lot of customers after dark because the store was one block off

Grand. It's one of the things I liked about working there. Most people went to the other 7-Eleven because it had a big sign and sat on the busy street. Not this one. I think it was a case of one franchiser trying to put another out of business. Sometimes I was so bored I'd pull out one of my textbooks and study. I hoped to be an engineer, but well…things happen. Good things, but not what I'd planned." His gaze floated to the wall of family photos. "Anyway, between dinner and nine, a few people came in and out. I knew a lot of them, including your brother. I said hello to him when he came in. I think it was a little after nine."

He cleared his throat and looked away, as if he were returning to the 7-Eleven again. "I gave some inaccurate information in that first statement, which I later corrected in the second one. I learned memories are tricky. I remembered a few other people came in after Richie and left before his killer arrived. But I was really shaken up that night, the first time I spoke with Detective Hubbard. When the guy showed up, I'd forgotten your brother was still in the candy aisle. Then everything happened so fast. He pulled out a gun and said something like, 'give me your money.' Just after I handed him the two hundred bucks from the register, Richie came around the corner. The guy turned and fired." Cruz looked up at Ari. "I'd be lying if I said I thought he killed Richie intentionally. If I'm certain about one thing, it's that he pulled the trigger as a reflex. I'm not sure he was even aiming at Richie. And once it happened, he ran outside into the darkness. I…I was so shook up. It took me a few minutes to call the police. And…I threw up in the garbage can. Once I finally got to the phone, I could barely hold the receiver." He closed his eyes and said, "I'll tell you this—until one of the detectives shared the coroner's report, I worried that those few minutes of inaction might have cost your brother his life. I was glad to know I didn't affect the outcome, as horrible as it was. I hope you understand that."

She nodded. He paused and she waited, recognizing that her objectivity had slipped away and she was completely engrossed in his story. She wanted him to add a sentence. She wanted him to suddenly say, "Wait a minute! I just remembered something!"

"That's all." She couldn't hide her pained expression, and he squeezed her hand. "I'm so sorry."

She batted away her tears and opened the folder of photos, centering her professionalism. "As you might imagine, I didn't know much about the investigation when it happened. Years later my father pulled some strings and obtained the crime scene photos. A police courtesy. I only looked at these the other day, and I noticed something." She withdrew the shots of the 7-Eleven interior and the close-up of the trading cards, the animal crackers swimming in the sea of Richie's blood. She worked every muscle in her throat to prevent herself from vomiting on the Cruzes' nice sofa. "Might I have a drink of water?"

"Of course," Cruz replied, scurrying to the kitchen.

When he returned, she gulped it down quickly and handed him the two photos. "I noticed Richie died holding the trading cards he wanted to buy, but he was also holding a box of animal crackers. Those were my favorites." Her voice started to break. She pointed at the other photo. "I remember the store vividly from my childhood. If you were standing behind the cash register, the candy aisle was to the left, but the cookies and crackers were in this center aisle. That aisle is directly in the line of sight with the register. At some point, Richie left the candy aisle and went to get the cookies. In your statement, you'd said he didn't leave the candy aisle, but he must have. I'm not doubting your story," she quickly added, "and I don't know if it means anything, but I thought maybe sharing that fact with you might help you remember something else."

He studied both photos and pointed to the far end of the candy aisle. "I'm guessing he must have gone around the back, along the wall with the cold cases. That would've been the fastest. I probably wouldn't have noticed if he was only there for a few seconds. That would confirm what I realized later, that other people came in after Richie. Perhaps I was ringing up a sale when he switched aisles?"

She nodded, realizing it was certainly a possibility. "Do you remember the little boy who walked around with a video camera that summer?"

"Glenn, right? He was a character. Had to always keep an eye on him when he came in alone. He didn't quite understand that he had to pay for everything."

"He was a good friend of Richie's. Did he come in that night? Maybe right after my brother?"

Cruz stroked his goatee. "I don't think so," he said slowly. "He came in earlier, around four thirty. The store was crowded and he wandered in by himself. Usually he was with someone, but not that time. He walked up and down each aisle like he was looking for someone, that viewfinder glued to his eye. He'd done that sorta thing before, but I always dismissed it because he wasn't doing anything bad. But this time he was bumping into people because he really couldn't see where he was going. He made a sound like a race car, but it got louder and louder. I confronted him and asked if he was going to buy something. When he shook his head, I told him to leave. He got mad and shook his head again and stomped his feet. I'll admit I was frustrated. It was hot. The customers were crabby. I told him to leave and not come back for the rest of the day. He left and didn't return." Cruz sat up straight. "Come to think of it, I'm not sure I ever saw him again."

"You may not have. After Richie's funeral, his mother came and took him back to California."

Cruz shrugged. "I can't imagine how remembering this would be helpful."

"It might be," Ari said. She pulled out the blow-up picture of the man in the plaid shirt. "I have a new piece of evidence that just surfaced." She handed Cruz the photo and his face went white. "This is him.

This is the guy," he said excitedly, his voice growing shrill. "Who is he?" Isolde appeared in the doorway with a dishtowel and Cruz pointed at the photo. "This is the guy, Iso."

She dried her hands and came to look at the picture. Ari imagined the killer had haunted the Cruz family almost as much as he'd haunted her own.

"Do you know his name?" Isolde asked.

"Not yet. This is new information, so it might take some time to run it through recognition software."

And first I need to give it to the police...

"You could solve the case!" Isolde cried.

She threw her arms around Cruz, who remained still, but smiling. Ari could tell he was generally stoic and unemotional, good qualities for a nuclear power plant worker. He looked at Ari curiously and asked, "Where did this come from? Was someone taking photos?"

"This is a still frame from a movie Glenn was shooting. He was out in the parking lot facing the store. The fact that you banished him explains why he didn't come in with Richie."

Cruz looked stunned. It took a moment before he regained his composure. He stared at the photo and frowned. "This is the guy, no question, but now that I see a photo, I don't think I did a very good job describing him to the sketch artist."

"That happens sometimes," Ari said gently. "Also, he wasn't wearing his ball cap until he entered the store. That could have distorted some of his features."

Cruz shrugged dejectedly. "Still..."

Isolde squeezed his shoulders. "Don't beat yourself up. You did the best you could. You were robbed at gunpoint and you witnessed a horrible killing..." She stopped herself and looked away. "I'm sorry."

"It's all right," Ari said. "Are you sure Glenn didn't come in with Richie that night? I'm asking because the video shows Richie meeting Glenn outside. Richie goes in, but then the video pauses. Eventually it starts again, just as the killer approaches the door."

"Are you thinking maybe Glenn snuck in to be with Richie?" Isolde asked.

"Perhaps," Ari said slowly. "That's one possibility. Or he might've ridden his bike up to the storefront windows and looked inside. Or, he might've just remained near the light in the parking lot, waiting for Richie to come out."

Cruz shook his head. "I think I would've noticed him if he'd come in. We weren't that busy, and he'd already made a scene that day. Is there more...footage?"

He was diplomatically asking if Glenn had captured the murder. "No. Right after he caught this moment, his reel of film ended."

"But at least he got this!" Isolde cried. "There is hope for justice."

CHAPTER FOUR

Since Ari was already on the west side of the valley and had no reason to rush home, she debated whether to stop by the Glendale Police Department. The second person most likely to answer her questions was Officer Grady Quigley, the police officer she'd met a few weeks prior, who'd shared he was one of the first responders to her brother's murder scene.

She headed toward the Glendale station, recalling her first encounter with a police officer who wasn't her father or one of his colleagues. She and Richie were walking through their neighborhood, returning home from a friend's house. She was ten and he was six. A black and white pulled up next to them and the cop in the passenger seat rolled down his window. He wore a smirk, as if they were breaking the law just by being on the sidewalk. "You kids know anything about a broken window on the next block?"

They both shook their heads, but Richie was the one who spoke. "No, officer, but we know lots of people in the neighborhood." He leaned closer to the window to read the officer's nameplate. "Whose house was it, Officer Deakins?"

Deakins' expression didn't soften despite Richie's concern. "That's none of your business, kid. This is a police matter, and I'm the one asking the questions."

"Well, you don't have to be rude about it," Richie replied. "I'm only trying to help."

Deakins' face turned red and he pointed at Richie. "You're the rude one, young man. I've got a good mind to call your parents."

"Okay," Richie said. "My father is Jack Adams, a grade-two detective with the Phoenix Police Department. He—"

"Officer, we didn't see anything," Ari interrupted. "I'm sorry if my brother was rude."

"I'm not being rude!" Richie argued.

She offered a thin smile and Deakins seemed to crack, pitying her for putting up with such a precocious smartass for a brother. And even at ten, Ari knew her good looks could work in her favor. "If we see someone suspicious, we promise to call."

"You do that," Deakins said. "And teach your brother some manners."

Before Richie could respond, the patrol car pulled away. Richie stomped his foot. "Why did you tell him I was rude? That's not true."

"Because he wasn't going to be nice to you. He doesn't like kids, and we weren't going to change his mind."

"But it wasn't true."

"Maybe not, but let's play our game. What if Officer Deakins was our friend? Why is he in a bad mood?" At first, Richie refused to answer her question. His face remained scrunched in a scowl and his arms crossed. "C'mon, Richie. Try," she coaxed.

"Maybe he had a fight with somebody. Maybe somebody spit on him, like that one guy spit on Dad."

She nodded. "All possibilities. Other ideas?"

"Maybe he didn't get his breakfast and his stomach is rumbling."

"You mean like when *you* miss breakfast and you're grumpy?"

He'd finally laughed. Richie's sense of right and wrong ran deep. He would fight endlessly if he believed—or knew—he was right. It got him into trouble sometimes, even at the young age of six. He often mentioned his father during conversations since he was proud of him. Jack had admonished Richie for invoking his name so much. Lucia had gone a step further, insisting Ari's role was to teach Richie compassion and protect him. And Ari had done a good job—until he died.

Lost in her thoughts, she missed a turn and found herself farther north than she'd intended. She pulled into a church parking lot to turn around. She knew the old 7-Eleven was just a few blocks away. Until recently she'd avoided the neighborhood—and Glendale—as much as she could. Then her friend Scott had asked for help a few weeks ago, and she'd spent several days driving the streets of her childhood. The memories randomly surfaced, and the oddest things triggered situations and conversations she'd forgotten long ago.

She chewed a nail, debating whether to detour to the 7-Eleven or just head for the police station. It was nearly six, so Officer Quigley's shift might be ending and she might catch him before he left. But it could be his day off. The pull to the murder site proved too great, and with a few more turns she was sitting in the old parking lot, staring at the boarded-up convenience store. "For Sale" signs stood at each corner, but Ari knew the location wasn't appealing to commercial investors. It was off Grand Avenue, tucked away next to a historic neighborhood. Whoever bought the property would be subjected to greater scrutiny by the community. She took a picture of one of the signs, wondering if the agent might be able to shed light on the current owner. All Ari knew was that the store had closed a few years after Richie's death. The original franchiser had lost interest in "the place where a kid was killed."

She pulled out the crime scene photos and walked the perimeter, determining the vantage point of each picture. A jogger and two dog walkers passed by on the opposite sidewalk, and each offered a wary glance. No doubt the property was a hangout for vagrants and drug peddlers. She smiled and waved at each one, hoping none of them called the police. She glanced to her right, in time to see a gray head of hair duck behind a rickety wood fence. Someone was watching her, and she thought it best to ignore him—or her.

She held up a photo of the east parking lot and the surrounding neighborhood. One thing was certain: the trees had continued to grow. Mulberry, bottle brush, and eucalyptus trees formed an array against the back fences that paralleled the sidewalk, their new leaves rustling in the breeze. Twenty-five years ago their sparse branches and narrow canopies didn't provide nearly the same amount of shade.

She headed to the north side, the back of the building. No light poles had been installed, but a small light cage sat above the rear door, its lightbulb broken long ago. She remembered a car parked here most days, but she'd been a kid whizzing by on her bike, her brother following behind. She hadn't been paying attention. Once in a while an employee hung out back on a smoke break, and sometimes he was joined by a friend. They didn't seem to be doing anything illegal, but she was young and probably naïve. She wouldn't have recognized a drug deal then. Now the back door was a fortress. Metal sheets were screwed to the doorframe to prevent squatters from entering. There was no door handle, as it would be a point of vulnerability. A short driveway connected the property to the side street that eventually snaked to Grand Avenue.

She walked to the south corner where the streetlight stood, Glenn's vantage point. It wasn't far from the front door, and he'd loved using the camera's zoom feature. She grinned, remembering his close-ups of nostrils, teeth, buttonholes, blades of grass—even the ridges of potato chips. Nothing escaped Glenn's lens. From here he had a great shot, hiding in the shadows, his subjects bathed in the store's interior and exterior fluorescent lights.

She caught quick movement to her right, and the head of gray hair disappeared again, only this time a hinge squeaked and the gray hair's gate opened. A diminutive woman in flowing lounge pants and a red T-shirt stepped outside. She wore a peace sign necklace made of dark wood and a pin that said BERNIE. Ari greeted her with a pleasant smile and her business card.

"I'm Nora Martinez. I may not look like a Martinez, but I married a proud Hispanic man," she added. She held Ari's card close to her face, ignoring the reading glasses dangling from a gold chain around her neck. "And you're Airy Adams?"

"Ari. It's short for Ariana."

"Cool," she replied.

Ari recalled seeing Nora Martinez's name in the pile of witness statements. Most were from neighbors, but none had been in the store, and most had seen or heard nothing. "How long have you lived in this house, Nora?"

She looked away but her jaws continued to move, as if she was lubricating her mouth before she spoke. "Fifty years, but I've got no interest in sellin', if that's why you're askin'." She blinked, momentarily drawing attention to her cornflower blue eyes. No wonder she didn't want to cover them with glasses.

"I wasn't fishing for another client. I used to live around here."

Nora stuck her fingers in her mouth for a brief moment. "Damn upper plate. Part of the joy of old age. Dentures." She sighed and said, "Adams. Had a tragedy in the family right here at this 7-Eleven. You're related?"

"Uh, yes. The boy who died was my brother Richie."

"I see." Nora turned and faced the store. "You a policewoman?"

"Um, no."

"I ask because the only people I've ever seen out here walking around with pictures were detectives." Ari gazed at Nora, who refused to make eye contact. "If you're related, you probably want to know what I said in my statement."

"Yes, I would."

She crossed her arms and raised her chin. "I'll tell you what I told them. I was home the night it happened. Had the back door open because it was so damn hot and we only had swamp cooling. I was playing solitaire when I heard the gunshot. I ran outside and tried to see what was happening through the fence slats, but it was dark so I couldn't make out much of anything. After the shot it was as quiet as quiet could be, for a few minutes."

She gave Ari a sideways glance and added, "Later on I learned I was the only one home on this block. People out doin' summer stuff or away on vacation."

"You said, 'for a few minutes.' Are you saying you heard something else?"

"I did, but nobody believed me. Don't expect you will either."

"What was it?"

"I heard a car start."

Ari couldn't hide her surprise. "A car? But the clerk, Elijah Cruz, said the gunman ran out. He never said anything about a car starting."

"I know. He said what he believed and I said what I *know*." She readjusted her upper plate again and faced Ari. "They dismissed my statement because I'm not afraid to report what I see. Back then it was a whole lot of drug deals. And today it's the same thing." She pointed at the building as if she could punch it and said, "Only thing that's changed is they boarded up the windows! People still comin' and goin' at all times of the day and night, makin' deals." She tapped Ari's stack of pictures with her finger. "And I got proof, too. I got my own pictures. Would you like to see them?"

"Sure," Ari said warily, somewhat concerned she was about to be sucked into a lonely lady's house where she would struggle to politely excuse herself. But curiosity won out, and she followed Nora through the back gate. A long platform, roughly two feet off the ground ran the length of the back fence that faced the 7-Eleven. It reminded her of a duck blind, with four chairs lining the platform, each facing a peephole. Nora ascended the stairs and pulled out a small square of the fence in front of the first chair.

"See, I put my camera lens right here. And then I just start snappin' away. I have different spots so I get the best angles. And…" She pointed to the enormous mulberry tree in the corner, a rope ladder gently swinging in the breeze. "Back in the day I used to climb up there and get some great evidence, but my climbin' days are over. After I fell off the ladder and dislocated my hip, my son told me if I didn't stop, he'd move me to an old folks' home." She looked at Ari shrewdly. "Do you think those still really exist?"

Ari struggled for an answer, impressed by Nora's elaborate setup. The celebrity paparazzi would benefit from her in their midst. "I think they're called something different now, like senior living centers. I hear they can be a lot of fun."

Nora grunted in disbelief and gestured to her platform. "What do you think?"

"You've gone to a lot of effort. Are your pictures inside?"

"Absolutely!"

Nora powered through the back door into her kitchen. A large, Hispanic man in his forties sat at the kitchen table eating a McDonald's meal. His black hair fell over his eyes, almost meeting his graying, bushy beard. He wore a dark brown polyester McDonald's uniform, and she surmised he'd just returned from work. He held a cell phone in one hand and his half-eaten burger in the other. He said a few more sentences in Spanish before offering, "Adios," and discarding the phone on the table.

"This is my son, Wolf." He offered a wary nod and piercing gaze with eyes the same blue as his mother's. "Ari's here to look at some of my photos. It was her brother who…died at the 7-Eleven."

Ari thought Wolf said, "I'm sorry," but his mouth was full of burger so she wasn't sure.

"Did you know him?" Nora asked.

He waited until he'd finished eating before he said, "Not really, but I think I saw him—and maybe you—in the neighborhood."

"Probably," she agreed.

"Are you reopening the case?"

"Technically it's never closed since it's an unsolved murder. I've found some new evidence, and I'm just poking around to see if it leads anywhere." She pulled out her image of the man in plaid. "Do either of you know this man?"

Nora nodded. "I do. Saw him talking to that day clerk, Mellow. A few times. I'm sure he's in some of my photos. What's his name?" she asked Ari.

"I don't know yet," she offered, astonished at this revelation.

Nora looked at Wolf. "You must know him." She stuck the photo under Wolf's chin.

He stared at the photo for several seconds. "Yeah, I knew him from school, but I can't remember his name. That was a lifetime ago." He stood and added, "If it comes to me, I'll let you know." She handed him her card, and he put it in his back pocket. He threw away his food wrappers and headed out the back door, mumbling, "Good luck on your search."

Ari wanted to ask him a few more questions, but he disappeared and Nora headed into a bedroom that had been turned into storage. Craft boxes were stacked in rows that nearly touched the ceiling. Each was labeled with a month and year, beginning with November 1968. A single box held two to three months of pictures. The wall was nearly filled, and Nora was working on the last row. Ari quickly found the box containing Richie's death, JUNE–SEPTEMBER, 1992.

"All of these photos were taken from your perch in the backyard?"

"Almost," Nora said with pride. "But when I go out, I always have my camera with me. And I have my own YouTube channel."

"I'm impressed. I'll have to make sure I subscribe."

"Wonderful!" Nora scurried to a roll top desk and handed Ari a business card. It simply read, *Nora Martinez. The Eye of Glendale.* "You can type that into the YouTube search bar and you'll find me."

"Can we talk some more about…that night? You said you had proof?"

Her smile disintegrated. "Of course," she said softly. She rolled her jaw again and headed for the box that included the day Richie died. "I need you to hold up the boxes above this one and I'll pull it out. Just don't drop 'em, or we'll be spending the rest of the night reordering the pictures."

"I'll be careful."

"Luckily, you're tall. That's an added bonus."

Ari positioned herself next to Nora, who pulled out the box and set it on a nearby table, while Ari slowly lowered the other boxes back into position. Her heart pounded. Perhaps all the answers to her questions were in that box. She knew it was doubtful, but it was impossible to rein in her hope that Richie would have justice.

She sat next to Nora, who slowly fingered the index cards that listed the individual dates included in the box. "Here's the date you're looking for."

She pulled out a small stack of pictures. The top photo depicted a black blob, a pinpoint of white light in the middle. The second picture was no better, and neither was the third. Ari uttered a small sigh.

"As you can tell, my photos weren't so great in the nineties, or the eighties or the seventies for that matter. Back then I was using a little Instamatic, the one with the flashbulb that popped off. Those were lots of fun. It wasn't until two thousand that I got a decent camera after my husband Mario died. That's Wolf's father. His life insurance came through. My Nikon was my favorite until we hit digital. Man, oh man, did that change everything."

"Well, let's see what you've got."

Nora sighed. "Unfortunately, they're not in chronological order. I usually keep them that way, but the police borrowed these after the…incident, and I can't remember if they returned them all. And to make matters worse, when I went to put them back, the stack of boxes came toppling down. My well-meaning nephew was helping me, but he was klutzy—and short." She gestured to the pile. "I know there were more, but truth be told, they probably weren't very good."

The photos taken in daylight seemed to fare better. In one, a young man leaned against the back wall, smoking a cigarette. He wore a small nameplate above his heart, so she guessed he was an employee taking a break. Another photo showed him outside talking to a scraggly person with long hair, and the next one showed him talking to a well-dressed man in a suit.

"That's interesting," Ari said.

"Uh-huh, that's what I mean." She pointed at the employee. "That guy was the day clerk, Mellow, a dealer. His real name was…" She closed her eyes and muttered in frustration, scolding herself for not remembering. Ari had seen her father do the same many times in the last few years. "Well, it's not coming to me, but Mellow was obviously a great code name for how he made people feel. As a teenager in the sixties, I knew drugs, okay? I thought we were hardcore, but the shit that's out there now, pardon my French, is unbelievable."

Ari gazed at Mellow. White guy with longish, blond hair pulled back in a ponytail. Like the mystery man in plaid, Mellow was rail-thin. "Are you sure he was a drug dealer?"

"Know it for a fact. When your brother…passed, and these photos came to light, I thought the police would charge this guy, but no such luck. I heard the cops talked to the man in the suit, but nobody had any evidence, and I just couldn't seem to get the snap right when they were making the exchange. It was frustrating. Totally."

"Is Mellow still around?"

"Nuh, uh. I don't think so." She whipped out her phone and made a call. "Wolfie, Mellow es muerta, sí?"

"Sí."

She hung up. "We raised Wolf to be bilingual. Mario and I met at a Cesar Chavez march." She snorted and added, "I'd hoped that would give him a leg up in job interviews, but that would've required him to *want* a career."

The rest of the photos in the stack were as dark as the first few—except for the last one. Amidst the darkness that filled most of the frame, there was a black spot with a band of metal.

"Is that the fender of a car?"

"Exactly! This is my proof. After I heard the gunshot, I jumped up from my solitaire game, grabbed my trusty Instamatic and headed for the fence. Back in those days, I didn't have the setup I do now. I just had an old metal stepstool. Anyway, I got out back as fast as I could, but my little niece had left her skateboard in the grass and I tripped. Got a whale of a sprain. I heard a car start. I climbed up the stepstool and started hitting the shutter, but I couldn't keep my balance on that ankle. My eye wasn't on the viewfinder. That's the best shot I got."

"I take it the police weren't interested in this picture?"

"Not in the least. The detective on the case…Horseshit? Somethin' like that. He sounded so damn condescending. Thankin' me for being a good citizen. But since the photo didn't have a time stamp and the make of the car wasn't identifiable, it was worthless. I asked him if he did any research or showed it to a car guy. He said yes, but I knew he was just livin' up to his name—Horseshit."

"I think his name is actually Hubbard."

"Horseshit to me. I knew he hadn't done anything with my photo because the killer was never found, and somebody else showed up at my door several years later." She cocked her head to the side. "His name was Adams, too."

"He's my father."

"Does he know you're here talkin' to me?"

"Not yet. But he will soon. He's out of town right now."

"Nice guy. Can't imagine what it would be like for a parent to lose a child."

Nora allowed Ari to borrow the box. Perhaps there were some other clues in the photos taken during the days leading up to Richie's murder.

It was dark by the time she left Nora's house and Wolf hadn't returned. After his hasty departure, she suspected he knew more than he'd shared.

She'd had enough sense to park near the streetlight, the same one Glenn had stood under when he filmed the last movie of Richie. As she approached her 4Runner, she heard a noise, like someone kicking metal. She quickly hopped inside and locked the doors.

The sound came from the back of the 7-Eleven. She'd noticed a few garbage drums by the back door earlier, and she guessed a homeless person was rummaging through the trash or starting a fire to endure the chilly April night. She made a wide circle and headed behind the building. Sure enough, a figure was leaning over one of the cans, giving her a view of his derriere. She headed to the exit and glanced at her rearview mirror. The man was still bent over the can.

"Not everyone is out to get you," she muttered.

For the next several miles she played back her afternoon—meeting Elijah and Isolde, talking with Nora the hippie, and Wolf's crystal blue eyes. Something was off and she couldn't figure it out.

She thought of Nora's words. *I can't imagine losing a child.* It wasn't any easier losing a brother, but she never would have said that to Nora.

Immediately after Richie's death, she'd gone into a deep depression. She wouldn't leave her room, and she missed the first month of the next school year. Her parents decided to leave Glendale and move to east Phoenix. She could start at a new school where no one would know her. After the move, it still took another two weeks before her mother's cajoling finally worked its magic and she left the new house. The well-meaning teachers offered understanding and sympathy, but there were missteps. The most blatant faux pas occurred when she was selected as Student of the Month. The principal asked her if she had any brothers or sisters at the school. She hadn't known how to respond and burst into tears. He'd later apologized after his secretary clued him in about Richie's death.

She pulled into her driveway, still reaching for the missing piece. She went inside and set the box of pictures on the edge of her dining table. When she turned for the kitchen, she caught her own reflection in the mirror and scared herself, thinking someone was behind her. She laughed—and the clue came forward. When she'd glanced in her rearview mirror as she left the 7-Eleven, she'd not only seen the man bent over the old garbage can, but the back end of a dark sedan. It seemed unlikely that someone would drive to an abandoned store without a specific reason. And why was a garbage can at a vacant building? Perhaps there was something in the can the driver was retrieving? Nora said the property continued to be a magnet for drug deals. Perhaps Ari had witnessed a drug drop?

Or perhaps someone is following me and I nearly caught them.

CHAPTER FIVE

Ari forced herself to ignore Nora's box until after her morning appointment with the Carpenters. Lorraine had smoothed things over with them in a way no one else could. She'd told Ari, "You got another chance. Don't blow it."

And she wouldn't. While it was impossible to sever her memories and not think about Richie, she could detach herself from his investigation by going to Southwest Realty to work. Forced distance was what she needed, and if Richie's case file and Nora's box were nowhere near her person, she could focus on the Carpenters.

She wasn't surprised by the stale smell that greeted her when she entered her office. She cranked open two of the large second-story windows and soon fresh air filled the space. She gazed across Grand Avenue at her other business, The Groove, an eclectic collection of buildings that included a terrific coffeehouse. She smiled at the parking lot, filled to capacity with Saturday customers. Once she retrieved her own steaming cup of coffee from the breakroom, she searched for the Carpenters' dream home. An hour later she had six more prospects, and two of them met all of the stringent criteria on the couple's checklist.

Her phone rang and she glanced at the unknown number. While she wished she could ignore the call, real estate agents didn't have such a luxury. Anyone could be a potential commission. "Ari Adams."

"Hey, babe."

Molly. "Hey, honey. It's so good to hear your voice. Why are you an unknown caller?"

"Because according to my client, Bo, there are no phones in nature—except for the outrageously expensive satellite phone the guide carries for emergencies. He collected everyone's cell before we started the hike into Bryce Canyon."

"You gave the guide your cell phone?"

"No freakin' way," she laughed. "I stashed it in my bra, and I told him if he tried to take it, I'd break his fingers. He decided I could keep it. Didn't matter anyway. Reception out here is nearly impossible."

"Where are you exactly?"

"We're at the lodge getting ready to head out."

"Are you coming home tonight?"

"No, that's why I'm calling you. It'll be tomorrow. Bo wants to meditate with nature for a day longer."

Ari could hear the sarcasm in Molly's voice. Bo Chang was CEO of a tech firm that had just hit the big time. He was horribly paranoid, believing that a rival was stalking him, so he'd hired Molly's firm, Nelson Security, and specifically Molly, to accompany him and his executive team on a "bonding mission," an outdoor retreat for his administrative team.

"How's everything at home? Did you find a place for the Carpenters?"

"I have some possibilities. Everything else…is fine."

"I heard that, Ari."

She smirked. *Damn.* "Heard what?"

"That hesitation. C'mon, babe. What is it? You haven't found yourself in the middle of another case, have you?"

She tried to decide where to start. Molly didn't have much time, and Ari struggled for a sound bite that would make sense and wouldn't spike Molly's blood pressure. She certainly wouldn't share that someone might be following her.

"Babe, stop cherry-picking," Molly said sternly. "Just tell me. In a nutshell. Go."

"You asked for it. Found one of Glenn's movies showing Richie's killer. Also found my father's personal copy of Richie's file. Now I'm interviewing various witnesses. That's it." She waited for Molly's response, but all she heard was the background chatter from the lobby of the Utah hotel where Molly was staying. Apparently, a woman was looking for a bellhop. "Honey?"

"Okay, I wasn't expecting that. My only question: have you turned over the movie to the police?"

"No, not yet. Dad's not due back for two more days, and I wanted him to see it first—and you, too. If we've waited this long for justice, what's a little longer?"

Molly didn't have an answer for that. "Unbelievable," she murmured. "Okay, but stay out of trouble. I'll be home late tomorrow. I love you."

"Love you."

She hung up feeling warm and tingly. While they had endured many challenges as a couple, including a serious breakup, they were stronger now than ever. Much of the credit belonged to Dr. Yee, their therapist, who had helped them unpack their individual suitcases of problems and anxieties, as well as their needs as a couple.

Feeling rejuvenated, she headed out to meet the Carpenters. They loved two of the houses, and she worked through lunch helping them write an offer on their favorite. As she sent the electronic documents to the seller's agent, she imagined there would be a few counteroffers back and forth. The Carpenters had asked for a lot and had lowballed the price. Still, it was forward motion. After she texted Lorraine with an update, she took a chance and called the Glendale Police Department, looking for Grady Quigley, the first officer on the scene of Richie's murder. She left a message on his voice mail, imagining it could take a while before she got a return phone call. As she prepared to head home, he called her back.

"I just finished my shift and was going out for a run. I could meet you someplace instead."

"I wouldn't want to interrupt your exercise regime," she said.

He laughed. "At my age, there's no regime. I just make time for it when I can. Let's meet at The Vine in thirty."

She headed to downtown Glendale. The Vine was the newest addition to the heart of the city, located in one of the oldest buildings surrounding Murphy Park. When she was growing up, the building had been an ice cream and candy store named Heavenly Delight, complete with a soda fountain and counter. Visiting there was a monthly occurrence for the Adams family. Her mother had an incurable sweet tooth for chocolate shakes, and her father marveled at how easily Lucia kept her trim figure despite her significant consumption of chocolate fudge ice cream.

Their visits were one of Ari's most cherished memories. Whenever something good happened to anyone in the family, they all climbed into the station wagon and went to Heavenly Delight after dinner. It happened after Ari's team won the soccer game, Richie was selected as Student of the Month, or Jack solved a case. It literally and figuratively became the cherry on top of a wonderful day. Whenever she thought of a perfect memory of her family, inevitably she landed on the four of them sitting in a Heavenly Delight wooden booth with its creamy white vinyl seats. And they were always laughing.

Fortunately, The Vine looked nothing like her childhood ice cream shop. She'd not been inside, but she'd seen the outside patio area, now designed as a Paris café with small round tables and petite chairs. The interior proved more urban with sandblasted red brick walls, industrial light fixtures, and a coffee bar that looked like it was made from a large, old tree. Sinewy green-painted vines flowed across the walls and floors, wrapping the entire place in a natural hug.

As she studied the drink board, someone tapped her on the shoulder. "Ari?"

She turned and Grady Quigley smiled at her. His short brown hair was glued to his forehead by sweat, and his running clothes seemed to hang on his tall, long-limbed frame. "I decided to jog over here. That's how I got my exercise today. Hope you don't mind if I'm a little smelly."

"Not at all."

They each ordered a latte and went outside. It was a rare day of mild temperatures and the patio was crowded. They found the last open table in the corner, and after her suspicions of being followed, Ari was grateful to sit away from public view.

Grady peered up at the front of the building. "Did you ever come here when it was the ice cream store?"

"Yeah, we did. I was just thinking about our visits. I always smile when I think of this place."

"Me too. This is where I proposed to my wife."

"Really?"

"Yup. I slipped the ring on top of her banana split. She almost ate it, but I stopped her in time."

They laughed, and Ari appreciated the levity. "Thanks for meeting me. I wanted to share something with you and take you up on your previous offer to discuss my brother's murder."

"Sure," he said, flashing the same sad smile she'd seen a million times. Richie's death was just that—so *sad.*

She pulled out the picture of the man in the plaid shirt. She didn't need to say anything else as Grady's pleasant face disappeared. "Is this the guy?"

"Yeah."

"How did you get this?"

She told him the story of Glenn's movie and he seemed to fade into his latte. He wiped a hand over his face and said, "I don't remember this kid. I can't believe this was there the whole time and it took twenty-five years to find it."

"My dad always says sometimes it's like that."

"We talked to everyone. We canvassed the neighborhood. I spoke to the Longs. You'd think they would've mentioned this."

"We should probably give them some grace. I'm not sure how much help they would've been. They were going through their own grief," Ari said, referencing the death of the Long matriarch.

"Yeah, that's right. Taglio, one of the detectives, kept me updated on your brother's case, and I promise you, this guy was never interviewed."

Ari finished her latte and leaned forward. "I believe you." She paused and said, "I came upon a copy of the case file that my dad has. Do you know anything about that?"

A look of surprise danced across his face and was gone in an instant. "No, I don't. It would be inappropriate for a civilian to have a copy of a police file. I'll pretend you didn't tell me that." He stared at her for a long beat. "What do you want to know?"

"Your first impressions. What you saw when you got there. How the detectives acted when they arrived on scene. Anything, regardless of how trivial it may seem."

His finger ran the length of a seam in the tablecloth, and he couldn't look at her. "I've thought about that night for most of my life. It was the first time I ever saw a dead child." He glanced at her, as if he'd said something wrong.

She nodded her encouragement. "I was with Tucson PD for a year. I remember the first time I caught a child abuse case. I understand."

"My partner was a great guy, Forrest Prayman. I always thought he should've been a preacher with a name like that, and he was great with witnesses. He died from prostate cancer a decade or so ago, but he would've been the guy to talk to." He shrugged. "Sorry you're stuck with me." He sighed and took a sip of his latte. "Anyway, we arrived on the scene a little after ten, and that clerk, Cruz, he was a mess. He'd dropped in front of the counter like a rag doll, sobbing. Forrest went to Richie and I went to Cruz. I could barely understand him. And one thing I've never forgotten… Cruz was surrounded by change."

"What?"

"Dimes, nickels, quarters. There had been a big plastic jug on the counter, collecting money for a girl's surgery. At some point, it had been knocked over and there was change everywhere. Some of it had rolled down an aisle. I got Cruz up and he told me about the man in plaid and how Richie surprised him. He shot him and ran. We secured the crime scene and eventually Floyd Hubbard and his partner Chris Taglio showed up and sent me outside. The crowd had started to gather. Then your dad got there. I don't know how he found out so fast, but he did. I had to restrain him. Hubbard made some remark about him going home. He was such an ass, Hubbard I mean, not your dad. He calmed down and followed Chris around as they surveyed the crime scene." Grady pulled his gaze from the tablecloth and looked at Ari. "I don't know how he did it, but you know, they talk about people flipping a switch. That's what your dad did." He snapped his fingers. "He went from parent to cop in an instant." He threw his chin toward the photo. "What did he say when you showed him that picture?"

It was Ari's turn to look at the tablecloth. "Actually, Grady, he doesn't know about it yet. He's out of town on vacation."

"Oh."

She sipped her latte while he drifted back to his own thoughts.

"Have Hubbard or Taglio seen it?"

She shook her head. "You're the first. I intend to turn it in to the police after my dad looks at it. Maybe facial recognition software will find a match."

"Possibly. He looks pretty young, though. If he had a juvenile record back in the nineties…"

She knew he was referring to the basement fire at the Glendale PD headquarters that had destroyed a large number of files before they could be scanned. Most of them had been juvenile records.

She pulled out the stack of crime scene photos and handed them to him. "What else do you remember about that night?"

He exhaled and flipped through them. When he reached one of the crowd, he tapped a stocky man with dark hair, who Ari guessed was in his mid-forties. "This guy gave me all kinds of grief. Can't remember his name, but he kept ranting about the drug deals. Said something like, 'maybe now that a kid is dead you'll actually do something about it.' I told him to go home or he'd be arrested. He left."

Ari thought of her visit with Nora. "I heard another neighbor say the same thing. That the 7-Eleven was often used for drug buys."

Grady nodded. "We had an active presence at this location, at least as much as we could. Funny, though, after your brother's murder, things seemed to quiet down there. And then the place closed about two years later."

"What about the investigation? You mentioned the neighborhood canvassing…"

"Oh, yeah. Me and most every other guy on Glendale PD. Nobody wants a kid's death to go unsolved. During the first month of the investigation, most of the unis gave up their day off to question neighbors and shopkeepers. There was a hotline for a while, too."

Ari sat up. She'd not found any information on a tip line in the file. "Any good leads?"

Grady searched his memory and shook his head. "Nothing ever panned out. It was weird because something should've broken. Glendale wasn't a big place in the early nineties, there was a sense of community. Now, we didn't have this photo, and frankly, the sketch we circulated doesn't look a lot like this guy, but people talk. There were so many of us asking questions that someone should've found a lead." He leaned back and took a breath. "An arrest shoulda happened."

"I know," she said softly. "What else do you remember? Anything about Hubbard and Taglio working the case?"

He closed his eyes, almost as if he were meditating. She watched the heavy pedestrian traffic along the sidewalk, the snowbirds taking advantage of the last few weeks of cool weather.

"About a week later I stopped by the squad room and Hubbard and Taglio were having one of their legendary discussions. Another detective told me they were arguing about an interview they'd just had with an old guy who'd been walking his dog a few blocks from the 7-Eleven right around the time it went down. He said the shooter had driven past him. Hubbard called him a loony cracker. Said he couldn't even figure out what day it was. Since Cruz said the shooter ran away on foot, Hubbard thought the dog walker was just seeing things. Taglio thought the guy was credible. Nothing came of it, and I suspect that was because Hubbard was the lead, and a lazy S.O.B." Grady cracked a smile. "But he got his."

"How so?"

"He's about three months from retirement now, but he's spent the last two years sitting behind a desk at the station. For years he was known for being a little too Dirty Harry when he arrested someone. Then he made the mistake of roughing up the mayor's kid. They gave him a choice: early retirement or a desk job." His smile turned devious. "You should pay him a visit and show him this photo. I'm sure he'd love to be reminded about one of his greatest failures."

"What about Chris Taglio?"

Grady winced. "That's a sad story. They gave him early retirement. He's got Parkinson's. He's still super sharp mentally, but physically he struggles. It sucks that some of the best people face the worst shit, you know?"

Ari immediately thought of her mother. She'd never forgive cancer for taking Lucia away from her. Nor would she forgive the man in the plaid shirt for taking Richie.

"Did you ever interview Nora Martinez?"

He cracked a smile at the mention of her name. "The hippie lady with the camera? The one spying over her fence?"

"Yes."

"Oh, yeah. We interviewed her a few times, at her insistence. Claims she heard the shot."

"And like your other witness," Ari added, "the guy with the dog, she claims there was a car."

"That's right. She had some blurry picture of a fender." He shook his head.

"I'm guessing she wasn't credible?"

"She might've been. I was the first one to talk to her. She was out at the crime scene perimeter. Called me over and said she had information, pictures of the killer, but she needed to develop her film. I got all of her contact information and took the camera from her. When I told Hubbard about her, he laughed until he cried. Said she regularly called the precinct, claiming she had photos of drug buys, but the pictures were always blurry or overexposed, or she'd chop off heads…" He waved his hand. "She might've seen something, but she has no credibility with Glendale PD."

"What about her son, Wolf?"

"Ah, yes. We interviewed him. He was a teenager then. He was at work when it happened, but he frequented the 7-Eleven a lot. Did you meet him?"

"Yeah. He looked at the picture and said he thought he went to school with the guy, but he couldn't remember him."

"Interesting." Grady pushed aside his empty latte cup and glanced at his watch. "Until you showed me this picture," he said, pointing to the photo of the man in plaid, "I would've put my money on Wolf for the killer."

Grady left Ari to ponder Wolf Martinez's involvement in Richie's death. Grady said he had no proof, just a hunch that Wolf was somehow involved. She finished her own latte and took a stroll around the park. She doubted the 7-Eleven drug trade had anything to do with Richie's murder. He certainly wasn't using drugs at the age of eight, and he questioned any family member who swallowed an aspirin about what was wrong with them.

After her second lap around the park, she decided she couldn't completely ignore the drug angle, since it was possible someone—a buyer or a dealer—might have some information about Richie's killer. Perhaps the man in plaid was a regular user, and after several visits to the 7-Eleven, he'd decided to rob the place for his next fix. Yes, Richie had nothing to do with the drug trade, but perhaps his killer did.

Before Grady departed, he'd told her Floyd Hubbard was working the front desk at the main precinct. "The mayor enjoys a walk after lunch. Sometimes she'll pop her head inside the doors just to say a taunting hello to him. If he weren't such a jackass, I might feel sorry for him, losing his standing and being put on display."

It was such a beautiful day, Ari walked the five blocks to the precinct. She was greeted by Hubbard when she came through the door, although "greeted" was too strong a word. His hard stare and unsmiling face sparked an instant desire to turn and leave. His military-style crewcut sat on the top of his square head like a patch of grass. He had enormous jowls, and Ari surmised a large belly rested on his thighs, hidden by the cement counter. *How many crimes go unreported because this guy is the first contact?*

"Sergeant Hubbard, I'm Ari Adams. I'm—"

"Adams. I know the name. What do you want?"

"I'd like to ask you a few questions about my brother Richie's murder since you were the lead investigator."

He smirked as if he'd swallowed something distasteful. "Why?"

Unwilling to be bullied, she met his hard stare with one of her own, and he backpedaled. "I meant that it's been so long without any new evidence."

She wanted to shove the picture of the man in plaid under his nose, but she restrained herself. While she imagined her father would immediately bring the photo to Glendale PD, she wasn't going to give it to them just yet, and she didn't want Floyd Hubbard to get credit for doing nothing.

"I've heard some things from my father," she lied. "I'd like to verify if they're true."

Hubbard clasped his meaty hands under his chin. He looked around conspiratorially. "Not sure if the old man is making up stories, huh?"

"Something like that."

"What do you want to know?"

"He said at the time of Richie's death, the 7-Eleven was frequented by drug dealers and users."

"That's correct."

"Did you ever tie the drug angle to Richie's murder?"

"No. It didn't have anything to do with drugs. Your brother was in the wrong place at the wrong time. That's all." When she didn't reply and continued to stare, he unfolded his enormous hands and splayed them on the counter, a glint of humanity shining through with the gesture. "Look, we knew drugs were being passed out back, but the center of it was the day clerk, a guy whose name I can't remember…"

"Mellow."

He nodded. "But when your brother came in that night, Elijah Cruz was the clerk on duty—a squeaky clean young man going to college and just trying to pay bills. He had nothing to do with that stuff, no priors, no juvenile record. For Christ sake, he was collecting money for his sick sister's cancer surgery. Had a change jug by the register."

Ari remembered the shrine to CeCe Cruz at Elijah's house. "What about Mellow? Did you ever make an arrest?"

"No," he sighed. "Unfortunately, your brother's death scared off the dealers. All of a sudden, the drug trafficking went to zero. I imagine there was too much heat, and the main dealer, whoever that was, got scared off. Mellow quit and left Glendale as far as I know."

"You're not sure?"

He bit his lip. "No. Taglio might remember." He waved at an officer coming into the building before he said, "I imagine your father knows. He staged his own investigation and was a huge pain in my ass."

"Do you blame him?" she spat.

He winced at her sharp tone. "No, I don't. I blame myself… for a lot of things."

She imagined spending time behind the front desk was monotonous and boring. He undoubtedly had many hours to reflect upon his mistakes and regrets. "What about the idea that the killer left in a car?"

"Never happened, no matter what that loony, hippie-woman says."

"Did you ever talk to Wolf?"

"We did. He was a suspect for a while, although he looked nothing like Elijah Cruz's sketch. But that didn't matter. Witnesses aren't for crap. Still, Wolf Martinez had an alibi that night. He was working at the Glendale Eight Drive-In at the concessions booth. Five co-workers saw him. Not the perp."

"Do you remember anything else? Hunches you might've had, leads that didn't pan out?"

"There was nothing *but* leads that didn't pan out," he snorted. He stretched in his chair, his rotund belly poking up from behind the desk. "The weirdest interview we did was with that disabled kid, the one who lived with the Longs? Did you know him?"

"Of course. Cousin Glenn."

"He spent the whole interview staring at us through a movie camera. Wouldn't say a word. At one point, he got so agitated that he jumped out of the chair and ran around the room, his eye never leaving the viewfinder. He pointed the camera up, down, left, right, in a circle, everywhere. I thought he was going to run into something and poke his eye out."

Ari remembered Glenn's frantic behavior when he got upset. She'd seen it a few times that summer. "Do you recall what made him so upset?"

He scratched his face. "It was something Taglio said, or maybe it was the cousin… Since he was a minor, he had to have someone over eighteen with him. His aunt had just died, and his uncle was in no shape to talk about a murder. So he was interviewed with his cousin…a girl, a real looker. Can't remember her name either."

"That would've been Blythe Long. I knew her."

"You might want to ask her."

Ari nodded and decided not to share that Blythe was dead. "Well, thank you for your time, Sergeant Hubbard."

"Why are you doing this? Why now?"

His annoyed tone pushed her temper to the edge. He wanted her to forget Richie. It would be so much easier for him. She caught herself just as she was about to throw down the picture of the man in plaid. Instead she remained cryptic. "I've heard some interesting details, Sergeant Hubbard."

He blinked and when he saw her sincerity, worry replaced his smug expression. "What details?" She turned away and he called, "If you're withholding information, Ms. Adams, I promise you, I'll find out."

She turned and met his stare. "And you'll do what, Sergeant? Arrest me? You have to admit you don't have the track record for making that happen, do you?"

CHAPTER SIX

"I had the dream again," Ari said to the therapist, "or rather a new ideation of the same dream. It was definitely the same theme."

Dr. Yee opened her journal and crossed her legs. "Go on."

Ari had not intended to have a solo appointment with her therapist, but then the nightmare happened and she desperately wanted to share it with someone. Since she was catching up on paperwork in her office, Dr. Yee had agreed to meet with her on a Sunday. Ari closed her eyes. "This time it was at the rodeo. Our parents took us every March when it came to the Coliseum. For some reason, in the dream Richie and I were in the ring and I was holding his hand. Suddenly one of those rodeo clowns appeared in front of me. I stared at his big red nose, and then he suddenly jerked forward, like somebody goosed him from behind. I jumped and let go of Richie's hand. I turned to look for him, but there was a stampede of horses behind me. I couldn't see him. I tried to run between them, but I couldn't find him. Then it all just disappeared."

"The clown, too?"

"He'd turned into my father."

"What happened next?"

"He pointed to the side of the ring. Richie was on the ground, motionless. I ran to him and tried to wake him. I shook him and his head bobbed from side to side. He was dead. I was crying. I turned back to my father, but he was gone. That's when I woke up."

"Wow. Very intense."

Dr. Yee leaned back. Her small frame made the overstuffed chair seem enormous. She rubbed her palms together with a faraway look. Ari stared at the delicate fingers and the simple gold band that adorned her left ring finger. Ari almost cracked a grin at her appearance: yoga pants and a T-shirt. Her shoulder-length jet black hair was tied back with a striped scrunchie. Molly would be sorry she missed the "weekend version" of Dr. Yee, the therapist, who, during regular office hours, was the epitome of fashion sense with an endless wardrobe. She turned to Ari with a sigh. "I'm debating how seriously to take this," she said candidly. "Were you screaming?"

"Yes, but I'm okay now." Dr. Yee arched an eyebrow and Ari added, "Really. Thank goodness Molly wasn't home to hear me. She doesn't need to deal with my issues. She's got enough going on playing bodyguard to the tech guy, and she just won the contract to do security for gay pride in June."

"Still," Dr. Yee pressed, "she's your partner. Doesn't she have a right to know you're suffering? She would want to know."

"I tell her. She asks every morning if I had another bad dream and I tell her the truth."

"Good. Does she know about your guilt regarding Richie's death?"

"You mean that if I'd agreed to go with him that night after he asked me, he wouldn't have snuck out and gotten himself killed? That guilt?"

Dr. Yee ignored her sarcasm. "Yes, that part."

"She knows. We're way past keeping secrets. That won't happen again." She looked at Dr. Yee and offered a wry smile. "I think she's counting on you to fix me."

Dr. Yee laughed. "You don't need fixing, but I am concerned about some of your choices. Why did you destroy the trust you'd built with your father by breaking into his desk?"

"Well, when you put it like that…" She rubbed her temples and chose her words carefully. Although Dr. Yee had told her repeatedly that she never judged, Ari couldn't suppress her desire to please Dr. Yee. She wanted to be the patient who was always improving, moving forward and changing her life for the better.

"Snooping at my father's house wasn't just about Richie. Not only is it likely that my father has kept secrets about Richie's death, I've recently learned he's not been forthcoming about the end of my mother's life."

"Meaning?"

"I'd always thought I was Mom's primary caregiver, her sole source of support during her last months. Apparently, he was involved too."

"I don't understand. You're upset because your mother chose to lean on *two* people while she fought cancer and not just you?"

"How do you do that?" Ari asked, annoyed.

"Do what?"

"Make me sound like a selfish asshole." Dr. Yee's silence was confirmation. Ari expelled a deep breath. "I thought Mom was on my side. After Dad disowned me, she left him. It was two against one."

"Two against one," Dr. Yee murmured. "Sounds like something you'd hear on a school playground."

Ari sighed, exasperated. "Yes, it sounds childish, but it's how I feel. You're the one who's always saying I should own how I feel. So, I'm owning it!" She swallowed her anger and paused. "Sorry. I didn't mean to yell. I thought I was past this with him. I thought I'd forgiven him for what he did to Mom and me—for what I almost did to myself."

"Ari—"

"I know. I know. He's not responsible for my suicide attempt. I own my life and it's my responsibility to make meaning of it." She looked away. "I thought…" She gazed at Dr. Yee with pleading eyes. She couldn't find the words.

"You thought you'd wrapped up grief and anger and put them away on a high closet shelf."

"Yeah."

"Did you ever imagine Richie's killer would be found?"

"When I was younger, I was sure my dad would figure it out."

"Why?"

"One night, about three weeks after the murder, I went to the bathroom for a drink of water. I overheard my parents talking in their bedroom. Late at night was their private time, and if I got up, I didn't bother to listen at their door. But that night my dad was very upset and his voice was a loud whisper when he said Richie's name. He was certain he'd find the killer and I believed him. It was the way he said it. He was so sure. That made me sure."

"And if he found the killer, it would ease your guilt?"

"Yes," she blurted. "Uh, no." She sighed. "I don't know."

"It's okay not to know. Even for you, Ari."

"I hate not knowing."

"Yes, I'm well aware. So, what happened over time, when your father didn't find Richie's killer?"

"I think his sense of defeat happened far more quickly than mine. I lost my last glimmer of hope when I joined Tucson PD and learned that the likelihood of solving a cold case decreases with each passing year. Witnesses can't remember details or they die. Evidence disappears or it gets corrupted."

"And now it's possible that after twenty-five years, you might solve Richie's murder, correct?"

"Maybe," Ari hedged. "I don't want to get my hopes up."

"Why haven't you turned over the photo of the man in plaid to the police?"

"I want Molly and my father to see it first."

"You could make a copy," Dr. Yee said mildly.

"I could, but I'd have to give the police the movie, too. I'm not ready to give that up just yet." When Dr. Yee continued to stare, she said, "It's the end of Richie's life. He doesn't know it, and he's so alive. That sounds so trite, but Richie loved every day. I watch that little piece of film, and I want to scream at the screen. It just can't be his end. It shouldn't have been." She leaned forward in her chair. "If I give the police that footage, they'll completely disrespect it."

"What do you mean?"

"They'll toss it into the evidence box, and until Richie's killer is found, I'll never see it again."

"You could make a copy of that too," she said.

"I don't know how to do that."

Dr. Yee let that go and asked, "Do you believe you can solve Richie's murder?"

"I don't know. It was a long time ago. The killer could be dead, already incarcerated for something else, or he could've disappeared to the Bahamas."

"And how does the killer's current state matter to finding justice for Richie?"

"I guess it shouldn't but it does. I want to confront him. I want to see him in handcuffs. Attend the trial. Hear the jury say he's guilty. And I want to watch the judge sentence him to life in prison."

"And what if you're deprived of any—or all—of those things? What if the man in plaid is dead?"

She shrugged. "I don't know."

"I think you do."

"No, I don't," she snapped. She sighed and sank into the chair, deflated. "I'm sorry. I haven't been thinking clearly lately."

"You haven't been thinking clearly, or your thoughts seem to be in disarray? There's a difference."

"The second one. You know I'm crazy about creating order in my life. This is like someone came into my office and re-arranged everything. They moved my filing cabinet, put the staples in a different drawer, and un-color-coded my Post-it notes. It's maddening. Everything I thought I knew or understood isn't *right*."

"That's because perception is truth. And regarding the subject of your brother's death, you've built your own truth, mostly based on information given to you by someone else, namely your father, a man who destroyed your trust. And now, to find the truth, you will be required to look into the past with him at your side. You'll need to pool your resources and work as a team."

"I've never done that with him."

"I understand. This journey will be new for both of you. You'll be living in the past, the place where grief and anger dwell. You not only gained new information about your brother's death, but about your mother's. There's not one mystery, there are two."

Dr. Yee closed her journal and Ari glanced at the clock. They still had ten minutes left. *Why is she closing her notebook?* Ari saw hesitancy in Dr. Yee's eyes. *She knows something...*

She swallowed to coat her dry throat. "I know you're the one who's supposed to ask the questions, but I'd like to know what you're thinking."

Dr. Yee set her journal and fancy pen on the end table. "Moving forward, I think it's important for you to remember that the relationship you had with your mother is nothing like the one she had with your father."

"Of course."

"From what you've told me about your mother, she was incredibly kind, intelligent, and protective."

"Yes."

"Then she would never have wanted or allowed you to shoulder her pain. No decent parent would, especially if there's a spouse to help."

"But they were divorced."

Dr. Yee cocked her head to the side but said nothing.

Ari studied the swirls in the carpet as she pondered Jack and Lucia's relationship. Neither had ever married again or taken a lover, as far as she knew. She imagined how scared her mother must have been those last few months. She'd never have wished for her mother to be alone if she'd needed someone.

"From what you've shared," Dr. Yee continued, "it sounds as though there was a financial need as well. The cost to fight cancer is outrageous. Is it really surprising that your mother reached out to your father?"

"No, but I'm surprised he could help. He was a cop. He made decent money, but he couldn't give her a hundred thousand dollars. We were never rich."

"Maybe there's another answer you haven't yet discovered."

She felt as though Dr. Yee had jarred her brain. When it came to her parents, she clearly had little objectivity. But Dr. Yee never offered a suggestion she couldn't explain. Ari was missing something.

Dr. Yee smiled at her puzzled face. "What about insurance? I imagine your father had decent health benefits?"

"But she couldn't receive benefits as his ex-wife. They were divorced." She stared at Dr. Yee, expecting a look of recognition, but it was as if Dr. Yee was expecting *her* to realize… "Oh, my God. They got remarried."

Ari walked through her front door but couldn't remember how she got home. She'd driven on autopilot from Dr. Yee's office, fragments of old conversations bursting forth, thoughts she'd dismissed or ignored, all clues pointing toward the truth. She was certain her parents had remarried, if for no other reason than to provide Lucia with health insurance. *How did I miss this?* Jack and Lucia were tremendously pragmatic people who had remained friendly after the divorce. Ari knew her father would've done anything for her mother. She'd asked for the divorce after he'd disowned Ari for claiming her sexual identity, and once he'd regained Lucia's trust, Ari imagined Lucia would have been comfortable asking to remarry, anything to make sure her death didn't saddle Ari with bills she couldn't pay.

Again, Ari found herself holding the bottle of scotch. This time she put it away and announced, "I can only handle one family drama at a time. Richie, you're up."

She settled at her dining room table with Nora's box of photos. It was one of those craft boxes with a label on the front and covered in an interesting pattern of puffy clouds. Dividers separated each day's photos. She pulled out the first stack of pictures, the index card dated two days before Richie died. She shuffled through the two dozen photos, finding few pictures worthy of Nora's meticulous organization. Her cheap Instamatic took rotten photos, and the camera's limited ability coupled with Nora's limited photography skills equated to blurry and overexposed pictures.

Ari refiled the stack of photos and went to the next date, the day before his death. She shook her head and sighed. "This will be an hour of my life I'll never get back," she muttered. Some of the photos were comical: pictures of the ground, Nora's shoes and the trees in her yard. Most were awful but a few depicted Mellow out back smoking and talking to people. Including the man in plaid. They weren't doing anything suspicious, but their relaxed body language suggested they knew each other. She set that picture to the side.

Toward the end of the stack, she found several photos of a young Elijah embracing a woman Ari imagined was Isolde. In one photo it seemed Isolde was crying and wiping tears from her cheeks, but Ari wasn't sure since the faces were distorted. It probably didn't matter. Isolde was a teenager, and teenage girls cried over the trivial and mundane.

She shivered as she picked up the photos taken on the day Richie died. Another photo depicted Mellow outside with a different young man, one who was definitely white—but not the man in plaid. They looked like they were just talking while they smoked.

"No crime there," she muttered.

Day turned to night in the next photo. Ari imagined Nora hearing the shot, jumping up from her dining room table, running outside, probably snapping the Instamatic's shutter like crazy. Ari held up the grainy photo of the silver band across a smudge of black, what Nora claimed was a car fender.

Ari tapped a finger on the photo on the table. Nora seemed rather sharp for a woman in her late seventies, so she would've been on her game twenty-five years prior. She was certain she'd heard a car start. And she wasn't the only one. The dog walker had heard it too. Perhaps Elijah got it wrong. Perhaps the killer had parked in the back, walked around to the front door, and after he ran out, Elijah was so distraught he didn't hear the car leave. Easy to imagine, although it forced Ari to readjust the series of events cemented in her brain that collectively made up "Richie's Murder."

She set aside the photo of the presumed car fender and perused the rest of the pictures in the box that covered the three days after Richie's murder. The next stack had one good picture. Mellow, the 7-Eleven's day clerk, extending his hand toward the hand of a young Hispanic man. While she couldn't see what was in the clerk's hand, she was almost positive the Hispanic man was offering up cash. Unfortunately, their faces were blurry. Ari envisioned Floyd Hubbard laughing at Nora and tossing the picture back to her. Such a photo might've warranted some extra attention from the beat cops, but there wasn't enough evidence for a warrant to pursue Mellow.

Ari glanced at the last photo in the box: a lovely shot of a leaf. She returned the last stack to its place, tempering her growing frustration. She knew Nora meant well, even if she was a terrible photographer. As she straightened the photos and index card dividers, she realized two pictures had slipped underneath the entire array.

Both photos were much clearer, and she guessed they were each taken with a much better camera, perhaps during "the magic hour," the time near sunset when natural light enhanced photographs. And the lighting certainly made the subjects easy to identify. In the first photo, a much older Wolf Martinez, probably in his late twenties, hugged a scruffy looking teenage girl against his chest. Her face was turned toward Nora, and she smiled as if she'd just found her Prince Charming. The second photo, much older than the first, depicted two teenagers exchanging a hand slap: Elijah Cruz and Wolf Martinez.

CHAPTER SEVEN

Ari was determined to wait up for Molly's arrival home and show her everything she'd discovered, but then Molly called at ten p.m. "Bad news, babe. We're just now boarding the plane after a four-hour dinner."

"That must be some kind of record," she yawned.

"Go to bed. I know we have a ton to discuss, but I won't walk through the door until two a.m. Get some sleep and we'll talk in the morning. My appointment with the gay pride committee is at one p.m., so we have all morning to talk, if that works."

But it didn't work. Ari had a breakfast meeting with the Carpenters to discuss their counteroffer. She hoped to quash a few of their ridiculous requests, such as removing the existing solar panels. The Carpenters were Midwest transplants who didn't understand the true financial value of solar in a place like Phoenix. She'd prepared some figures illustrating the amount of money they would save on the electric bill by using solar energy.

Her alarm went off at six a.m., but she smacked the snooze button. Molly cuddled against her, softly snoring into her hair.

Waking her would be completely selfish, and it would suck away
the hour of prep time she needed for her breakfast meeting. So
instead of lounging with Molly, she grudgingly slipped out of
the embrace and prepared for work.

When she went into the dining room with her coffee
in hand, she immediately noticed fluorescent sticky notes
tacked everywhere with messages scribbled in Molly's hasty
handwriting. She'd apparently abandoned her suitcase at the
doorway and engaged in a self-guided tour of Ari's research.

Most of the notes were questions or suggestions for next
steps. *Have you spoken to Chris Taglio? Where are the unopened
packs of trading cards? Who gave your dad this information?* And
attached to the photo of the man in plaid, Molly had written,
Need facial recognition ASAP! Know anyone?

Molly had included a smiley face after the question as a sad
joke. Of course, Ari's father could and would use his clout to find
the name of Richie's killer, but Molly was also referencing the
fractured relationship between herself and her former Phoenix
police partner, Detective Andre Watson. After Molly had left
the force, they remained close and helped each other with
investigations—until Molly lied to him. They were currently
not speaking to each other, but Ari knew they would make up
eventually.

She laughed when she read the sticky note attached to Nora
Martinez's fender picture. *What the hell is this?* Despite her
exhaustion, Molly had even taken the time to watch Glenn's
movie. The sticky note affixed to the film reel simply read, *Wow.*
Ari wanted to watch the movie again, but if she did, she'd be
sucked into Richie's world, and her preparation for the meeting
with the Carpenters would suffer.

Her gaze landed on Molly's note about Chris Taglio, Floyd
Hubbard's partner. After her breakfast meeting, she planned to
stop by his senior center, which happened to be just a few miles
from the restaurant where she would meet the Carpenters. She
gathered her father's notes and the information specific to Chris
Taglio, along with a legal pad half-filled with her own notes.
Molly had marked a page with a pointing arrow.

The arrow pointed to Nora's statements about the constant drug dealing occurring at the 7-Eleven and Mellow's involvement. Ari had written, *Elijah=no*, since Jack didn't believe Elijah was involved. Molly had stuck a question above Ari's note: *Are you sure?*

"Elijah might be involved," Molly re-emphasized on the phone a few hours later.

She'd just woken up, and Ari managed to catch her for a quick call. Ari wiggled free of her suit jacket and tossed it on the passenger seat. It was only April, but the temperatures had flip-flopped into the nineties. She was hot and her temper was smoldering, since her marathon breakfast with the Carpenters had proved to be a battle of wills. Someone told them to play hardball, and they couldn't see reason, regardless of how often she attempted to show it to them.

"At the very least," Molly continued, "I'll bet he knew the deals were happening. He may not have been selling, but I'm sure a few customers came looking to score when he was on duty."

She knew Molly was right, but the idea of Elijah being anything but a good Samaritan wasn't a change in the narrative she was ready to accept.

"Babe, are you there?" Molly asked.

"I am. Rough morning. I'm on my way to see Chris Taglio."

"Good. I'll be interested to hear what he says. On another topic, when does your dad get home?"

"Later today."

Molly sighed loudly. She understood the twisted knot that was Ari's and Jack's relationship, the knot they'd successfully untangled over the last few years.

"Call me later," Molly said before she offered, "I love you," and disconnected.

Molly's sigh spoke volumes, but Ari wasn't ready to think about what she would say to her father. As much as she needed his help to solve Richie's murder, she was equally curious about his relationship with her mother. But discussing it with him would lead to anger, grief, and possibly hatred. She'd *hated* Jack for several years. It had consumed her life in so many ways, and she couldn't afford to let it happen again when they needed to focus on Richie.

"One family drama at a time," she reiterated.

Chris Taglio's senior center, Desert Oasis, was a campus of multiple buildings, offering various levels of care. Her father had left his map printout and directions to Taglio's building with his notes. What he hadn't mentioned was the need for an appointment. The security guard who stepped out of his little shack to speak with her explained as much when her name wasn't on his list. She nodded and listened politely while she concocted a story about being a niece just visiting for one afternoon. He didn't buy it and told her rules were rules. Her gaze fell to a tattoo on his left arm. *Pablo 1992-2014.*

"Who was Pablo?"

He blinked and glanced at his own arm. "My brother."

She showed him the Dodger cap smudged with blood that she now carried in her purse. Then she held up the part of Richie's file she'd brought and explained why she needed to see Chris Taglio. His gaze remained glued to the Dodger cap after she'd finished babbling. He turned away, and for a moment she thought he was dismissing her. Then the parking gate ascended.

"Thank you," she called, but he wouldn't look up.

She found a parking space and studied her father's notes about Taglio's exact location. She imagined the security guard was only the first of several obstacles between strangers and the residents of Desert Oasis. Most likely she faced more layers of scrutiny, but if she acted as if she belonged and knew where she was going, perhaps no one would notice her.

She studied the photo of Taglio attached to his initial crime scene report. Twenty-five years ago, he was thirty-eight, Ari's age, but he looked much older, as heavy jowl lines creased his cheeks and crows' feet extended to his temples. Ari guessed the daily grind of police work was responsible. Her father had written a few editorial notes about Taglio. *Sharp. Intuitive. Funny.*

"I guess I'll see for myself."

She glanced at her map once more and headed toward a set of double-doors labeled *Assisted Living Wing*. If Taglio required help with certain basic needs, then the Parkinson's had most likely worsened since her father's last interview with him five years ago. The doors whooshed open in front of a receptionist's counter. She couldn't see the receptionist behind two deliverymen who stood between them, which meant the receptionist couldn't see her. She darted down the first corridor, a patient wing. She only needed to make a left and then a right to find Taglio's room. She nodded at two orderlies, turned right—and nearly ran into a nurse carrying two vials of blood in one hand and a clean bedpan in the other. What Ari noticed first was her creamy pale skin, and then her soft brown eyes, her eyelashes bathed in mascara. Nurse Schaller was embroidered on her neon orange scrubs. "May I help you?"

"No, I'm headed to Chris Taglio's room, number one sixty-eight?"

"And who are you?"

She pulled out her card and held it up. "I'm Ari Adams. My father and Chris are old friends."

Nurse Schaller's eyelashes flicked toward the card but she didn't allow Ari to pass. "You're a real estate agent. Mr. Taglio planning on buying a condo?"

"No, this is a personal matter."

"Do you have an appointment?" Her tone implied she was certain Ari did not.

She took a breath and prepared a story that dabbled in the realm of truth. "Actually, I—"

"It's all good, Nurse Schaller."

They turned and acknowledged Chris Taglio, who stood in his doorway. He was dressed in khakis, a golf shirt, and green pullover sweater. He looked like he was ready to hit the links, except for his shoes—a pair of black slippers. His hands were in his pockets, and Ari could tell his arms were slightly shaking.

Nurse Schaller motioned to Ari with the bedpan. "Do you know this woman?"

"You bet I do," Taglio said with a wink. "Come back later, Nurse, and I'll croon you a tune."

Nurse Schaller snorted and walked away without another word. Taglio smiled at Ari and said, "I apologize if that comment sounded inappropriate. Nurse Schaller and I banter regularly. It's how we avoid killing each other." Ari smiled. "You're Jack's daughter."

"Yes. I'm Ari. There's been a new development in my brother's case, and I'd like to ask you some questions."

He directed her to a loveseat in a corner of the spacious room, which looked more like an apartment. A small kitchenette, a regular twin bed, and a dinette set filled most of the square footage. A jigsaw puzzle covered the dinette tabletop, and three different Sudoku puzzle books sat on the coffee table in front of the loveseat. What was noticeably missing was a television. Taglio's body might be betraying him, but his mind was not.

He lowered himself into a worn recliner and stared at her. "You look like your mother. That's a compliment."

She knew she was blushing. "Thank you. I wasn't aware you knew her, but of course, that makes sense. You probably talked with them several times after Richie died."

"Listened is more accurate," he replied with a sad smile.

"What do you mean?"

He coughed, and when he covered his mouth, she saw how badly his hand shook. Only when it stilled against the recliner's armrest did he continue. "Our job was to listen, but my partner was one of those guys who always had to show he was in charge. Had to be number one, you know?"

"I heard. My father included several unflattering editorial comments in his file about his interviews with Detective Hubbard."

Taglio belly-laughed at the understatement. When he caught his breath he said, "Did your dad ever tell you that he almost got into a fistfight with Hubbard?"

"Really? No, that's not in his notes."

"Yeah, your dad came in screaming one morning about a month into the investigation. Right before a squad huddle so everybody was there. He'd just interviewed Nora Martinez, and she'd shown him her picture of the fender." He paused and asked, "Have you seen that photo?"

"I have. It's blurry," Ari added diplomatically. "I understand why the police might have discounted it."

"Well, your dad didn't. He shoved it in Hubbard's face and started shouting that there were now two witnesses who said they saw a car after the shooting. Told Hubbard he needed to get off his lazy ass and find justice for his son. Hubbard was ready to blow, but then your dad started to cry." Taglio looked at her with tears in his eyes. "Who could get mad at him for that? After their confrontation I decided to help him. Well, that's when *we* decided to help your dad."

"Who's we?" she asked, already sensing she knew the answer.

"Me and Grady Quigley, the first officer on the scene."

"I've met him. I know Richie's death deeply affected him."

"It did. He had a year-old son when your brother died. He was so disturbed, the shrink had him pulled from the field. Sent him to the evidence room."

"Ah. That was helpful."

Taglio offered a mysterious smile. "It was." He threw a glance about the room and added, "Floyd Hubbard tanked your brother's case. I tried to get him to look at other possibilities, other suspects, but he wasn't much interested in my theories. I'll never admit it publicly because Glendale PD has been really good to me."

"I'd like to hear your theories."

He nodded. "And I'll share them. But first I want to know what you've found."

She pulled out her picture of the man in plaid and detailed the contents of Glenn's movie. He didn't interrupt and his gaze never left the picture.

"We could've used this twenty-five years ago. You said the cousin, Glenn, shot this movie?"

"Yes, do you remember him?"

"Oh, sure. It's hard to miss a kid riding a bicycle with a movie camera stuck to his eyeball."

They both laughed. She'd completely forgotten how Glenn steered his bike with one hand while holding the camera in the other. He'd only crashed once that summer and had managed to protect the camera as he hit the ground.

Laughing worsened Taglio's shakes. She moved on quickly and said, "Floyd Hubbard told me Glenn wouldn't say anything when you interviewed him, but at some point, he became agitated and ran around the room. Do you remember that?"

"Vaguely."

"I knew Glenn rather well, and he only exploded when he struggled to process something important or someone angered him."

"Then it could've been because of Hubbard," Taglio snorted. "He was always irritating witnesses."

"Perhaps," Ari conceded, "but do you remember what was said right before he blew up?"

She waited and watched as the shakes overtook most of his body. Eventually he stood up and walked behind the couch, which seemed to calm him. He eventually looked up and said, "It happened late in the interview. Well, it really wasn't an interview anymore. We realized he wasn't going to answer any questions, so we talked to the cousin, the pretty girl?"

"Blythe Long."

"Yeah. She was telling us what she knew about the 7-Eleven." He bit his lip and looked away. "It was something she said. Then he jumped out of the chair and flew past us. She kept talking like it was nothing. I guess she was used to it, but we weren't." He shook his head. "It's not coming to me right now, but I'll think of it."

"Do you remember seeing Glenn the night of the murder?"

He narrowed his eyes. "I can't remember." Then he slapped his knee. "Wait. Yeah, I saw him that night. And the next day, too."

She pulled out the crime scene photos and showed him one of the crowd. "He's not in this photo, but Elijah Cruz kicked him out of the store earlier that afternoon for being obnoxious. But the movie footage shows Glenn talking to Richie just a little while before he died."

Taglio stared across the room. His face twitched and he scratched his nose. "It's difficult to summon memories you never thought were important." He tapped the far left of the crowd photo. "He was over here. I pointed out to the photographer that he wasn't getting the whole crowd in his shots, specifically Glenn, but he assured me he was. Obviously not."

"So, Glenn was there at the scene. You're sure?"

"I am. Had the camera to his face. And when I looked at him, he turned his bike and rode away. I went back there the next afternoon. Wanted to see the place in daylight. When I pulled up, he was sitting on his bike in front of the lamppost." Taglio stroked his cheek and looked at Ari. "You know what?"

"What?"

"He didn't have his camera. I saw his whole face, and it was all scrunched up, a cross between rage and agony. I walked toward him, but he bolted away. I told Hubbard we needed to find him, and he said to let the unis take care of it when they canvassed the neighborhood. But they never located him. I'm the one who found him for the interview."

"I'm not surprised the unis didn't talk to him. That store was in a different neighborhood. Richie preferred to go there because he swore they got better trading cards."

They both chuckled at the glorious naiveté of a child. Taglio motioned for the other photos, and he laid them across the coffee table. He picked up each one and studied it as if he were looking at it for the first time. Then he reordered the whole stack in chronological order. He held up a close-up of the trading card display and pointed at one of the pegs suspending a row of cards. The odd arrangement showed cards missing from the middle. "Your dad said Richie always picked his card packs from the middle of a row, right?"

She smiled. "Yes, he thought it brought him good luck." She shifted in her seat and asked delicately, "Do you know where those unopened trading cards packs are? I didn't see them with the other…stuff you gave my dad."

"Quigley thought it best that we not empty the entire box of evidence. As far as I know, they're still in the basement at headquarters. Did you see the fingerprint report?"

She shuffled through the papers she'd brought and shook her head. "No. I'm fairly certain I'm operating with an abridged file. My dad's out of town, and he hasn't brought me up to speed. What does that report say?"

"Those trading card packs he'd chosen had three sets of fingerprints on them: his own, the day clerk's because he stocked the display, and an unknown—a child. Hubbard dismissed that third set, saying that any kid meandering around the store could've touched them." Taglio shrugged. "He could be right, but I disagreed. I always maintained there was a fourth person in the store, and now you're telling me Glenn was nearby, filming before the murder. Maybe I was right."

"There's something else," Ari interjected. "There's a break in the filming. Glenn greeted Richie, and after Richie rode toward the store, Glenn paused the film."

"For how long?"

"I can't say in terms of seconds or minutes, but he started filming again just as the killer approached the door."

"So maybe Glenn snuck into the store when Cruz wasn't looking." He paused and scratched his cheek. "You know, Cruz changed his story along the way and said people came in between Richie's arrival and when he was held up. He might not have noticed Glenn."

"If Glenn snuck in, he wasn't there for very long. He had to leave in time to get back to the parking lot and record the killer's entrance."

Taglio rubbed his hands together, unaware or uncaring of how severely he trembled. "Something's not right. Do you have my notes?"

"I do," she said, handing a small stack of papers to him.

He groaned as he scanned the pages he'd written decades before. "I'll need some time to re-read and process all this. I'm questioning the time frame, and our young filmmaker makes me question it more." He picked up a photo of the candy rack and pointed again to the empty space on the peg. "Not many shoppers reach for stuff in the middle or the back."

"Right. Usually you just take the first thing you see, unless it's been opened or damaged."

"Exactly. I think Richie pulled off those packs from the middle and showed them to somebody. And I'm thinking that person is Glenn. He's the key."

CHAPTER EIGHT

After Ari found her father's secret hiding place in his desk, she'd vowed not to interrupt his vacation. She checked her watch. He and Dylan had landed back in Phoenix fifteen minutes ago. They were most likely still standing at baggage claim, bored and waiting for the carousel to load. Surely a text wouldn't be too intrusive. *Found what you wanted me to find. Meet?*

It only took thirty seconds for a reply. *Give me two hours. Go here.* She stared at an unfamiliar street address out in Laveen and a five-digit gate code. Google Maps confirmed it was a Quick and Safe Storage location, matching the bill she'd found at his house. A shiver of excitement gave her goose bumps.

Two hours was just enough time to race home, retrieve the movie projector and Glenn's movie, and head back out west. Her heart raced and twice she had to let up on the gas when the speedometer crept to eighty-five. She didn't want a ticket, and if she were stopped, she doubted she could provide a coherent explanation to the officer. This was a moment when she should be *allowed* to speed. In fact, she wished all the cars would get the hell out of her way. She'd spent the last week predicting how she'd feel when the moment came to share the movie with her father. Then he'd raised the stakes by planting the file, somehow knowing she'd go looking for answers eventually.

She pulled up to the Quick and Safe Storage keypad, and while the gate slowly whirred to life, she checked the directions to the unit number on his text. It was inside the main building, no doubt air-conditioned to protect the evidence from the summer heat. She imagined he'd planned to arrive first, and her hunch was confirmed as she rounded the corner and found his Subaru Outback parked next to a door. She typed in a second code and the lock clicked. Her boot heels echoed as she followed the signs toward unit nine-sixty. A wide accordion garage door appeared closed, except for the two-inch space at the bottom. If this was his version of an office, he was violating his storage contract and didn't want scrutiny from other tenants, security cameras, or drones that might hover around an open door.

As she reached the door, he hoisted it high enough to duck under and hug her. He was taller by a few inches, and there wasn't an ounce of fat on his rock-solid physique. He defied all geriatric stereotypes, and she could only hope she looked as good when she neared sixty.

"How was Rocky Point?" she asked.

"Relaxing."

"Everything good with you and Dylan?"

He cracked a wide smile. "It's great." The pleasantries aside, he stuffed his hands in his pockets and leaned back on his heels. *He's nervous.* Whatever was behind that door would catapult their relationship into a completely different place, and historically, change equated to difficulty for them. They had never been the picture-perfect father and daughter, both struggling to live up to what the other imagined. She could tell he was searching for words. The underlying excitement of finally capturing Richie's killer was tempered by the agony of reliving and rehashing Richie's death. Up until the last week, the possibility of justice had been nothing more than a hope that grew more distant each year.

She asked mildly, "How did you know I'd come looking for answers about Richie?"

"Because you're my daughter," he said automatically, as if he'd prepared his response long ago. "You've always been curious—about everything. Richie barreled ahead, ready to try anything, but you studied and asked questions. I knew eventually…" He finished the statement with a shrug.

"How did you find this place?"

"I rented this space years ago, when it was owned by one guy. He was ready to sell the whole place to a corporation, but I convinced him to sell it to me."

"You own this storage company?" She was dumbfounded. He'd never once mentioned owning property other than his house. But it demonstrated how he kept things private.

"Yup. Kinda interesting. I'll tell you about it some time."

But that time wasn't now. "What about when you moved to Oregon?"

"I left it. Chris Taglio and Grady Quigley each have a key. That way if a lead ever broke, one or both of them could take everything back to the evidence room at Glendale HQ while I got on the first flight home." He gazed at the door and added, "But I never got that call."

"Why do you get a bill each month?"

He looked surprised for a split second, then pleased. "It keeps me humble," he joked.

She resisted the urge to pull out the movie and projector, waiting until his round of Show and Tell concluded. He'd obviously planned for this moment. The letter in the desk was proof he'd intended to fold her into the investigation, but only if she wanted to be involved.

"I guess the best way to start is just to show you what I've been doing for the last few decades," he said, raising the accordion door.

Sunlight streamed inside and filled the enormous space, which was much larger than a standard unit. She could see where he'd torn down walls between several units to create his own finished workroom, including overhead lights. Each of the three walls served a different purpose. The crime scene photos covered the wall closest to her, including the ones of Richie she'd banished to the back of her file folder. She stepped to the east wall, his murder board. At the center was Elijah Cruz's sketch, surrounded by pictures of Cruz, Wolf Martinez, Mellow, and three other scary looking men wearing identical white tank tops. Their arms sported dozens of tattoos and "WHB" was inked into each man's neck. *Westside Homeboys.* A yellow index card beneath the respective photos indicated the bald man was Jesus Santiago, the serious one in the middle was George Delgado, and the man who looked almost dashing except for his scary artwork, was Damian Cortez.

The back wall was Jack's brainstorming area. The photos, documents, and questions he'd displayed validated her early impressions. A sticky note affixed to the crime scene photo of the trading card rack read *3rd Set of Fingerprints? Glenn?* He'd highlighted certain passages from the reports by Hubbard and Taglio and drawn arrows to pictures of other players: Nora Martinez, Wolf Martinez, Grady Quigley, and Warner Krueger, who she suspected was the dog walker and the other person who had heard a car leave the parking lot. She was disheartened to see a sticky note slapped to his photo that read *Deceased.*

One side of a rolling board was covered in cork. Dozens of color-coded notecards formed a timeline of events, beginning with the night of Richie's murder. A row of folding tables cut the space in half. Files, papers, notes, phone messages, and interview transcripts plastered the surfaces. An outsider would see chaos, but Ari knew it all formed a logical progression toward an answer, one that had eluded them for a quarter of a century. *Maybe I have the clue we need to finally solve this.*

As she scanned the space, calculating the thousands of hours Jack had worked the case, it suddenly occurred to her that Glenn's movie might have both a positive and negative effect. Jack would be ecstatic that Richie's killer was revealed, but he might also be resentful that Ari swooped in and solved the mystery he'd toiled over for a few decades.

When her gaze turned back to him, he asked, "Do you need time to vent? Ask questions about how this came to be? I'm guessing you came looking now because you went back to Glendale to help Scott Long, right?"

She didn't answer and instead turned and faced the horrible photo of Richie lying in his own blood. Since finding the note that day in her father's house, she'd formulated a litany of questions worthy of an interrogation. They were at the ready, and he'd given her permission. She could spend the afternoon grilling him, making him feel guilty about leaving her out. But as her gaze remained riveted on her little brother's glassy brown eyes drained of life forever, she no longer cared about her father's transgressions. Instead of answering his question, she strode to the offending photo and turned it face down. The only thing that mattered now was justice.

"I need to show you something," she said and ducked under the accordion door.

She returned with the projector and the movie. While she prepared it, Jack flipped the rolling board and revealed a blank whiteboard on the other side. He parked it eight feet away from the projector. When it was ready, she glanced at him. Sweat covered his forehead, and she didn't think the slightly humid temperature in the storage unit was to blame.

She started the film and stepped behind him. She couldn't bear to see his face while they watched. When Richie rode up to meet Glenn, her father gasped and reached for the table. His shoulders arched as he wept. But his tears vanished at the sight of the man in plaid. He marched toward the whiteboard for a better look but halted when the movie disappeared. He whirled around, his eyes demanding an explanation.

"I found this a few days ago when I was packing up the movies Scott Long loaned to me while I investigated his mother's death. There are several movies of Richie from that summer. I'll show them to you sometime. This was the last one I found. Totally by accident...or maybe not," she added.

He managed to mumble, "Play it again...please," as he grabbed a folding chair and sat down.

She complied and he made the same request at the end. She played it six times. As she turned off the projector he propped his chin on his upturned palm, deep in thought. She bit her lip and refrained from blurting the many questions crowding the front of her brain. Her father needed processing time. He was at the place she'd been just a week before—probably a worse place. He'd been following the case for years. She couldn't imagine all of the theories, hunches, and rabbit holes he'd investigated, all leading nowhere.

"Have you shown this to anyone else?"

"No, I was waiting for you." She pulled out the still-frame photo of the man in plaid and set it in front of him. "I did, however, print this, and I've shown it to Elijah Cruz, Grady and Chris. They were shocked to see it, especially Elijah."

He studied the picture critically, wearing a fierce look of hate at the man who'd killed his son. "Maybe we'll get lucky," he said. "I'd love to be the one to slap handcuffs on this guy, but I'd be happier to learn he's been rotting away in a cell somewhere, not able to hurt anyone else's child."

"Me too. But before we give up the film, there's something you should see."

She played it again and stopped at the moment before Glenn had paused. She explained the break in time and the theories she and Chris Taglio had shared.

"The third set of fingerprints," he said. "They really could belong to Glenn."

"Or maybe he just stood outside, waiting for Richie." She shared with him Cruz's memory of kicking Glenn out earlier that day. "I remember Glenn as one who followed rules. If Cruz told him not to come back, I don't think he would've gone back inside."

Jack frowned. "Then that third set of prints could belong to a random kid. But we need to talk to Glenn—or rather, you need to talk to Glenn."

"Agreed. Do you want to take the film to the IT team now, and we can come back to this…"

She gestured at the wall of suspects. While she wanted to hear his thoughts about the investigation, she knew it might be for naught if, in fact, she'd found the clue that solved Richie's murder. If they could close the case by the end of the day or week, the contents of the storage unit would be nothing more than an interesting footnote. Then, as they packed up the massive amount of research and information, some of which would likely be used in a criminal proceeding, Jack could share all of the interesting anecdotes he'd collected over the years. She'd love to hear about the day he was escorted out of the Glendale police station after raging at Hubbard. And solving Richie's murder would also allow them to broach the other family topic weighing on Ari's mind: the death of her mother.

"Let's take the film in together," he offered. "The tech guys will want to pull their own still frame to hunt for a match."

Ari's phone chimed with her emergency tone. She glanced at the display. "Someone just broke into my house," she exclaimed. Before Jack could comment, the security company called to inform her they had dispatched the police.

They hurriedly decided to split up. Jack would take the film downtown while she drove home and called Molly, who would have received the same security alerts. He touched her shoulder before she hopped into the SUV and asked, "Remember when I was burglarized?"

"Yeah, a long time ago. Your patio door lock was jimmied, right?"

"Right. I never told you any of the particulars, but I've always thought it was related to Richie's murder and my investigation."

"Why?"

"It happened just after I followed up on a lead about the day clerk, Mellow. I'd connected him to Westside Homeboys, the local gang. I re-interviewed a number of people—cops and witnesses—about the drug traffic through that 7-Eleven. A week later Mellow was stabbed and killed in prison. Then I got robbed." He shrugged. "It might've been coincidental, but I don't think so."

She remembered reading Jack's notes about Mellow's death. "Do you think the man in plaid orchestrated his stabbing? And your burglary?"

"Maybe, but it could also be someone else affiliated with the case. Someone who has a lot to lose."

"Someone like Floyd Hubbard."

Jack didn't answer. "I don't want to accuse a brother in blue, but it's awfully coincidental that you've been hit just as you find the biggest lead we've ever had on the case. Does Hubbard know about the photo?"

"No, but he knows I've found something," she admitted.

"Watch your back." He patted her shoulder and headed toward his car. As she exited the storage facility, her phone rang. *Molly.*

"Babe, you're not going to be happy, so I wanted to prepare you."

Ari groaned. "How bad is it?" she asked, imagining her new midcentury-modern living room couch pillows sliced and white stuffing strewn across the floor.

"The good news is the damage is confined to the solarium." She winced. Her books. Molly's piano. "Whoever broke in wasn't stealthy. They took one of the decorative boulders from the backyard and hurled it through the glass."

"Oh, God. Is your piano okay?"

"Yes. Perhaps the burglar is a lover of the arts. He or she didn't touch my piano. Or damage the artwork or books. And your mother's jewelry is still here."

"What did they take? My dad suggested the break-in might be related to Richie's case. He was burglarized when he got a hot lead several years ago."

"Well, I'm certain our burglary is tied to Richie's investigation. From what I can tell, the only thing missing is your notes and photos of the case. The dining room is empty."

She felt sick to her stomach. She didn't care as much about the crime scene photos or her father's notes, as he had everything at the storage unit. But she'd lost most of *her* notes.

"What about the evidence bag with Richie's baseball cards?" she blurted.

"Those are gone, babe. I'm so sorry. What else do you have with you?"

"I brought the movie, the projector, and two of the photos from Nora Martinez's box. And I've been carrying around Richie's hat."

"Well, that explains it then."

"Explains what?"

"Like I said, nothing else appears to have been taken, but I can tell every room has been searched—quickly—but definitely searched. I'd bet you a commission that whoever was here was looking for that movie."

CHAPTER NINE

Ari cried when she saw the shattered solarium wall. The vandal was sending a message. She thought of the garbage picker she'd seen as she drove around the 7-Eleven. If she had been tailed, the perp probably followed her home. Normally she was keenly aware of her surroundings, but since she'd found that movie, she'd been dazed, stuck in a fog that wouldn't lift. Everything else was a pestering distraction.

Molly came around the side of the house, talking to a uniformed officer, her six-foot frame towering over him. Her curly blond hair touched the collar of her Nelson Security polo shirt and her black cargo shorts displayed her tanned and muscular calves. When she saw Ari, she excused herself and pulled Ari into a hug. "I'm sorry."

Ari took a deep breath and nodded. "What do we know?"

"Not much more than what I said on the phone." She led her away from the house. "I didn't tell them about the copy of Richie's file. I doubt whoever gave your father a copy did so with the blessing of the Glendale PD. Didn't want to get a good Samaritan in trouble."

"Agreed. Too many questions to answer."

"You know what this means?"

"What?"

"Somebody's worried. He knows the movie is the key."

That was true. They headed across the lawn and Molly stopped. "Oh, shit," she mumbled.

Andre Watson, Molly's former police partner, approached, smoothing his navy tie against his crisp white dress shirt. His tailored gray suit hugged his lean frame, and the shine of his shoes reflected in the afternoon sun. His somber expression matched Molly's. Until they repaired their fractured relationship, their professional interactions would continue to be strained. But it would take time to regain the trust they had lost, and neither was ready to start a conversation, leaving Ari as the go-between.

"Hi, Andre," she offered, pulling him into a brief hug.

"Sorry about your house. You just get it redone and something like this happens," he said, referring to the remodel that had occurred after a bomb exploded in her garage during an investigation.

They both looked at Molly. "Hey."

"Hey." He turned back to Ari. "Any idea who did this or why?" From his smirk, she knew that *he knew* it was a rhetorical question.

"Yes, I have an idea. You'll find out more when you see my dad. He's downtown talking to the department's IT team. I came across a movie that was filmed just a few minutes before Richie died. There's a moment when the killer turns toward the camera. I'm betting whoever broke in here was looking for that."

He blinked several times and asked, "Are you serious?"

"Yeah."

She recounted how she came across the movie, and he only shook his head in reply, speechless. His gaze landed on the huge hole in the solarium wall. "So this is probably the same guy or one of his associates."

"Possibly."

"It could be someone with ties to the murder that we haven't connected yet," Molly added.

Andre met her stare and nodded his agreement. "Someone who got away with murder twenty-five years ago and wants to make sure that doesn't change." He opened his iPad and tapped some notes. "If your dad has the movie, then whoever did this left empty-handed. Anything else missing?"

She hesitated a moment too long, and his eyes narrowed. *Why couldn't the investigating detective be someone else?* "Yes. I was starting my own investigation and I acquired some of the reports and witness transcripts," she said slowly. "I also had my own notes."

His tapping stopped and he glanced from Ari to Molly and then closed his iPad. "I see. I appreciate, Ari, that you're telling me the truth and trusting me to make decisions about this information."

"Oh, for God's sake," Molly spat at his dig at her about their previous case. "It's not the same, Andre. I was protecting you. I didn't want to put you in a bad position."

"I don't need your protection."

Ari held up a hand. "Stop, please. I can't add this stress right now. I need you both to work together and help me. Help Richie."

Andre sighed and the tension between them diminished. "I can do that. Maybe we'll find a print somewhere inside. And when I'm done here, I'll text your dad and see if there's anything I can do to help identify the guy on the movie."

"Thank you."

He headed back toward the house without acknowledging Molly. "I really hope the two of you kiss and make up soon," Ari told her.

"I know. We need each other," Molly acknowledged. "I'll reach out."

Ari looped her arm through Molly's and they strolled to the front yard. A handful of Ari's neighbors had congregated on the sidewalk. She couldn't remember some of their names, but she'd waved or said hello to all of them over the past year in the hope of making amends for disturbing the peace with her explosion. Mrs. Trotter, the self-appointed community busybody and Ari's next-door neighbor to the west, motioned for her and Molly to join them. Mrs. Trotter was in her mid-seventies and usually battling some sort of ailment, real or imaginary. Somewhat overweight, she wore stretchy jeans and a yellow T-shirt. Her all-white hair was held back by a pink headband, revealing clusters of liver spots on her cheeks. Today her right hand grasped a cane, but Ari knew better than to ask about it since she didn't have time for a twenty-minute chat.

"Hi, Mrs. Trotter. Hi, everyone. You all know my girlfriend, Molly, don't you?"

They nodded and Mrs. Trotter squeezed Ari's arm. "I just spoke with Detective Watson, the handsome gentleman who looks like Denzel?"

"Yes?"

She pointed to her upstairs window that faced Ari's yard. "Fortuitous as it might be, I was cleaning the blinds when I saw someone scale your back fence. He picked up one of your decorative rocks, hurled it into the solarium and marched inside." She sighed and said, "You might want to reconsider your landscaping choices, dear. You're making it very easy for thieves."

Ari bit the inside of her cheek. "I'll think about it. What else did you see?"

"Unfortunately, not much. Your alarm screeched when the glass broke, and I ran for my cell phone downstairs. I figured it couldn't hurt to have two 9-1-1 calls on the books."

"Absolutely. Can you describe the person you saw?"

"Somewhat. He *or she*—don't want to assume it was a man in this age of equality—wore dark pants, a green baseball cap, and a blue plaid button-down shirt."

"Did you say plaid?" Molly asked.

"Yes. I'm sure of it. One other thing. He had a red bandanna sticking out of the front pocket of his pants."

"Did you see anything else?"

"No," she said primly. "It took some time to retrieve my phone and make the call. I'm not as nimble as I used to be, and I've got to be extra careful on the stairs." She turned to Ari and added, "You know, I had that hip surgery last year."

Ari nodded. Mrs. Trotter had regaled Ari with a detailed account of her surgery and the predicating accident on her back steps that had hospitalized her. Ari hoped she wouldn't rehash the incident, as Molly didn't possess Ari's patience to listen to her retired neighbors.

Mr. Carter, who was ninety and lived directly across the street from Ari said, "Ms. Adams, you sure do attract trouble. I've lived here fifty years, and this has always been a quiet street until you moved in."

"Hush, Robert," Mrs. Trotter scolded. "We've had plenty of excitement over the years, or have you forgotten the alcoholic wife-beater, the man with the vicious Doberman, and Mr. Christmas with his two hundred and fifty thousand exterior lights?" The other neighbors mumbled agreement, silencing Mr. Carter.

"What'd they pinch?" asked a short, stocky woman wearing a golf shirt and PING visor. Ari thought her name was Sue, but she wasn't sure.

"Just the usual," Molly lied. "A little jewelry, laptop and tablet. Stuff that can be easily sold."

"Probably for drugs," Mrs. Trotter suggested. She removed her hand from Ari's arm, as if releasing her from the conversation. "I promise I'll keep my eyes peeled, as we used to say."

"I appreciate that. Thank you." She addressed the rest of the group with a sincere smile. "Hopefully nothing like this will happen again. You all have a nice day," she said as she and Molly waved goodbye and scurried to the front porch before Mrs. Trotter could say anything else.

"Do you think Richie's killer is my burglar?" Ari asked.

Molly leaned against a porch post and crossed her arms. "It would be a hell of a coincidence. As I recall, the Westside Homeboys carry red bandannas."

"I don't understand how a gang would be involved in Richie's death, unless he was just collateral damage." She groaned. "I hate that term."

Molly stroked the side of Ari's face. "I know, babe."

Andre strolled out the front door with a uniformed officer. "I'll be in touch," he said to Ari as he left.

Lorraine's ringtone sounded. Ari hoped the Carpenters hadn't complained to Lorraine about the counteroffer. "Hey."

"Bad news, chica."

Here it comes. The Carpenters fired me. "What is it?"

"I'm on my way to the office. The alarm company just called me. We've had a break-in."

"Hold on one second, Lorraine." She said to Molly, "Go stop Andre before he leaves. He needs to head over to Southwest. There's been a break-in."

"Shocker," Molly mumbled, pushing off the porch post and calling to Andre.

"My house was burglarized," she said to Lorraine. "Andre's here, and we're sending him over to the office. I'll follow shortly and Molly can stay here."

"Chica, what's going on?"

"The really short version is that we could be close to solving my brother's murder, and somebody is panicked."

"Ah! Mi dios!" she gasped. "No wonder you've been distracted…"

Lorraine continued to exclaim as Ari watched the exchange between Molly and Andre, both of whom displayed combative body language.

"Did you hear my question, chica?"

"Uh, no," Ari murmured. "Lots going on here."

"I asked if there's anything I can do to help."

She turned away from Molly and Andre and walked to the side of the house. "Actually, there is. What do you know about Westside Homeboys?"

"Personally, not a lot, but it would only take a few phone calls. Why?"

"I'd like to talk to someone who knew what was happening in Glendale around the time Richie was killed. Any chance you might know someone who knows someone?"

"Absolutely, chica. If there's one thing most crews respect it's *la familia*. If there's an old banger who knows what happened, he'll tell us."

CHAPTER TEN

"Meet Kelly Owens," Jack announced as he unceremoniously dropped the picture of the man in plaid on Ari's dining room table.

Molly and Ari closed their laptops and set aside their research on Westside Homeboys. Jack had been gone the rest of the day, and after Ari's anxiety peaked at the three-hour mark, Molly suggested they do some homework on the gang that had ruled the east Glendale territory.

Jack tossed his phone on top of the photo and dropped into a chair, sullen.

"What's wrong?" Ari asked hesitantly. "He's not our guy?"

Jack squeezed her hand. "He still could be Richie's killer, but this is more complicated."

"What's his story?" Molly asked.

"It's interesting," he replied, opening his notepad. "Born March 27, 1971. So he was twenty-one when the shooting happened. He has no arrests in Phoenix, but he's got a long record in Glendale for shoplifting and possession."

"Sounds rather typical," Molly said.

He raised his index finger. "Just wait. About seven months before Richie's murder, in January of '92, Owens was arrested with two other guys, one of whom had ties to Westside Homeboys. Charge was burglary of a house that belonged to a known rival of WHB. All three of them did thirty days. Fast forward to May. Huge bust at Glendale High School thanks to an officer posing as a student. Owens was one of the dealers caught on film selling pot to kids at a track meet."

"Oh, wow," Ari said. "On school grounds. Isn't that automatic jail time?"

"Usually," Jack agreed, "and for everyone else, it was. But not for Kelly Owens."

"He was the informant?" Molly suggested.

Jack smacked the table. "Ding, ding, ding. Exactly."

"Whose informant?" Ari asked hesitantly.

Jack folded his hands and propped his chin on top of them. "Detective Floyd Hubbard questioned Owens. I think Owens worked with him."

"What?" Ari cried. "Dad, why aren't you coming unglued about this? What if Hubbard's been protecting him all this time?" She looked at Molly, who also seemed stunned by the news.

"Hold on, honey," he said. "As much as I dislike Floyd Hubbard and think he's a lazy SOB, I don't think he's been hiding him. In fact, after Richie's death, Kelly Owens disappeared. Vanished. He has no criminal record after August 1992—anywhere. Nothing. No bank account. No income tax filings. No credit. That's why I've been gone so long. Andre and I checked every database we could think of. There was a missing person's report filed by his sister Kacy, two weeks after Richie's murder. She was interviewed by Chris Taglio, but her brother never turned up." He paused and frowned. "Andre said nothing was taken at your office. Just a smashed window?"

She grimaced. "Yeah, the window smasher had the decency to leave Lorraine's office and all the other workspaces alone. He figured out which office was mine and made a cursory run through it. Probably was in and out in less than two minutes."

"At least he's a courteous thief," Jack offered.

"But he's getting desperate," Molly said solemnly. She stared at Ari. "I'm handing off some of my work to my associates and securing *you*." She tapped on her phone, and Ari guessed she was texting Buster, her second in command.

"Good idea," Jack agreed.

"This is unnecessary," Ari scoffed.

"I don't think so," Molly said as she sent the text. "We don't know what's going on here. Whoever got away with Richie's murder is running scared." She pointed at Owens's picture. "If this guy has been hiding in plain sight for the last quarter of a century, not only is he brilliant, but he's going to protect himself. He probably has a life, maybe a good job—and kids." She caressed the back of Ari's neck. "He'll fight to keep his freedom, and we'll fight for justice…for Richie. I'm in this with you and your dad. No arguments."

She smiled at Molly. "Okay." She looked over at her father. "What's next?"

He shook his head and folded his hands. "I'm not making that decision. You are. We're here to support you. I'll guide you through what I've found, work my resources as best I can, and do whatever legwork you give me, but this is your show, honey. I had twenty-five years to catch this guy and I couldn't get the collar. You need to take the lead. You have fresh eyes and you've found the most important clue. I defer to you."

She couldn't hide her surprise. It was the nicest thing he'd ever said to her. She studied the murder wall they'd recreated with Jack's photos and information from the storage shed, rationalizing that Ari's burglar wouldn't make a repeat performance. "I think we need to find out as much as we can about Kelly Owens."

"Agreed," Molly said. "We need to talk to his sister if she's still around."

"She is," Jack said. "And we should go over to Glendale High and get a look at their yearbooks. See if we can learn anything more about his associates. Maybe find some of his teachers who might still be alive."

"I'm disappointed," Ari said. "I showed Chris Taglio a picture of Kelly Owens, and he said he didn't know him. I thought Taglio really wanted to find Richie's killer. But he lied."

"I don't think Chris lied," Jack disagreed. "He probably took Owens's missing person report without Hubbard and never made the connection."

"He told me he liked Wolf Martinez as the doer," Ari said, "until Wolf's alibi checked out."

Jack wagged his finger. "I always suspected he was more involved than he let on."

Molly reached for the file on Wolf. "Are we sure his alibi is solid? If he worked concessions at a drive-in, I'm guessing his boss was a college kid and his colleagues were his friends, people he knew in school. They all might have lied."

"You have a point," Ari said.

Jack nodded. "Let me check that out again."

"Oh, no," Ari groaned.

"What?" Molly asked.

"I'll have to tell Nora Martinez her box of photos was stolen."

Jack's eyes widened. "Do you still have that photo of Elijah and Wolf?"

Ari rummaged through her bag and held up the two photos that fortunately had not been stolen. "Yup. I've got it."

Molly plucked the second photo of Wolf and the teenager from her hand. "What's this?" She studied it closely and said "Ew. Seriously? Wolf Martinez the man dating a teenager?"

Jack motioned for the photo and Ari handed it to him. "Nora Martinez gave this to you?"

"Not intentionally," Ari replied. "I don't think it belonged in that box. And I don't think it has anything to do with our investigation, but it certainly illustrates how creepy her son is."

"And he hangs out with Elijah," Molly added. "See? I don't think Elijah is quite so innocent."

"I disagree," Jack interjected. "Everybody put him through the ringer. That guy is clean." He turned to Ari. "He may have known Wolf, and he may have adopted a 'don't ask, don't tell' notion about the drugs going through the store with Mellow, but I doubt Wolf and Elijah were exchanging money for drugs."

Ari nodded her agreement. She didn't like Elijah for the perp. She folded her hands and asked, "What can you tell us about that night? I've wanted to know for years, but I didn't want to know. Does that make sense?"

"It does," Jack said. "Your mother was in the living room reading and I was in my office working. It was just like any other night. You were watching TV, and we thought Richie was with you since he wasn't in his room."

He paused and she looked down at the table, remembering their fight in her room. They'd been whisper-shouting, Richie begging her to go. He knew if she would accompany him, even though it was after dark, Lucia and Jack would acquiesce. Once he realized he couldn't wear her down, he'd stormed out of the room, and for the first time in his life, he'd snuck out of the house, a fact she didn't know until her mother knocked on her door and woke her up. She'd told Lucia he should be in his room, and her mother told her to go back to sleep. It never occurred to her that Richie would disobey their parents.

"I was lost in my work," Jack continued. "I had no sense of time. Your mother appeared in the doorway, panicked. She said, 'Richie's gone. You've got to go find him right now.' It was after ten thirty. You'd fallen asleep on your bed and ten thirty was late, even for Richie." He looked at Molly. "Richie would stop and talk to people wherever he went. And not like an annoying kid. He would ask people questions and get them to talk about themselves. But those chance meetings always made him late. We had to cruise the neighborhoods more than a few times. We always found him on the sidewalk chatting with someone, usually older neighbors walking their dogs. It was hard to get angry with him because the neighbor would jump in and take the blame. Tell us Richie was just listening to their stories." He smiled and his lip trembled. "I grabbed my keys and was headed out the door when the kitchen phone rang. I'll never forget the look on your mother's face when she picked up that receiver. She had incredible intuition, and there were tears in her eyes already as she answered. Chris Taglio was the one who called. Then she burst into tears. I ran to her and all she could say was 'Richie' and 'Go to the 7-Eleven.'

"I've never driven so fast in my life. When I saw the flashing lights, I knew. I'd forgotten my badge and the officer working the crowd wouldn't let me through. I was screaming and Taglio ran up and escorted me in. He was talking as we walked into the store, but I don't know what he said. I automatically headed toward the candy aisle. That's where he was. I saw his beautiful curly head on that disgusting linoleum floor. All I could think of was how defiled he looked. His pure little self, lying on that filthy, goddamn floor. I leaned against the beer case and cried. Taglio put his hand on my shoulder and suggested I go home. I faced him and shook my head. Then I turned on cop mode. He explained their theory, and he took me out back. When we returned, they'd removed Richie's body, so I figured the coroner had been there before they called me, but they didn't want to move him until I'd had a chance…to see him."

"Did you talk to Elijah Cruz?"

"No, but I saw Hubbard interviewing him outside. Really grilling him. Cruz was pointing to the road and explaining how the perp—Owens—had fled. He looked really shook up. I didn't realize he was the night clerk. I thought he was a witness. He wasn't wearing a uniform and his left cheek was smeared with dirt. He didn't look like he'd been working. Turns out he'd slipped in a mudhole running out to greet the cops."

Ari pulled out the crowd shot she'd shown Chris Taglio. "Do you remember seeing Glenn there? According to Taglio, he was sitting on his bike over here." She pointed to the far left of the photo.

He stared at it, his gaze scanning each of the faces. "I remember watching the crowd, wondering if the killer had returned." He groaned. "I can't remember, honey."

"Did Taglio give you the file? He alluded to me that he had."

"Him and Grady Quigley, but not until several years later. Quigley never left the evidence room and became the grand poohbah of the place. He copied the file and gave me Richie's hat and baseball cards. By then a decade had passed. No one was looking for Richie's killer. No one even remembered his death." Jack met Ari's stare. "Except us."

"How come he didn't give you the unopened trading cards?" Molly asked.

Jack cracked a smile. "Taglio and Quigley are great guys through and through. They kept those cards because they were truly evidence, and that third set of prints needs to be admissible, if there really was a fourth person in that store. Chris always believed—every time I spoke with him—that I'd find Richie's killer. He wanted to make sure we had the ammunition when we needed it."

"You need to talk to Glenn," Molly said to her. "Put that on your to-do list."

"I'll call Scott," she replied, referring to her childhood friend and Glenn's cousin. She reached across the table and squeezed her father's hand, suddenly feeling very close to him. "I don't remember anything from that night. You and Mom didn't tell me anything until the next morning."

He squeezed her hand and pulled away. He stood and faced the gallery of photos on her wall as he spoke. "No. We had to process it first. I came home and your mother was still sitting on the floor underneath the phone. She didn't want to wake you up. We spent most of the night just sitting on the front porch crying."

"I remember the phone kept ringing. It woke me up once or twice."

"That was Taglio. To Hubbard's credit, they started looking for the killer immediately. He kept calling with updates. They rousted a whole bunch of people, including some of the Westside Homeboys. Nobody claimed to know anything." He turned, waving his index finger. "Wait, wait. I remember something. There was a guy…"

Jack dove into a stack of his files he'd retrieved from the storage shed. He slid the bottom folder out and thumbed through the pages. "Here it is." He scanned the interview and nodded. "David Rubens, fifteen. One of the unis talked to him.

He'd just moved to Glendale to live with his aunt after getting expelled from his school in Gilbert. His cousin, the aunt's son, was a Homeboy. Interviewing officer was Tomas Garcia. He conducted the interview in Spanish, which is probably why Rubens opened up more to him. Rubens told him WHB had expanded their business and were offering high-interest loans to gamblers and users. He wondered if the killer was robbing the 7-Eleven to make a payment or pay off his loan."

"Literally robbing Peter for Paul," Molly murmured.

"Not a group of people I'd want to owe," Ari said.

"It says here that Rubens also knew Mellow." Jack's cell rang and he dropped the folder onto the table before excusing himself.

"We need to interview him ASAP, if we can find him," Molly said. "Westside Homeboys was involved in the drug trade, and I'm thinking Mellow is at the center of the 7-Eleven contact."

"I'll text Lorraine. She's reaching out to her more unsavory connections." Molly raised an eyebrow, prompting Ari to add, "Don't worry. I'm not meeting a group of gangbangers in a dark alley."

"I wouldn't put it past you if it meant justice for Richie."

"True," she conceded, "but I reckon most of the Homeboys from the nineties are dead, in jail, born again, or just too old for the game."

"It doesn't mean they're not dangerous." When Ari shrugged, Molly put a hand on her shoulder. "Promise me you won't interview any gang members without me or your dad present."

Ari looked away, one of her "tells" when she was about to lie. Molly brushed her fingers along Ari's jawbone and turned her face so they could stare into each other's eyes. "Promise."

She smirked before she said, "Yes. I promise."

Satisfied, Molly nodded and got up. "I have to meet with Buster and catch him up on all of Bo's expectations."

"Is this guy worth all of the effort?"

"For a million a year, yes. But I've never met anyone so paranoid. He's a huge pain in my ass, but his contract will ensure my employees all have health benefits for another year."

She kissed Ari on the head as Jack reappeared. "I have to go, too. There was another murder downtown." He was part of an ongoing investigation into the murder of homeless men near the arena, and he thought they might get a break soon.

"Go," Ari said. "Both of you. I'll talk to you later."

The front door closed and she wrapped herself in the silence around her. She savored these moments as of late. In the past, helplessness had polluted any vivid memories of Richie, tainting what had been joyous or humorous. *But now there's hope for justice, it's okay to think happy thoughts…*

The brother-sister bickering had dissolved long ago, and she couldn't remember most of the fights or arguments, although her father periodically reminded her that she and Richie had some "humdingers." *I only remember the last one—when I refused to go to the 7-Eleven with him.*

That August night she'd refused him, even after he begged, and she'd completely forgotten why she'd been so stubborn and unwilling to go—until last night. Right before she went to sleep she remembered Floyd Hubbard mentioning Blythe Long, Glenn's cousin, and sister of her best friend Scott. It was because of Blythe that Ari had decided to stay home that night.

That summer ended horribly but it had begun wonderfully. Ari had developed a massive crush on Blythe—her first girl crush and the first step toward acknowledging she was gay. It would still be four years before she looked in the mirror and declared herself a lesbian, but that was the summer of discovery. She'd spent as much time as she could at the Long house. She was there to see Scott, but she often arrived just as Blythe wheeled out the gardening box or pulled up with the groceries. Ari always offered to help, and Blythe cheerily accepted. If she had any idea that Ari was half in love with her, she never let on.

They had several talks about music, college, and women's rights. Blythe possibly viewed herself as an older sister figure to Ari since she was nearly nineteen and Ari was only twelve. Once in a while they talked about boys. Blythe was definitely straight, and Ari played along just so she could keep spending time with her.

During one of their talks, Blythe mentioned she loved the new TV show *In Living Color*. Ari had never seen it and vowed to watch it. She thought it was scheduled on Tuesdays at nine thirty, so when Richie asked to her to go to the store, she said no. He couldn't understand why watching a TV show was so important, and she couldn't explain it to him. He'd snuck out and been murdered, and the irony was that she'd gotten the time and day wrong. The show wasn't even on.

The next morning when she padded out to the living room and saw her parents sobbing, wearing the same clothes they'd worn the night before, everything trivial—her crush on Blythe, TV shows, strawberry ice cream, and the rest of her shallow and superficial pre-teen life—meant nothing. For a long time, everything meant nothing.

She jumped when mariachi music wailed from her purse and groped around for her phone. "Hi, Lorraine."

"Hola, chica. I have a name. Jesus Santiago. He was a Westside Homeboy lieutenant from the late eighties until they sent him away in ninety-six. Apparently, he found God in prison. Now he works at a shelter for battered women. He's the muscle when an alleged batterer comes looking for his woman. Big guy from what I understand. My contact says he's the nicest former gangbanger you'll ever meet."

She glanced at Jesus's picture on her dining room wall. He didn't look so friendly in the nineties. "Well, that's great," Ari said, "but I just promised Molly I wouldn't meet any former gangbangers without backup. What are you doing tomorrow morning?"

CHAPTER ELEVEN

Ari heard the bell tinkle over the front door of Elsie's, a breakfast dive in west Glendale. She peered over her menu and smiled at her co-broker and friend, Lorraine Gonzalez. Lorraine's shiny red-lined lips curled into a broad smile as she sashayed across the diner, her hips trapped in a tight A-line skirt. Her black hair, pulled back tightly and held with a clip, contradicted her sexy look. She carried her designer handbag in the crook of her arm, and she sported a sparkly emerald on the ring finger of her right hand, a gift from her beau, who happened to be their other business partner.

"Hola, chica," she said, sliding into the booth. Her smile faded into a look of concern. "If I'd known you were involved in your brother's case, I would've taken the Carpenters off your hands."

The waitress appeared with Lorraine's customary cup of coffee and engaged her in a minute of small talk. Lorraine made friends everywhere and their company, Southwest Realty, flourished because of her referrals and extensive client base.

Ari counted herself lucky that Lorraine had lured her away from her previous boss, a horrible womanizer. She'd acquired a mentor and a great friend all in one phone call. Lorraine's smile vanished again when Peggy the waitress left.

"I didn't want to give you the Carpenters," Ari said. "You're dealing with those commercial deals. Your plate is full."

She waved a manicured finger. "Doesn't matter, chica. Familia first. Always." She took a sip of coffee and glanced out the front window. "I wanted us to meet before Jesus arrives so you can fill me in."

Ari explained everything from the moment she found Glenn's movie to the break-in at the company. She wrapped up the story with, "I'm so sorry that happened, Lorraine."

"It's not a big deal. They didn't take anything. Trust me," she snorted. "I've been robbed so many times in my life. This was a blip. Nobody got kidnapped or shot, so it was okay."

Ari knew Lorraine had grown up in South Phoenix. Her father and brothers had been gang members, and it was her mother who'd shielded her from the life, wanting something better for her daughter. With the help of the parish priest and the blessing of Lorraine's father, they'd found the money for Lorraine to attend business school.

The front bell jingled again and an enormous bald man entered. Despite his attempt at respectability with his green polo and khakis, he still looked like a gangbanger with a teardrop under his left eye and tattoo sleeves on both arms. He stroked his goatee as his suspicious eyes scanned the diner, alarming customers who stared back at him. Lorraine held up a hand and his face broke into a smile, softening his look. He joined them and Lorraine made introductions as Peggy returned with another cup of coffee and took their orders.

"Thank you for meeting us, Jesus," Lorraine began. "Do you remember the murder?"

He frowned. "Yes." He gazed at Ari with respect and sincerity. "My sincerest condolences."

"Thank you."

"You probably don't know this, but the Homeboys sent flowers to your brother's funeral, anonymously, of course."

"They did?"

"Your brother was known to us."

Her heart raced, and for a moment she feared everything she believed about Richie was untrue. Could the Homeboys have somehow turned her eight-year-old brother into a drug runner? "How?" she managed to ask.

At the sight of her frightened expression, Jesus held up his hand. "Not what you're thinking. Your brother was in class with the little brother of Damian Cortez, the second in command of WHB at the time. The brother's name was Manny. Did you know him?"

"His name sounds familiar. Perhaps he came over to our house?"

"He did. Many times. They were good friends and shared a love of *Star Wars*."

Ari nodded. "I remember now. They would watch the movies on Richie's VHS player, stopping every five minutes to make up their own dialogue and scenes. It was really clever. Geeky, but clever."

Jesus laughed. "Yes. Your brother was Manny's only friend. He had a cleft palate, and many of the children made fun of him, but not your brother. Richie was always kind to him, more than kind," he added. "He stood up for Manny and told the other kids to leave him alone. I heard one time he almost got into a fight with someone who was picking on Manny."

She felt tears pooling in her eyes. "That sounds like him," she whispered. Lorraine squeezed her hand and she smiled.

"Manny was devastated when he was killed," Jesus said. "Damian wanted revenge, but George, the leader of the Homeboys, wouldn't allow it because of your father. Jack Adams was also known to the Homeboys. We didn't respect a lot of cops, but we respected him." He paused and said, "Well, some of us respected him. Many of the boys just thought all cops stunk. But George knew if he went after Richie's killer, Jack would go after him. George couldn't risk it."

"That's understandable. Richie inherited his strong sense of right and wrong from my father."

Peggy appeared with their breakfasts, and once they started eating, Jesus continued. "Well, Damian did some digging. Nothing that got him in trouble with George, but he searched and searched for the killer. He intended just to get a name and location and call it in anonymously to the police."

Ari set down her fork and faced him. "Jesus, I got the impression from my dad that the Homeboys stonewalled the investigation. I don't mean to offend you," she added quickly.

"You're not. It's true that we didn't help your father. There were other activities that prevented us from doing so." He shook his head and sipped his coffee. "Just know there were conflicted emotions. Even gangbangers have a heart."

"What did Damian find?" Lorraine asked.

He wiped his goatee with his napkin and said, "That's the crazy part. He got a name almost immediately, a white guy who ran with us sometimes named Kelly Owens."

"Yes," Ari said, her voice cracking as she held her temper. The Homeboys had known the identity of her brother's killer for the last twenty-five years—and nobody in law enforcement could acquire that information.

She pulled out the still photo and Jesus nodded. "Yeah, that's him."

"We heard he was an informant for Glendale PD."

He shook his head. "That's what they thought. Actually, he was playing both sides. He fed information to the cops, but only what George wanted them to know."

"How does a gringo wind up in Westside Homeboys?" Lorraine asked.

"He wasn't really one of us. After we found out he was an informant, we shook him down once in a while. He was a low-life user and not much else."

"But how did you get his name?" Ari asked. "And where is he now?"

"I really don't remember how we got his name. I'll have to think about that."

"Could you ask Damian?" she pressed.

He frowned. "No, he's gone. Killed in a drive-by ten years ago. As for Kelly, that's the weird part of the story. He disappeared. After that night, nobody could find him. And Damian looked. Even though George had forbidden him from getting revenge, he looked—for Manny's sake. I'm guessing if he'd found him, Owens would've had some kind of accident, nothing that could connect the Homeboys. But as far as I know, he never got the chance."

Ari finished the last bite of her French toast before she asked, "So why do you think he tried to rob the 7-Eleven that night?"

"I think he wanted money to leave town. I heard the police figured out he was playing both sides. The guy wasn't that bright. After he accidentally shot your brother, I'm thinking he ran. Maybe he drove down to Mexico or went to live off the grid. I don't know."

Ari sighed. She hated the idea that Kelly Owens may have gotten away with her brother's murder. "Did he owe the Homeboys any money? I heard they'd branched out to money lending."

"That's true. They offered some loans for a time," he said, air-quoting the word *loans*. That became...problematic, and George wanted out of it."

Lorraine poured them all some more coffee. "Why?"

He folded his hands in front of him and looked around the diner before he whispered, "George got spooked. He'd loaned money to a really bad dude, a guy making meth. He was pretty ruthless and not afraid of George." He paused and glanced at both of them. "The Homeboys never got into meth. Pot, sure, and cocaine. But not meth—because of that dude. He gave George a sample as part of his payment. Sent George on the worst trip ever. He totally freaked. Waved a gun around, completely paranoid. He put the gun to his head and threatened to kill himself."

"Was it bad stuff?" Ari asked.

"It was just bad for *George*. Once he came off the high, he cut all ties with the meth maker, who paid us back in a month. Then he stopped handing out loans. Really freaked him out."

Lorraine dabbed at her lips carefully so as not to smudge her lipstick. "Do you have a name of this meth maker?"

"Only a nickname. El Lobo."

Lorraine looked at Ari. "How's your high school Spanish?"

"Good enough to know lobo translates to wolf."

Ari called her father immediately after Lorraine and Jesus left the diner. Holed up in her SUV, the engine humming and the AC blowing, she started the conversation with, "Did you have any idea your son was connected to Westside Homeboys?"

"What?" Jack cried. "That's impossible."

She reminded him of Manny and told him everything that Jesus had said. All she heard was silence when she finished. "Hello? Are you there, Dad?"

"I'm here. I had no idea. I wonder if Richie knew who Manny's brother was?"

"Probably not. I imagine Damian would've shielded his little brother to some extent, and I'll bet Manny was bright enough to leave a cop's kid out of it."

"I'm surprised Damian let Manny come over and play. Jesus Christ," he proclaimed. "This puts a whole different set of possibilities on the table. Over the years I've tried to talk to some of them, but they always clammed up." He sighed and she could tell he was frustrated. The information should've come to light during the investigation, but they had been missing the key—the identity of the shooter. Only when Ari was able to open the door to Kelly Owens's identity, could the clues fall into place.

"There's more." She told him about El Lobo. "During the nineties, I think Nora Martinez's son Wolf was involved with a meth lab, at least for a while. Can you run him and see what you find?"

"Sure. I'll have some time in a little while. But it's unlikely a high school kid was a meth maker. Maybe the runner, but I'll bet there was an adult or several adults at the top of the food chain."

"Makes sense. How's the case coming?"

"The killer got sloppy and left a thumbprint. We might have an arrest soon." He was whispering, so she guessed there might be a reporter nearby. "What else are you up to today?"

"Scott Long is meeting me for lunch, so between now and then I'm going to sweet talk my way into Glendale High and look at their yearbooks. Hopefully, I can learn some more about Kelly Owens. Did you get me an address for his sister?"

"Crap. Forgot. I'll do it now and text it to you," he said and hung up.

She crossed the train tracks into west Glendale. While the city council had spent money renovating the downtown, the oldest residential area had grown decrepit, housing the community's poorest residents. Phoenix had incentivized its historic neighborhoods with grants and tax breaks. Glendale had not. She turned into Glendale High's visitor lot and parked in front of the modern administration building. The entire school was surrounded by wrought iron, and the front entrance could be locked down in an instant for an emergency. Since school shootings now happened all the time, gaining access to a high school campus was like visiting prison. She drummed the steering wheel and thought of a story that would win her access. She guessed the truth was still the best story she had, and if that didn't work, she'd come back with her dad—the former cop.

Fortunately, that proved unnecessary. The smart school receptionist summoned the School Resource Officer, Don Oswald, who, after hearing she was related to Richie and knew his friend Grady Quigley, escorted her to the school library. He passed her off to Betty Fairchild, the librarian and the most senior employee in the entire district.

Ari surmised she had to be in her seventies, simply because she'd served the school district for nearly fifty years. She wore a mauve blouse and gray slacks, and her white hair formed delicate curls around her head. Her handshake was strong and her gestures forceful. Ari assumed a librarian would be timid and docile, so she wasn't expecting the booming voice that ordered three boys to get back to work. They immediately sank back into their research.

She winked at Ari. "That's how you make it here for fifty years."

"I guess so," Ari said with a smile.

After Officer Oswald excused himself, she led Ari to a workroom. Along the far wall were rows and rows of yearbooks. "Glendale High was founded in nineteen eleven, a year before statehood." She pointed to the upper left corner of the top shelf. "We didn't start a yearbook until the nineteen twenties, and I came on board in nineteen sixty-seven. By then we were missing some books from the thirties and forties, and I went on a mission to recover them from the families of past students. I'm proud to say we now have every yearbook in our possession." She smiled broadly, but her gaze shifted to the research area and the three students, who again were laughing and joking. "Excuse me. I have to deal with some naughtiness."

Ari watched as she charged past the circulation desk toward the students. "I'm glad I'm not them," she murmured. She expected Mrs. Fairchild to scold and yell, but instead, she leaned over the biggest joker and picked up the book he was supposed to be reading. She flipped through some pages and asked him some questions. He nodded and she went to the next student and did the same. When all three were finally back in study mode, she returned.

"So many of these children lack the abilities to be successful and the concentration skills needed for reading. It all changed with computer games."

"I agree."

"Now, who are you looking for?"

"Kelly Owens, probably class of eighty-nine, but—"

"He didn't graduate," Mrs. Fairchild interrupted. "I knew him well. He dropped out at the beginning of his senior year. Had to leave school and go work."

"Wow, I'm impressed. You have a terrific memory."

Mrs. Fairchild gestured to the workroom table and they sat down, the librarian choosing a chair that gave her a clear view of her students, who were still on task. "You always remember the ones who touch your heart in some way."

Ari glanced at the clock. She needed to meet Scott Long in less than an hour. She decided to spend the time talking with Mrs. Fairchild and ask to borrow the yearbooks. "Why do you remember him so clearly?"

Mrs. Fairchild adjusted her glasses and sighed. "For several reasons. First, he was held back twice in elementary school. He came to Glendale High at sixteen. The only freshman who could drive. He could barely read. A nice boy, but lost." She glanced at the table of students, who were whispering, hovering on the edge of inappropriate behavior. "So many of them are lost."

"And the other reasons?"

"He was raising himself for the most part, and his little sister. The mother was a drunk or a drug user. Can't remember which—as if it mattered. He was taller than the other kids in his class so he wasn't bullied, but he didn't have any friends. He was incredibly jumpy and easily spooked if someone yelled at him." She gazed at Ari and said, "The library is a refuge for many students. They come here to escape their teenage years. Some kids come in the first day of freshman year and don't leave until they graduate. The books are their friends."

"I believe it. Was Kelly that way? You said he couldn't read well."

"No, he didn't come to read. At first he just came to sit in the air conditioning, so I put him to work. He liked it. Every day he would shelve books, deliver copies to teachers, update the overdue list...anything I asked. I used to call him my LIT, Librarian-In-Training. He thought that was a great nickname. Once we trusted each other, he let me help him with his reading. Then he started to do better in school. Eventually made the Honor Roll. I was so proud of him and started to imagine he might have a future. He actually had just borrowed his first book for pleasure reading, *The Lord of the Flies*..."

She bit her lip and looked away. "Then he showed up one morning about a week into his senior year, carrying the book. Said he needed to return it. That's when he handed me his withdrawal form. I cried in front of him. Then he cried. He said he had to go to work. He was way past the compulsory education age, so there was nothing anyone could do. I told him to come and visit me from time to time, and he did for a while. And then a year passed, and I realized I hadn't seen him." She gazed at Ari thoughtfully. "I think that was somewhere around the time your brother was killed."

"It was."

Mrs. Fairchild stared at Ari, expecting her to explain.

"What if I were to tell you that Kelly Owens killed my brother—by accident?"

Mrs. Fairchild continued to stare, but she offered no emotion. It was as if she'd turned to stone, except for the gentle rise and fall of her chest. She took a deep breath and exhaled. The air in the room filled with peppermint. "An accident I would believe." She reached for a piece of paper and a pen from the middle of the table. "Do you have the name of the prison where he is incarcerated? I'd like to write to him."

Ari shook her head. "Mrs. Fairchild, no one was ever arrested for my brother's murder. Up until a week ago, we didn't even know Kelly was involved."

"I don't understand."

"We only recently learned Kelly was at the scene. According to the clerk, he came in with a gun to rob the store. My brother came around the corner, and Kelly turned and fired. You mentioned he was easily spooked. That makes sense in this case. The clerk said it was probably just a reflex, but he ran out. No one has seen him since."

Mrs. Fairchild scratched her temple, processing. Ari guessed she'd ruined Mrs. Fairchild's opinion of Kelly Owens. A bell sounded and the three students grabbed their things and left.

As if their departure was a cue, Mrs. Fairchild rose and went to the rows of yearbooks. She pulled three from the shelf and placed them in front of Ari. "I'm trusting you to return these. Please leave your name and phone number on the piece of paper, so I know how to contact you in the event you need a reminder." She paused and swallowed before she said, "I can't imagine what it would be like to lose your brother in such a horrible way, and I hope with all of my being that these books can help you find his killer. But after five decades of working with teenagers, I know with every speck of my being that Kelly Owens would never shoot someone and run away."

CHAPTER TWELVE

Ari pulled up to the valet stand outside Joyride Taco and checked her watch. She was only ten minutes late after becoming tangled in the Glendale High lunch traffic. Mrs. Fairchild might be absolutely positive that Kelly Owens was an upstanding citizen, but Ari doubted the well-meaning librarian could know the other side of her students, the one that appeared after school was over. Ari had known many kids who behaved differently once they were free of the school setting.

She found Scott Long sitting on the patio sipping an iced tea. He wore a dark blue suit, and his brown hair was peppered with smatterings of gray. She knew that as the CEO of a data tech company, he only sported a suit on important meeting days. They were the same age and had been good friends until Richie's death and her family's move to the east valley. They had lost touch but had reconnected a few months prior on Facebook.

He gave her a hug and soon the waitress appeared. Once she left with their orders, Scott threw his hands up and said, "Tell me what happened."

She'd only shared the short version on the phone, so she detailed what she'd found on the movie and some of the evidence that suggested Glenn might be a witness. As she ventured deeper into the story, he looked away, nodding periodically so she knew he was still listening. She asked, "What do you remember about that night?"

He met her gaze. "I've been gathering memories of that time ever since you called. That was such an awful summer," he said.

She knew he was referring to Richie's death and the death of his own mother, which had occurred a few weeks before Richie was killed.

"So much of everything after Mom's death is a blur. The house was insane and sometimes Glenn hopped on a bicycle and rode off when he couldn't stand the screaming anymore. A few times I went with him."

"Was your dad arguing with your siblings?"

Scott nodded and chewed on some ice. "Blythe and Carlin, the twins, were in his face all the time, understandably so. Our mother had just died, and our father was bringing his mistress into the house before Mom's headstone was even finished. I didn't understand what was happening, but my brother and sister were nineteen, so they got it. Carlin got so mad one night he threw a glass against the dining room wall.

"Either no one was talking or everyone was yelling. Not much in between. The day Richie died I was coming home from a sleepover. By then Glenn was driving me crazy, so whenever I had the chance to go somewhere else, I took it. Blythe felt sorry for me so she drove me wherever I wanted to go. When I got home that day, Carlin said something about Glenn getting kicked out of the 7-Eleven." He paused and looked at Ari for confirmation. "Is that right?"

"Yes, the swing shift clerk, the one who was on duty when Richie died, told me that Glenn was there in the afternoon making all kinds of sounds and annoying customers."

Scott rolled his eyes and laughed. "Those sounds were something else."

"Oh, yes. Remember his foghorn?"

"I woke up to that foghorn!"

They both laughed as their taco lunches arrived. Once they'd started eating, Ari asked, "Do you think Glenn understood what it meant to be banished? Do you think he would've snuck into the store, even though he'd been told to stay out?"

"I think he'd have understood. He'd have been uneasy about returning if someone had been harsh with him, which I'm assuming is what happened?"

"Yeah, Elijah, the clerk, admitted he lost his temper."

Scott lathered his taco in hot sauce and said, "But here's the thing. Even if he was uncomfortable and knew he wasn't supposed to go inside, if Richie wanted him to, he might've done it. Maybe not for anyone else, but for Richie…"

"They found a third set of fingerprints on the trading cards Richie was holding when he was shot. My dad wonders if the prints belong to Glenn."

Scott froze, his taco halfway to his lips. "Seriously?"

"You probably don't remember, but Richie used to pick the cards—"

"From the middle of the rack," Scott finished. "I remember that." His eyes narrowed. "You know, there's another possibility. Richie taught Glenn that trick, and more than once I saw Glenn doing the same thing, even when Richie wasn't around. Do you remember that Glenn started his own trading card collection that summer? Sometimes, even when he didn't have any money, he'd stand at the trading card racks and touch the ones in the middle that he wanted to buy. He just touched them, as if he were claiming them for his own."

She leaned back in her chair. "I'd forgotten that. It's weird. I've been rehashing these memories for the last month. You'd think by now I would remember all the little details."

He took a sip of his tea before he said, "Don't be too hard on yourself. We were kids who faced two of the worst childhood traumas. I don't know about you, but I spent a year with a shrink." He snorted and added, "After what you uncovered about my mom's death, and that she was actually murdered, I'm back in therapy."

"Me too," she admitted. "So possibly Glenn touched those same cards earlier in the day, maybe even a different day when he was there without Richie. Of course, those fingerprints could belong to a completely different kid."

Scott shrugged. "But it's just as likely Glenn went in with Richie."

"Well, the timeline gets complicated. He filmed Richie going into the store, but then there's a break. He paused it. So, maybe he pedaled his bike to the front and snuck in to join Richie. Elijah admitted that other people came in after Richie, so it's possible Glenn got by without Elijah noticing him. But then the movie starts again as the killer goes into the store. Glenn was standing in almost exactly the same place as he was when he started filming. So if he went in with Richie, he would've left quickly and returned to the parking lot."

"Maybe he tried to go in and Elijah booted him out again."

"Possibly, but I think Elijah would've remembered that."

"So maybe Glenn just stood there waiting for Richie to come out. Maybe he saw Elijah through the window, thought he'd get in trouble again, so he rode back to the light post? Proximity was also a big thing with Glenn. If he sensed danger or anger, he backed up."

Ari realized they had exhausted the possibilities. She wiped her hands on her napkin and threw it into the empty taco basket. "Do you remember a guy named Wolf? Probably about Blythe's age?"

Scott groaned. "Do I ever. He came around a lot, but not so much that summer. He had it bad for Blythe. One time we were walking down the street, and he pulls up in his car and starts to howl at her, like a wolf."

"Did he think she'd laugh or was he trying to harass her?"

"I don't know. He was creepy. He always looked like he was snarling at me."

"He probably wanted you to disappear so he could be alone with Blythe."

"Like she'd ever give him the time of day." He suddenly sat up straight. "I remember he scared the shit out of Glenn about a week after Glenn arrived. We were hanging out in the front yard, and Wolf's car comes barreling down the road and screeches to a stop in front of the house. It was just me and Glenn, but he was looking around for Blythe. Of course, Blythe had warned me never to tell him she was home. So I told him she was gone, and he looked over at Glenn who had the movie camera against his eye. Wolf started growling and baring his teeth like he was a rabid wolf. Glenn got scared and backed up. He fell over our trash can. I'll admit it was funny and I laughed, but Wolf roared and slapped the steering wheel. He thought it was hilarious." Scott paused and said, "But it reminded me of the night Richie died. When I went to bed, Glenn wasn't home. I told Blythe. She went out looking for him and I went to sleep. When I woke up the next morning, Glenn was in the other bed, and Blythe was sitting next to him. She was asleep sitting up. Later she told me about her evening looking for Glenn. She said she ran into Wolf. She—"

Ari held up a hand. "Hold on. Sorry to interrupt, but your sister saw Wolf Martinez in the neighborhood on the night Richie died?"

He thought carefully before he said, "Yes. I'm sure of it."

"Interesting," she murmured. "We'd heard he was at work. Go on."

"Blythe found Glenn around one a.m., cowering behind the trash can at the side of the house. He was shaking. And you know what else she said? She said something like, 'This is the same way he was when we found Mom.' She connected the two events."

"Like he'd seen something that spooked him?"

"Yeah. Maybe he saw something that scared the crap out of him."

Ari sighed. "I feel so bad for him. He endured two tragedies that summer."

Scott nodded. "He never came back."

"Do you know where he is now?"

Scott shook his head. "I heard he settled in a group home once he turned eighteen, but I've heard nothing since. Mom was the connection to that side of the family. I could ask Carlin. He might remember the city in California where they lived."

"Good." Then Ari laughed. "Uh, I just thought of something else that might be helpful. His last name."

Scott also laughed. "Yeah. I doubt you'll be able to find someone named Cousin Glenn." He looked sheepish. "I don't know his last name. Carlin might remember."

"And he was autistic, right?"

"Yes, highly functioning. I would guess he's in some sort of adult living situation. Unless his mother changed miraculously, she had no idea what to do with him. And now she'd be in her eighties, if she's alive. He'd be thirty-five, I think."

"That sounds right. He was ten and Richie was eight. Did you ever see him after that summer?"

"No. We might've if Mom hadn't died. His mother, my aunt, came for the funeral and took him home. I remember Carlin and I were charged with packing up the boxes of movies he'd made and storing them in the basement. Who would've thought we'd packed away evidence to help solve Richie's murder?"

"I know. Sometimes a case breaks at the oddest time. My dad always talks about patience."

"Well, I think your family has been patient enough. I'll find Glenn's contact information. I'll call the award kids if necessary."

Ari knew he was referencing his stepbrothers, who were referred to as the "award kids" because they'd been named after children's literary awards, Newberry, Caldicott and Nobel. "I'd appreciate it. I'd hate to drag Glenn into this, but he may be an eyewitness and the only person who really knows what happened that night."

They paid the bill and walked out to the valet station, agreeing to meet for lunch more frequently. "Who knows?" Scott joked. "We might become adult friends."

"I'd like that," Ari said, offering him a hug.

His Porsche rolled up, and before he climbed into the driver's seat, he leaned over the top of the car. "One more thing. I distinctly remember Blythe telling me and Glenn to stay away from Wolf. She called him the worst kind of drug dealer."

"What do you think she meant?"

"I'm not sure, but if Blythe said it, then it was true."

Ari would've been content to sit in her car and spend some time noodling—her father's word for thinking—but when the valet handed her the keys, she had no choice but to vacate the lot. Unsure of what to do next, she pulled into a nearby shopping center and parked in an isolated space away from the harried customers, most of whom were well-dressed business people running errands on their lunch hour. Cars jockeyed for the spaces being vacated, and their drivers moved swiftly to the stores and restaurants with great purpose to beat the ticking time clocks back at their respective places of employment.

She should be moving just as fast, but there were several different directions from which to choose. Often when she had too many tasks to perform, she found herself sitting somewhere, thinking about everything else—except those important tasks. It was overwhelming, but she knew the feeling would pass, or more likely, she'd get a sign showing her what to do first.

"And what is it I need to do?" she asked, acknowledging that another good reason for parking away from everyone was to avoid looking like a crazy person talking to herself.

She glanced at the yearbooks on the passenger seat. She needed to go through them to see if she could learn more about Kelly Owens and his associations. She needed to revisit Floyd Hubbard and find out why he didn't tell her Owens was his informant. She needed more information about Wolf, and she probably needed to confront him. If Blythe saw him in the neighborhood, then he left work, at least for a short time. She needed Elijah to explain his relationship with Wolf. When her father texted her the contact info for Owens's sister, she'd pay her a visit. Lorraine said she would find David Rubens, if he was still around. And she'd be making a quick trip to California to see Glenn...

Her three interviews that morning with Jesus, Mrs. Fairchild, and Scott, had created more questions and provided few answers. Jesus and Mrs. Fairchild knew different personas of Kelly Owens. No doubt he'd changed between the time he'd left high school and the night of Richie's murder. During those two years it seemed he'd thrown his lot in with the Westside Homeboys and worked a deal with the cops. If his world had been about to implode, he could've been desperate enough to rob a convenience store and run away with the money.

And there was Wolf. Assuming he was El Lobo, he'd been making meth, most likely with someone older and experienced in the drug trade. While opioids and heroin certainly rivaled meth on today's streets, in the early nineties, meth was a favorite. She thought of one of the picture she'd found: Wolf talking to Elijah in the back of the 7-Eleven. Could Elijah have been a meth user? His life had taken an unexpected turn and he'd stopped going to college. She'd assumed his decisions were tied to Isolde's pregnancy, since he'd defined the life changes as good in the long run. Perhaps he'd been addicted to meth and gone into recovery? If he'd been a client of Wolf's, how would Wolf have reacted to losing a customer, someone who might turn him in to the police?

"And what does any of this have to do with my little brother?" she exclaimed. She shook her head and groaned. She was making this too hard. "Occam's Razor."

The Colbie Caillat song "Brighter than the Sun," filled the cab, and Ari smiled. *Molly.* "Hey, babe."

"What's going on?" Molly asked.

"Thinking about Occam's Razor."

"Hmm. So you think you're making this too complicated?"

"I don't know. All I truly care about is justice for Richie. I'm not out to nail drug dealers or ruin Floyd Hubbard's upcoming retirement by exposing him as a lazy cop. I don't care about anything except solving Richie's murder."

"But you're finding it's entwined with something larger and more complex."

"Apparently." She told Molly about the hole in Wolf Martinez's alibi and Kelly Owens double-crossing the police. "It seems he was feeding the police whatever information the Westside Homeboys wanted him to."

"Was this according to the ex-gangbanger you met this morning?"

"Yeah."

"Well, that might've been his take on the situation, but cops really lean on their informants. I think you just found another plausible explanation for Kelly's disappearance."

"What do you mean?"

"If Hubbard strong-armed Owens, and he revealed some information the Homeboys didn't want leaked—"

"Then the Homeboys might've killed him."

"Correct. I had a few dealings with them when I worked in the gang unit. They didn't always confine their murder and mayhem to their own territory, or even their own city. Allegedly they were responsible for a few drive-bys in the eighties and nineties, but no charges were ever brought against them. And they were known to be ruthless about disloyalty. It's possible Kelly Owens isn't missing. He might be dead."

CHAPTER THIRTEEN

As Ari predicted, she received a sign about what to do next: present the seller's counteroffer to the Carpenters at four o'clock. With only two hours to prepare, she headed back to her office at Southwest Realty and studied the offer. It was fair and she would encourage the Carpenters to accept it, but she had a feeling they would counter again.

She used the time before their arrival to search the Glendale High yearbooks for Kelly Owens. She quickly realized it would be a short search. Each index only listed one page where his face could be found—a class picture page. She opened each book to the respective page and studied the three pictures of Kelly Owens. His frosh picture showed a happy, cherubic kid, still clinging to the edges of pre-teen innocence. By sophomore year, his smile was gone and he looked suspiciously at the camera. His hair was longer and he sported an earring. His junior photo clearly showed the tell-tale signs of drug abuse—gaunt cheeks and longer hair that covered most of his face, except for one eye that was partially closed. He'd arrived at picture day stoned. She set the photo from Glenn's video next to his junior picture.

He'd trimmed his hair, probably to get a job, but his face looked the same.

She decided to skim each book, index be damned. She'd served as an officer in her high school yearbook club, and she knew indexes were rarely accurate. While yearbook staff members attempted to index each student with every photo in which he or she appeared, it was impossible to place names with every person in the crowd shots.

There wasn't a candid photo of Kelly anywhere in his freshman yearbook. She thought she might've found one shot of him sitting at a pep rally in his sophomore yearbook, but she couldn't be sure. Next to him was a dark-haired boy. The possible-Kelly was leaning toward the dark-haired boy, whose face was partially blocked but looked a lot like Wolf Martinez. She hurriedly flipped the pages of his junior yearbook. She almost skipped the club section, since Kelly didn't seem to be a joiner, but she remembered how much more involved she became in school after she knew more people. Richie, of course, would've been in everything his freshman year if he'd lived that long. He would have reveled in the high school experience.

She blinked away the forming tears and dragged her gaze across row after row of smiling students assembled for each club photo. Her gaze halted at a familiar face—Elijah Cruz. His arm was wrapped around the girl next to him, Isolde Tovar. She was looking at the camera, but he was gazing at her—with love. He held something in his hand, a black and white eight by ten head shot of a girl, who looked slightly familiar. "CeCe, his sister," she murmured.

Ari glanced at the club name—MECHA. She remembered the acronym stood for a long Spanish phrase. It was a club to support Hispanic heritage. She read through the names listed under the photo—and found Wolf Martinez. Third row, fifth in. While other students mugged for the camera, he looked straight at the lens, a serious expression on his face.

Two other names in the MECHA group stood out: George Delgado and Damian Cortez. She found the duo in the top row, huddling in the middle. She wondered if their placement was significant. Her yearbook adviser had always told her to study group photos carefully for inappropriate behavior by students, like flipping off the camera. She found something the Glendale High yearbook staff had missed: George Delgado, the leader of Westside Homeboys, flashed a gang sign at waist-level. Only those looking for it would've found it.

She pulled out a piece of paper and started drawing circles, a method Molly had shown her long ago. A separate circle for Elijah, Isolde, Wolf, George, and Damian. They all knew each other in school, and George and Damian were known gangbangers. She knew Elijah and Wolf knew each other from Nora's photo of them meeting at the back door of the 7-Eleven. She imagined Isolde floated on the fringes as Elijah's girlfriend.

She stared at Damian, whose brother Manny had been Richie's friend. Her memory had finally crystallized and she remembered both of them. Damian, driving an old Chevy Nova, had dropped Manny off at the Adams's house several times. He'd waved to her once or twice, and she recalled being creeped out by the way he looked at her. She guessed Blythe Long must have felt the same way when Wolf Martinez gazed at her.

Her phone beeped. A text from her father, providing Kacy Owens's phone number. She composed a quick text to Kelly Owens's sister, introducing herself and asking for a short meeting. "Maybe we'll both have time this evening after I meet with the Carpenters." She hoped by vocalizing the idea it would come true, and the Carpenters wouldn't eat up three more hours of her life with another counteroffer.

She added circles for Kelly Owens and Mellow. Somehow Kelly had involved himself with the Homeboys, but Mellow was a dropout and a few years older than all of them. She'd read Jack's file on him and confirmed he was a California transplant with a juvie record. He'd moved to Tucson a month after Richie's death, once Hubbard and Taglio had cleared him of any wrongdoing. He had an airtight alibi for the night of the murder: he was sitting in St. Joseph's hospital with a sick friend. A year later, after landing in Tucson, he would be caught selling heroin and sent to the Florence Correctional Facility, where he was knifed by an inmate, who happened to be a former Homeboy.

His murder had conveniently occurred just as Jack uncovered another lead. Mellow's assailant had offered no defense as he was already serving a life sentence without parole for murdering a rival gang leader.

She scanned the other five photos on the MECHA club page. One showed Elijah leading a club meeting, and the other four photos were taken at a car wash, the number one moneymaker used by high school clubs in the eighties and nineties, before gas stations worried about liability. One photo showed Isolde in a revealing tank top standing on the corner holding a homemade sign that said, *Support MECHA! Help CeCe.* The picture Elijah had held in the official club photo was glued to Isolde's poster.

Another photo showed the car wash helpers huddled around the poster. It was a much larger and diverse group than just the two-dozen official MECHA members. Ari guessed there were sixty people in the photo, including white students and African-Americans amid the many Hispanic students and a few adults Ari assumed were the sponsors. She squinted to see the faces since the camera was several yards from the group to ensure everyone was included.

"Damn it," she murmured, retrieving her magnifying glass. Slowly she scanned the faces, some of which were easier to see than others. A tumble of blond hair obscured a face Ari was certain belonged to Kelly Owens—and next to him was Wolf Martinez. She rationalized they might not know each other very well, except for the faint "bunny ears" Wolf offered behind Kelly's head. Rarely did anyone do that to a person he or she didn't know. There it was. Wolf and Kelly were friends. Elijah and Wolf knew each other. Kelly knew the Homeboys, but not Elijah and Isolde. Was that possible? How could Elijah not recognize Kelly? Granted, he looked much different than he had during high school. And there was a two-year gap between the time he dropped out and the night of the robbery. She rubbed her temples and groaned. None of this had anything to do with Richie, at least not directly. She closed her eyes and thought again of Occam's Razor just as Molly called.

"Are you still thinking of Occam's Razor?" Molly asked.

Ari chuckled. "Actually, yes. How ironic. I've looked through these yearbooks, and several of the players are connected to the Homeboys. The simplest version of the story is that Kelly Owens robbed the 7-Eleven to get enough money to leave town. I'm guessing the cops were on to him as a two-timing informant. Richie's there and gets shot. Kelly bolts out of the store and disappears."

"That's simple," Molly agreed. "Too simple, really. Do you know how hard it is to erase yourself?"

"That's now. Back in the nineties, before social media and cell phones, it would've been easier. Crossing the border wasn't difficult either. You didn't need a passport to get into Mexico. He could've jumped in a car and driven south, all the way to South America."

"Is that where you think he is?"

"Possibly." She sighed. "Maybe not. I don't know. Hopefully after I talk to his sister, Kacy, I'll have a better hunch. Dad got me her number and I texted her, asking for a meeting. Are you coming to Cali with me to interview Glenn?"

"Definitely. I'll be home later tonight and we can make the arrangements. Did Scott call you with Glenn's address, and perhaps his last name?"

"Not yet. But I've got plenty to follow up on here, and there's still my real job."

"Just be extra careful, babe. Whoever broke into the house and your office might be getting desperate. If the perp is the same one who had Mellow shanked, he's got friends and he'll pull whatever strings are necessary to keep his freedom. Even if he's in South America."

Molly hung up and Ari finished preparing the documents for the Carpenters. Her phone beeped just as a car door shut. She scanned Kacy's message and her eyes widened.

I'd b :) to talk to you. What happened to your bro was horrible! Can u come to Rudy's Cabaret @ 10? Do you want to see the letter I got from Kelly?

Ari offered little resistance to the Carpenters' insistence on another counteroffer. For the moment, she just wanted them gone. Fortunately, they had tickets to the symphony and were in a hurry. Ari had them out of her office in forty minutes.

When Molly heard Ari was venturing to Rudy's Cabaret, a strip club in a sketchy neighborhood, she insisted on accompanying her. And when Ari wanted to make a quick stop at Nora Martinez's house to talk with Wolf, Molly insisted Buster, her second-in-command at Nelson Security, join them. While Ari knew Molly could hold her own in any situation, she was grateful to see Buster, a hulking former bodybuilder and former Marine, at the wheel of a black Escalade when they picked her up at her office.

"You look beat," Molly said as she climbed into the backseat.

Ari nodded. "Have you ever wanted a client to just go away?"

"We get at least one of those every few months," Molly retorted. "There's a reason some people need security."

They all laughed and Buster glanced at her through the rearview mirror. "Hey, Ari. Look at my smile." His front tooth was no longer missing. During his stint with the Marines, a member of the Taliban had smashed him in the face with the butt of his rifle, dislodging his front tooth. Apparently, he had a new implant.

"Looks terrific, Buster."

As they motored back to Glendale, Ari told Molly about the letter Kacy received from Kelly and showed Molly her circle diagram and how the players overlapped. "Most everyone involved was connected to Glendale High, except the day clerk, Mellow."

"And he worked for the Homeboys?"

"Right."

"Any chance he was a conspirator in Richie's death?"

Ari shrugged. "I think anything is possible. I'm wondering if someone has been helping Kelly all these years."

"Doubtful," Molly snorted. "It's so difficult to hide anymore. People can't even keep their own individual identities safe. Now," she said, "if someone were able to ship him off to a relative who lived in parts unknown where he's living a new life, that's a possibility."

"Like witness protection?"

"Sort of."

"You don't think Hubbard set something like that up for him, do you?"

Molly shook her head. She squeezed Ari's arm and said gently, "Honey, I know Richie was the world to you, and I understand that solving his murder will bring you great peace…"

"But?"

Molly seemed to falter as she searched for words. "But it's highly doubtful his killer had the same value to the authorities as Richie had for you. I don't think there's a big conspiracy here, not one involving an eight-year-old. Even most felons have codes when it comes to kids. I think whatever you discover, including the identity of the person who pulled the trigger, will be disappointing and tragic." She paused and added, "Just like it is now. I'm sorry if I sound cold. You know I'd do anything to bring back your brother."

Ari caressed Molly's cheek and gave her a soft kiss. "I know."

They kissed again, their lips yearning for more. Molly pulled away first. She glanced at the back of Buster's bald head, his gaze fixed forward, staring at the thick evening traffic. Then she leaned close to Ari, placing her lips against Ari's ear. "We need some alone time to clear our heads."

Ari grinned. "And you think that will help us solve Richie's murder?"

"It will give us fresh perspective," Molly whispered. "A mind-blowing orgasm can reassemble all of the puzzle pieces to form a new picture."

"I see."

They settled against each other, holding hands for the rest of the drive. Having Molly near her would need to be enough for now.

Buster rolled to a stop in front of the Craftsman bungalow that belonged to Nora Martinez. Lawn lights framed the front yard. The grass was trimmed and a brick path led from the sidewalk to cement steps. A row of rosebushes sat across the front of a wide porch that covered the length of the house. The lights were on in the living room and she saw Nora through an open window, sitting in a rocking chair, knitting.

"I'm surprised she's not out back keeping watch from her perch," Molly cracked.

"It's still chilly. I'm sure it's hard on her," Ari said.

Buster leaned over the front seat. "Where do you want me, Boss?"

"Go around to the back gate. If anyone tries to leave, escort him to the front."

"Got it."

Buster headed to the end of the block, and once they were sure he was in position, they strolled to the impressive wooden front door which included a beautiful lead glass insert of a rose. A piano concerto played inside so Ari rang the bell twice.

"Did you say what Nora or her husband did for a living?"

"No. I just know they were both activists."

Molly pressed the bell again and said, "This is an expensive front door and that landscaping wasn't cheap either. Drug money could buy a lot."

They waited several counts, and when no one answered, Molly knocked. The music's volume decreased, and Ari thought she heard Nora talking to someone. Eventually the front door slowly opened to reveal Nora, who was decked out in a floral printed shirt and matching lounge pants. She looked at Molly quizzically until her gaze traveled to Ari. Then her face brightened.

"Ms. Adams, hello. What a surprise." She opened the door. "Please come in, both of you."

They stepped inside and while Molly introduced herself, Ari glanced toward the archway that led into the kitchen. She remembered the staircase to the upstairs was beside the kitchen, and she distinctly heard footsteps on the second floor despite the competing symphony.

"How can I help you, dear?" She glanced at Ari's empty hands. "You aren't bringing back my pictures?"

"Um, that's an issue we need to discuss. I'm so sorry to tell you this, Nora, but someone broke into my house a few days ago and stole several things related to my investigation, including your box of pictures."

Nora gasped and her hands flew to her face. "It was stolen?"

"I'm afraid so. I've filed a police report."

"Do you think your brother's killer took it?"

"It's possible. Again, I'm very sorry, and I hope you understand. We will do everything we can to get it back."

Nora nodded and motioned for them to sit on the couch. "It's all right. As you know, most of the pictures weren't very good. Can I get you anything to drink?"

"No, thank you," Molly said. "We're actually here to talk to your son. Is he around?"

At the mention of Wolf, Nora's expression turned wary. "No, he went out."

Molly looked confused and pointed up. "Hmm, that's funny. It sounds like somebody's upstairs."

"It does?" She cocked her head upward, but the previous noise had disappeared. "I don't hear anything."

"Maybe I was wrong. Where did your son go?"

A sudden commotion erupted from the kitchen area and Wolf cried, "You're hurting me, man!"

Nora jumped up from her chair as Buster appeared with Wolf. He had one hand at the back of Wolf's neck and his arms pinned behind his back. Nora grabbed a poker from a rack of fireplace supplies and swung it over her head. "You let go of my boy right now, or I'll kick your ass into next Thursday!"

Molly grabbed for the poker but was too slow. Nora brought it down as Buster shot to the right, still holding Wolf. The poker just missed his bicep by inches. Instead it connected with a glass tabletop that instantly shattered. Ari wrapped her hands around the stem of the poker and wrenched it from Nora.

"Stop!" Nora cried. "Who are you people?"

Ari looked at Nora. "We're exactly who we say we are, and we're trying to solve my brother's murder." She pointed at Wolf. "Your son has some valuable information, and we need to talk to

him. Most likely the police are going to question him as well."
She turned to Buster. "Let go of him, please, Buster."

"Only if he promises to sit down like a good boy."

"Get off me, motherfucker!" Wolf spat, still twisting and
trying to escape Buster's steel grip.

Buster pushed him to the couch and stood over him, his
hands on his hips. "Stay there." He turned and pointed at Nora.
"And you, lady, sit down. I ain't never walloped a woman. Don't
be the first."

Ari shivered at his tone, which had the desired effect. Nora
sat on the sofa cushion next to Wolf. Buster motioned to the
two of them and said to Ari, "Your show."

She took the chair opposite mother and son. "I don't
understand what just happened." She looked at Wolf. "Why did
you run away when the doorbell rang?"

He stared at her, his gaze never leaving her face. "I'm not
talking to you."

"Did you kill my brother?"

"What?" Nora shrieked. She pointed a crooked, arthritic
finger at Ari. "He had nothing to do with that."

Wolf remained stoic and didn't answer the question.

"Did you know Kelly Owens?" He crossed his arms and
didn't reply. "Is it true you ran a meth lab during the nineties
and used the 7-Eleven as a distribution point?"

"Of all of the cockamamie stories I've heard in my day,"
Nora interjected, "this is the worst one." She stood. "You can't
come in here and make accusations! I'm calling the real police if
you don't leave right now."

Nora withdrew her phone from a pocket in her lounge pants.
Wolf remained frozen in place, his dark gaze focused on Ari.

"Hold on," Molly said, taking a step toward Nora. "I don't
think you want to do that. If the police arrive, we'll be forced
to explain our suspicions, and that could make life incredibly
difficult for Wolf."

Nora looked to Wolf for guidance. Her hand holding the
phone trembled. Although her resolve had cracked, Wolf's
had not. He remained motionless. He hadn't even blinked. He
wasn't sweating, twitching, or breathing heavily.

"You need to leave," he said softly. "You are no longer welcome here and are now trespassing. Technically, your goon," he said, motioning to Buster, "is already guilty of kidnapping me."

"Bullshit!" Buster shouted.

Wolf ignored Buster, and Molly set her hand on Buster's arm, urging him to remain calm.

"I don't understand why you won't talk to us," Ari said, as Wolf's gaze returned to her. "The only reason someone wouldn't help find a child killer is if he was one himself. And according to the case file, you were at work. You couldn't have killed my brother, at least not directly. Please help us," she begged.

He blinked and she thought for a brief moment her emotional appeal had coaxed him to talk. But when his eyes narrowed to slits and his mouth formed the slightest hint of a smile, she knew he delighted in her pain. Rage emerged. She wanted to leap across the coffee table and plug her thumbs into his eye sockets, blinding him forever. His smile intensified as the corners of his mouth turned up, and she realized her face telegraphed her feelings. And he liked it.

"We're going," Molly announced, her hand cupping Ari's elbow and lifting her from the chair.

Unable to resist, Ari whirled around and said to Wolf, "Just so you know, an eyewitness saw you that night in this neighborhood. You may have been at work, but at some point, you slipped away."

He blinked but his expression remained stony.

They headed outside and the front door slammed ferociously behind them. Ari guessed the beautiful glass rose had cracked as Wolf Martinez got the last word.

Once they were back in the Escalade, Molly said, "Drive to the end of the block and turn the corner so we can see the front of the house and a view of the 7-Eleven. I want to see if either of them leaves."

Buster complied and they sat in the dark, watching and waiting. The street remained quiet. Ari gazed at the abandoned building, the harsh glow of the nearby streetlamp distorting everything it illuminated. This case was like the lamp. Distorted.

Everything was somewhat out of focus due to the two and a half decades of time that had passed.

After five minutes, Molly said, "Let's go. It's nine forty-five."

Buster pulled away and Ari glanced once more at the seedy place that occupied too much space in her brain.

Molly sighed. "What the hell was that? Nora was nothing like you described."

"I know," Ari agreed. "She's an ex-hippie. A pacifist, I thought. She was a kind, old lady who wanted to help. Thought it was horrible for a parent to lose a child."

Molly wagged her finger. "And that was the issue. Tonight wasn't about your brother. It was about her *son*." She clapped Buster on the shoulder. "Glad you got quick reflexes."

"Me too, Boss."

Ari replayed the moment when Nora had grabbed the poker. There hadn't been a second of hesitancy. No warning. "I can't believe she went after you like that, Buster."

"I can," he replied.

She remembered some of the stories he'd told about fighting in Afghanistan and Iraq. An old lady with a poker was nothing.

Molly put her arm around Ari. "We threatened her child. We learned something important tonight. Nora Martinez will do anything to protect her son."

"Do you think she helped with the meth dealing?" Ari asked incredulously.

Molly gazed out the window. "No, I don't. But she was probably complicit. I'm sure she turned a blind eye if she found out."

Ari shook her head. "I think it's the opposite. If she found out, I bet she did everything she could to keep him out of jail, including lying to the police, destroying the product, threatening the dealers—whatever. I know it sounds crazy, but if killing Richie saved Wolf from jail, I think she would've done it."

"I agree," Buster said.

Molly looked at her thoughtfully. "Good point. I'd love to know what Wolf's father did for a living."

"I'll find out," Ari said.

Molly pulled her closer. "I know we've been talking about Nora's surprising behavior, but Wolf's reactions made me sick to my stomach. I certainly understand why Hubbard and Taglio liked him for the doer. I can't believe he smiled when you begged for his help."

"I can, Boss," Buster said. "I watched a Taliban soldier laugh before he beheaded a crying old woman."

"That's horrible, Buster," Ari cried.

They pulled up to a light and Buster turned to look at her. "Yes, it is horrible. She was an innocent civilian. But he was not. That's why I shot him between the eyes right after it happened. He was dead before her head stopped rolling."

CHAPTER FOURTEEN

Kacy said she'd meet them at the front door promptly at ten p.m. She had a strict twenty-minute break, so they needed to be on time or pick another day. Buster eased the Escalade into the crowded parking lot at precisely nine fifty-nine.

"Stay behind us," Molly instructed Buster. "I don't want her spooked."

"Got it, boss."

As they approached the front door, they noticed a blonde wearing a skintight, lime jumpsuit. Her enormous breasts, dotted with glittery sequins, spilled into the V created by her only partially zipped front. Her heavy makeup hid some of the lines forming around her mouth, and her blue lipstick created a focus point for her face. She was talking with one of the bouncers, but their conversation ceased as she looked them up and down, her fake eyelashes batting incessantly. "Which one of you is Ari?" she asked.

"I'm Ari. This is my partner, Molly. Thanks for talking with us."

"Sure."

She waved at the bouncer and strolled to the back of the building near the delivery entrance. She said over her shoulder, "Like I told you on the text, I only get twenty minutes so we gotta talk fast." Once they were ensconced in the shadows, she pulled a piece of lined notebook paper from her back pocket and unfolded it. "I assumed he was dead until I got this letter about fifteen years ago. It was right around the ten-year anniversary of his disappearance. I took it in to that cop who talked to me the first time, and he made a copy of it, but nothing happened."

"They probably thought it closed the missing person case," Molly said.

Ari struggled to see the faint blue ballpoint print against ten years of creases. He'd only written four lines: *Hey squirt! Just wanted you to know I'm ok. Needed to get out, but I'm sorry I left you and Mom in a jam. I'll send money real soon. Maybe I'll catch you later.* He'd signed it with just a K.

Ari noticed a smudge around "sorry," and she realized it had been written with an erasable ballpoint pen. She hadn't owned one of those in years.

"Are you sure that's his handwriting?" Molly asked.

She nodded. "He always called me squirt, and I recognized the way he wrote his 'K.' He had a loop on it like a girl, and I always teased him."

"How much older is he then you?"

"Three years."

"I understand your mother passed," Ari said gently. "How did she respond to the letter?"

Kacy reached for a cigarette in her jumpsuit pocket and lit up. After she'd taken a drag she said, "Momma didn't care. She was off in her own world. Kelly and I raised ourselves, or really, he took care of me. He was a good brother." She stared at the decrepit stucco building and said, "I'm glad he's not here to see this." She said it as a fact, but her voice quaked. It was a difficult claim to make when the truth was her brother had abandoned her.

"Has he ever tried to contact you again?" Molly asked.

"No. But you know what's weird? There's been times when I'll be standing in the checkout line at the grocery store and I think I see him in the next line. Or I'll hear somebody talking on the bus and it sounds like him." She glanced at Ari. "Is that stupid?"

"Not at all," Ari said. "It happens to me, too."

"One time I was at a concert out at Desert Sky Pavilion. It was all heavy metal bands, Kelly's favorite. I came out of a Port-A-Potty, and I saw this guy crossing the grass, headed toward the stage. His hair was long and he had a beard. I tried to follow him but I lost him. I even started shouting, 'Kelly!' All these other people looked at me funny but I didn't care. I missed a lot of the show, running up to people and asking if they'd seen him. I carry some old photos of him on my phone," she added. "A few people sent me off in different directions, but I never found him. It probably wasn't him at all."

"Tell us about his friends," Molly said. "Who did he run with?"

"Nobody, really. He was basically a loner. He tried to fit in and gave into peer pressure."

"Can you give us an example?" Ari asked.

"Yeah. He bragged the Westside Homeboys made him an honorary member. When I told him that sounded ridiculous, he pulled out a red bandanna from his back pocket and pointed at a dark smudge. He said it was blood and George, the leader, gave the bandanna to him." She twirled a finger in the air. "Big whoop-di-do, you know? They weren't his friends. They used him."

"Did you know he was acting as an informant for the police?"

She blinked. "What? Are you serious?"

Ari nodded. "When he got busted for selling at the track meet, the Glendale police gave him a choice—go to jail or be an informant. He chose the latter."

Kacy looked away, biting her lip. "He must've done that for me. Man, I never would've thought he'd have the guts."

"Explain that?" Molly asked.

She offered a shrug and dropped her cigarette to the ground. "Like I said. Kelly was a loner. People made him really nervous. Everything made him nervous," she said. "Our mother used to call him kitty cat because he'd jump if there was a loud noise or if she raised her voice at him. I can't imagine him telling the cops about the Homeboys, knowing they'd kill him if they found out."

Ari glanced at Molly before she added, "It's interesting you mention these qualities, because the Homeboys did find out."

Kacy's eyes widened. "Did they kill him? Is that why he disappeared?" She frowned. "But he sent me the letter. If he was dead, how could he write to me?"

"We don't know," Molly said. "It sounds like Kelly struggled to stand up to people, so it's not surprising that he tried to please the cops and the Homeboys."

"What do you remember about the days leading up to his disappearance?" Ari asked.

She shrugged. "I've forgotten a lot of it, but it was in my statement. Kelly had just landed a job with a brake place. He bragged about all the money he was going to make. Get us out of the shithole we lived in. I was nearly eighteen, and I wanted to believe him. Mom was no good to us. She hardly worked and whatever she made went up her nose or in her arm if she had enough."

"Why would he think he'd make a lot of money working for a brake place?" Ari pressed.

She raised a sculpted eyebrow. "That doesn't make a lot of sense, does it?" She blew a stream of smoke into the dark night and added, "I knew he'd been dealing drugs. If he hadn't, I think we would've starved. But it was never big-time. He just sold weed to high school kids."

"Is there a possibility he planned to go deeper into the drug business?" Molly asked.

She reacted as if no one had ever asked her that question. Then she shrugged. "I suppose."

Ari checked her watch. They still had a few more minutes. "Did you know Elijah, Jesus, Damian, George, Wolf—"

"I know—knew—Wolf. I don't know the other people you said, but Wolf and Kelly were tight all through school, at least until Kelly dropped out. He could be a scary dude."

"How?"

"Just the way he looked at me. Like a wolf. Like he was going to eat me. He asked me out once." She laughed. "Kelly came unglued and told him I was off-limits. I was starting to fill out. Well…" She paused. "I was maturing, except for these babies." She cupped her breasts lovingly. "These cost me a small fortune but were well worth it." She put her index finger under her chin. "Come to think of it, Wolf was the first person who told me I needed to get a boob job. Kelly heard him say it and socked him in the jaw."

"Sounds like Kelly defended you," Ari said.

She glared at Ari. "Like I said, he was a good brother."

"What if I told you that he shot my brother?"

Despite the acres of makeup holding her face together, her expression fell, and she aged immediately, the hard road of her life literally written on her face. "That can't be," she whispered.

Ari withdrew the still photo from her purse and handed it to her. "Is this him?"

She took a look and closed her eyes, her shoulders heaving forward. She couldn't speak. She just shook her head.

"A boy made a movie outside the 7-Eleven, just a few minutes before my brother was shot. Your brother was the last one to go inside before Richie was murdered. And the clerk, Elijah, has already identified Kelly as the shooter."

Kacy leaned against the wall, as if she might faint.

"Are you okay?" Molly asked.

"Of course I'm not okay," she spat. "You tell me the person I loved more than anyone else in the world, killed a little kid and left town, not bothering to tell me goodbye. He lets me think he's dead for a decade before he bothers to let me know he's fine." She shook her head fiercely. "I am definitely not okay!" She paced in her fury and suddenly stopped. "Wait, where in the hell would he get a gun?"

"Probably off the street," Molly suggested. "Or one of the Homeboys could've given it to him."

She shook her head. "No, that doesn't make sense."

"Why, Kacy?" Ari asked gently.

"Kelly despised guns. They made a loud noise." She rolled her eyes. "Sorry, I forgot an important fact. Kelly had a hearing problem. Whenever there was a loud noise, it was twice as loud to him. He hated balloons because he worried they would pop." She chuckled and added, "The only kid who didn't want balloons at his birthday parties." She looked from Ari to Molly. "What you're saying about Kelly firing a gun doesn't add up to me. Are you sure he's the killer?"

"Not a hundred percent," Ari admitted.

"You know, Kacy, he may have carried a gun just because the Homeboys wanted him to," Molly said. "The clerk at the store believes Kelly shot Ari's brother by accident, like a reflex."

"You're sure he talked about coming into some big money?" Ari pressed.

"Yeah, I remember that." She pulled out her phone and checked the time. "I've got to get back. This whole thing is so weird and horrible." She offered a sad smile to Ari. "I'm so sorry about your brother. I can relate." She took Ari's card and headed through the back door of the club.

Molly slung her arm around Ari's shoulder as they slowly walked to the front. "What's eating at you?"

"The part about the money."

"Me too."

"If he really was coming into money to help the family, then that blows apart the theory that he was leaving town."

"Not necessarily," Molly said. She stopped walking and put her hands on her hips. "What if both were true? Maybe he was going to rob the 7-Eleven and send some of the money to Kacy once he got settled?"

Ari groaned. "Well, if he was a devoted brother and intended to send money to her, the fact that she hasn't received any correspondence or money from him supports the idea that he's dead."

"Could be."

They found Buster chatting with the bouncer. They waved goodbye, and once they'd settled into the Escalade, he said, "Boss, I got something from that guy, Houdini."

"The bouncer's name was Houdini?" Molly asked.

Buster grinned. "Yeah, he makes all the low-life customers disappear." They all laughed and Buster steered the Escalade behind the club, near the location where Molly and Ari had met Kacy. "I want to check something," he said, "back here where the employees park."

They crawled past a row of cars that ran the continuum of wealth: beat-up jalopies like an old Datsun B210, nondescript sedans, and beautiful luxury cars, including a sleek, silver Lexus and a sporty yellow Corvette. Buster pulled up behind the Corvette.

"This is what I wanted to see," he said, pointing at the Corvette.

Ari glanced at the vanity license plate, *MZ TNT*. "What does that mean?"

Molly rolled down her window to get a better look. "I'm guessing it's a reference to fireworks?"

"Yeah, Boss. According to Houdini, the lady can blow your world. You know…" Buster shifted uncomfortably in his seat and coughed.

Ari threw him a lifeline. "We get it, Buster. Who does this car belong to?"

"Kacy."

Molly whipped her head around. "Kacy Owens owns this car?"

"Yup. According to Houdini, Kacy's got money."

"From where?" Ari asked.

"Nobody's really sure. A lot of her coworkers kid her about it, asking her if she's got a sugar daddy, or if she's working as a high-priced call girl. She just laughs 'em off and never answers the question."

Molly rolled up her window. "Does Houdini have a theory? When we drove up, he and Kacy seemed like best friends."

"They're friends with benefits. Neither wants a relationship, and he knows she has other lovers, but they're close. He's asked her about the money and why she's working at a titty bar, but all she's told him is that she's not doing anything illegal. He believes her."

"Maybe Kelly is sending her money, just like it said in the note," Ari wondered.

"That's what I'm thinking," Molly agreed.

"Could be," Buster said. "Houdini said one time she slipped and almost gave him a name. She'd been saying 'he,' so Houdini knows it's a dude."

Molly leaned forward. "Did you ask him about the conversation leading up to the slip?"

"I did. He couldn't remember exactly what they'd been talking about, but a lot of times they talk about their childhood and growing up, so if she'd been talking about her brother, it would make sense." He pulled away from the Corvette and headed toward the road. "One other thing that's important. A couple of times she's been late to work because she had to stop and meet someone. The manager is super uptight about clocking in for your shift. One of those times was a few months ago. She was so late that she'd already been called to the stage. She ran in, flung her purse at Houdini, and booked it to the time clock while taking off her clothes. The snap on the purse popped open and he saw inside."

"What did he see?" Ari asked.

"A big wad of cash."

Ari glanced at Molly. "We need to take a much closer look at Kacy Owens. I thought she looked genuinely upset by our visit, but maybe she's a terrific actress."

"Yeah. Maybe she's been hiding Kelly all these years."

CHAPTER FIFTEEN

"We have a sale!" Ari couldn't suppress her joy, but she quickly apologized to Lorraine for shouting into the phone.

"No worries, Chica. If I were you, I'd be cracking open a bottle of champagne. Since it's eight a.m., have a mimosa," she said, laughing. "Changing topics. I hope you don't mind, but I did a little detective work of my own."

"Oh?"

"Yes. I called Rachelle Billups, the agent listing the old 7-Eleven site, and she gave me an earful."

"Really? What did she say?"

"She's the sixth agent who's tried to sell it. It seems to be a white elephant nobody wants, but this agent told me, in the strictest of confidence, that she's beginning to think the owner really doesn't want it to sell."

"Who's the owner?"

"That's interesting. The owner is the Krist family. You know them?"

"Weren't they involved in several civil lawsuits? And there was talk of racketeering charges?"

"Uh-huh. There was talk, but nothing came of it. This property is just a blip on their financial spreadsheet, but what I learned on my own is that they have a quiet arrangement with the Cortez family."

"Wait, Cortez as in Damian Cortez?"

"Close but not quite," Lorraine corrected. "Cortez as in Manny Cortez, your brother's friend. Remember, Damian is dead, but Manny took over the family's business. They own a huge event empire called Celebración. It's patronized by most of the Hispanic community in Maricopa County. They do wedding dresses, quinceañeras, catering, music, the works." Lorraine paused and whispered, "I've heard, though, that it's also a front for money laundering. Profits of which come from drug pushing. That's just a rumor, but, you told me that some of the Glendale neighbors still believe drugs are being sold around that building, right?"

Ari thought of Nora's comments and the guy bent over the garbage can. "Yeah, the woman I talked to says it's still happening. So, you're suggesting that nobody's trying very hard to sell the land."

"Exactly. It sits on the edge of a historic neighborhood that has strict codes. I think potential buyers are being scared off, and frankly, it's not in a good location anyway. According to Rachelle, there have been few bites."

"Why is it even on the market then?"

"Rachelle thinks the Krists are just trying to look like they're doing something to keep the historical society off their back."

"And the Cortez family is fine with that, so the Krist family is fine with that as well."

"It seems that way."

Ari wondered if any of the present-day drug activity had a connection to the past. Were any of the same players still involved? She knew Glendale was a generational community, and sons and daughters who grew up there tended to stay and raise their own families, sometimes in the same houses, sending their kids to the same schools. "What do you know about Manny Cortez? Have you met him?"

"Once, actually. He's very personable. I'm not sure whether he handles the ruthless side of *la familia*, but I liked him."

"Do you think he'd talk to me?"

"Probably. I'll make some calls."

They said their goodbyes as Lorraine dashed into a client meeting.

Ari set aside thoughts of Richie for the moment, closed her eyes and said a little prayer, hoping the rest of the Carpenters' purchase went smoothly. Real estate deals could fall apart for a variety of reasons, and they were still a long way from a closing and receiving the keys.

And the timing couldn't be better. They were entering the inspection period, which meant Ari's responsibilities would lessen for the moment, and she and Molly could take a quick day trip to California and visit Glenn Vershaw, also known as Cousin Glenn.

Scott had sent her a text the night before with Glenn's last name and location. He was living in the Compass Residential Group Center in Riverside, California. His caretaker was a man named Moreno, and Scott promised to make an introductory call. Since it was after eleven, Ari dialed the center's number, hoping Scott had contacted someone. Fifteen minutes later, after she'd been transferred four times, explained who she was to three different administrators, and got hung up on twice, she finally reached Moreno.

She started to explain once more and he interrupted. "I know who you are." It took her a moment to understand him through his thick Mexican accent. "Glenn has mentioned you many times."

"Oh, really. I'm surprised. I only knew him—"

"For one summer."

"Right. I can't believe he remembers me."

"He does," Moreno said flatly.

When she was sure he wasn't going to offer any other information, she said, "My friend and I were hoping to come by tomorrow for a short visit. Would that be possible?" He didn't reply, and she finally said, "Mr. Moreno?"

"I'm not sure it's a good idea, but I'm not sure it's a bad idea."

"I don't understand."

"Glenn rarely speaks. Did he ever speak as a child?"

"He never talked to me. He was always holding a movie camera up to his face. He'd wave usually, or he'd sometimes point at things. Sometimes we heard him laugh or growl when he was angry, but I never heard him talk. My brother Richie might've had some conversations with him. Has Glenn mentioned what happened the night Richie died?"

"In his own way. When he came to Compass, he brought a photo with him. It was a picture of him as a boy with two other boys and a tall girl. The four of them were standing in front of a large rosebush. On the back, in a woman's handwriting, were the names Scott, Richie and Ari."

She vaguely remembered the photo. Blythe had taken it after an hour of cajoling Glenn to be in it—without the video camera pressed against his eye. He finally complied, but when Blythe instructed them to say cheese, Glenn barked like a dog. The final result showed three smiling kids and one with his mouth wide open, shaped like an O. "What does he say about the photo?"

"Well…he names the four of you, and then he points to the boy I assume is your brother, and says, 'dead.' Over and over. If I don't take the picture from him, he'll poke it incessantly and eventually melt down."

"How does he respond when you take it away?"

"He's still agitated but only for a few more minutes. It can take an entire day for him to recover after a meltdown."

"When he has one, does he say anything else other than 'dead'?"

"Sometimes, but it's random words. Some cause greater anxiety than others. That's what I meant when I said your visit might be a good idea and a bad idea. Yes, he might have some answers to solve your brother's case, but those answers will probably trigger an emotional meltdown."

"I understand, and I feel bad about upsetting him, but I think it's a price worth paying if he can help find my brother's killer. Don't you agree?"

While Moreno didn't answer her question directly, he scheduled the visit. No doubt he'd realized she would use whatever leverage was necessary to access Glenn's memories, including a subpoena to interview him and a warrant to search his belongings. She didn't relish the idea of taking Glenn to the breaking point, but it might be the only way to unlock his brain.

And then there was the movie. Prior to handing it over to the Glendale Police, her father had made a DVD, and Ari uploaded the contents to her iPad. She planned to show it to Glenn, but decided not to mention that fact to Moreno, rationalizing that forgiveness really would be preferable to permission. If Glenn flipped out over a picture, seeing Richie alive in a movie could possibly send him on a psychological bender. Still, whatever guilt she felt about Glenn's pain, vanished when she thought of Richie's life, extinguished before he could grow up to be a man.

She'd agreed to meet her father for a late picnic lunch. Afterward they would pay Floyd Hubbard a visit. Jack wanted to confront Hubbard, but Ari insisted on accompanying him, lest the meeting turn into a brawl. Hubbard had lied to them, claiming he didn't know Kelly Owens. While she agreed with her father that Hubbard was the worst kind of cop, she felt they still needed him to fill in pieces of the puzzle they didn't understand.

She pulled into the main parking lot of Encanto Park, one of the Adams family's favorite spots. They'd enjoyed countless picnics, canoe and paddle boat rides in the lagoon, and trips to Kiddieland, a junior amusement park that sat at the edge of the property. She crossed the bridge, heading toward the duck pond. She remembered the time she and Richie had capsized their canoe. They had run aground, facing the wrong way. They couldn't agree on what to do, so they both paddled fervently, spinning in a circle, shouting at each other, until they turned over. It had been a long, cold drive home, and their parents had used the incident and the car ride to lecture them on teamwork.

She found her father sitting at a picnic table along the shore. He was fiddling with his phone, and even though he still looked dashing, he also looked tired. His shoulders were hunched, and his chin was propped on the upturned palm of his left hand, as if he was trying not to fall asleep. He'd set out a hoagie, drink, and chips from McGurkees, one of Phoenix's oldest sandwich shops. "Is that what I think it is?" she asked.

He nodded. "Your favorite, the hero."

"Heaven," she said, unwrapping the sandwich and breathing in the wonderful spicy smell of Italian salami. While she continued to gorge herself on the rare treat, he looked around, barely eating his own hero. "What's wrong?" she asked between bites.

"Stuck in memories," he replied sheepishly. "Sorry."

"Don't be. I was just thinking of the time we capsized the canoe."

He cracked a half-hearted smile and chuckled. "That was quite the day."

"What are you thinking about?" she asked hesitantly. She wasn't sure she wanted to know, as it could set off another crying spell—for both of them. She'd cried more in the last few weeks than she had in years.

"I was thinking about the time we came to this very spot, and your mother had made an apple pie. Remember what happened?"

Ari laughed and said, "We were playing Frisbee and didn't notice the squirrel that jumped on the table and nibbled on the crust."

"It wasn't just the crust. He'd picked up one of the apple chunks between his little paws."

"Richie saw him first and yelled, but when Mom saw him, she chucked the Frisbee at him and knocked him and the pie off the table. She always had a great arm," he said proudly. He gazed toward the lagoon. "So many memories."

"Yeah."

He coughed and said, "So what have you learned?"

She apprised him of her conversations with Kacy Owens, Lorraine's information about the 7-Eleven site, and her upcoming visit with Glenn. He couldn't maintain eye contact, and she wondered if he was really paying attention or still lost in the memories of the park. She finished and returned to her sandwich. For a long while they ate in silence, listening to the quacking ducks and geese and the buzz of a distant lawnmower.

"Dad?"

He shook his head, as if he couldn't slough off whatever was bothering him. He dropped his half-eaten sandwich and covered his face with his hands. She touched his forearm. "Hey, it's okay. This is all overwhelming."

He rubbed his eyes and took her hand. He suddenly looked older, and she finally saw the crow's feet at the corners of his eyes and the creases in his forehead. She wondered why she hadn't noticed his aging before. *He was always perpetually young, until Richie died.*

"I don't expect you to fully understand now, but when you get older… When more of your life is behind you than in front of you, you have a different perspective on mistakes and loss. You see the connectivity of everything." He looked at her and said, "I fucked up with all three of you."

She didn't object. In her case it was absolutely true. When she was twenty-one, he'd banished her from the house for being gay. Lucia had left him as a result. Ari knew he also felt responsible for Richie's death. She allowed him his feelings and merely squeezed his hand to reply.

"If I could go back," he started, "I'd do so much differently. I know you understand how sorry I am for being such an asshole when you came out. Did you know I joined PFLAG?"

She blinked. "No, I didn't."

He nodded and wiped his face with his napkin. "I've actually met a lot of fathers for a cup of coffee and a conversation when they discover their child is gay."

"And what do you tell them?"

"Mainly I just listen, but if one of them asks, I say don't do I what I did."

She abandoned her sandwich and joined him on the other side of the table. She hugged him and he started to cry. A straight couple walking a little mutt offered a concerned glance but kept going.

She pulled him tighter and he whispered, "I miss Richie and your mom every day."

"I do too."

He pulled away, his expression earnest. "Do you know why I pushed you away?"

"I'd always assumed it was because you were homophobic."

He shook his head. "I knew gay cops. Lesbian detectives. Hell, I promoted them."

Now she was genuinely curious. "I'd always thought you wanted me to be Richie, and I couldn't live up to him. He was such a good person."

He patted her shoulder. "You are too, honey."

"But I'm not Richie."

"No," he said firmly. "And that's good. That's wonderful."

"Then, I don't understand. Why did you hate me?"

"I didn't hate you," he said, but his tone was sharp. He looked away and said, "But you messed up my plan."

"What?"

He rubbed his hands together and seemed more uncomfortable than she could ever remember. "Keep in mind that what I'm telling you now is the result of several years of therapy."

"You went to therapy?" She knew she sounded shocked so she added, "I mean, that's great. When was that?"

"About two years after you came out, and then again later when I realized I wasn't as okay with our relationship as I thought. Anyway, the therapist helped me see that we can't force our lives into a certain order. That might sound obvious, but I'm an order kinda guy."

"I know," she deadpanned. "I get it from you."

"Richie dying. Not in the plan. Your mother's cancer. Not in the plan." He offered a half-smile and stroked her cheek. "I put all my hope for order on you. I never suspected you were gay. Yeah, you didn't want to play dress up or have parties with your dolls, but you didn't want a boy's haircut or trucks for Christmas. You were more... What's that word?"

"Androgynous."

"Yeah. I always pictured you in the white wedding dress, a handsome guy on your arm. Having kids. I needed you to be the order in my life, and when you weren't... Your mom warned me not to pigeonhole you. I think that was her way of softening the blow once you finally told me." He checked her expression. "When did you tell her?"

"About four years after Richie died. When she went into remission."

He gazed upward, and she guessed he was working the timeline. "Makes sense."

It would be another few years after she told Lucia that she would attempt to tell her father and their lives fell apart. He exhaled and propped his chin on his clasped hands, thinking.

"Dad, can I ask you something about Mom?"

His gaze flicked toward her. "Sure, honey."

"Did you and Mom get remarried?"

He sat up—and she had her answer. His look of surprise didn't convey shock about the question, but rather, shock that she'd figured it out. "How did you know?"

"Well," she sighed. "Since we're talking about therapists... My therapist figured it out."

"What?"

She shook her head. She wasn't explaining this well. "While I was looking into the death of Scott Long's mother, I met some people who knew you and Mom. They'd seen you together long after I thought you were apart. It didn't fit with the timeline of your divorce."

His expression sobered. "Honey—"

"Dad, I'm not mad, well, at least, not anymore. Now that I've had time to think about it and work through it with Dr. Yee, I understand. You always loved Mom. She always loved you. Her medical bills would've destroyed us both."

He returned to rubbing his hands and looking at the ground. "At first it was just for the insurance. We both told ourselves it wasn't about love." He couldn't help but look up and smile. "But it was always about love. Sorry if that sounds sappy. And I'm sorry we kept it from you. If it makes you feel any better, I wanted to tell you, but your mother convinced me it wasn't the right time. You wouldn't have understood."

Her mother wanted to hide it from her. She let that fact swirl in her brain, toppling over what was left of her understanding of her parents. "So the day Mom died...when hospice called me..." She looked at him, tears streaming down his face. "You couldn't be there with her. Otherwise, you would've had to tell me the truth."

He nodded and wiped a hand across his face. "Actually, I came here after the nurse called. She knew you weren't aware that your mom and I were back together. So you went to her and I parked myself here—until the nurse called me a few hours later and told me she was gone."

"I'm so sorry."

"Don't be."

She knew she was trembling as guilt roiled through her.

"Honey, are you okay?"

"No. There's something else I've never told you. About the night Richie died—"

"He asked you to go with him before he snuck out." Her jaw dropped. His expression softened. "Your Mom overheard the two of you arguing." He pulled her close and kissed the top of her head. "You okay?"

"Yeah. I need to think about this, though. Can we talk about it some more, maybe after all of this with Richie is over?"

"We can talk about anything you want."

She nodded and they got up and collected their trash. They walked back to the parking lot, and she saw that he'd parked next to her.

"Do you know how to get to Hubbard's house?" he asked.

"I do. Are you sure about confronting him at his house on his day off?"

He crossed his arms. "I am. We're going to corner him. Quite possibly he'll slam the door in our faces, but I think he suspects this is coming. Maybe he'll be more inclined to talk with us on his turf."

"I hope you're right. And could you run Kacy Owens's financials? I'd like to see if we can figure out where she's getting all this money. Also, we wanted to know what Nora Martinez's husband did for a living. He was an activist for Hispanic causes, but we don't know his day job."

"Will do." He pulled out his wallet. "I've been meaning to show you this."

He withdrew a visibly ancient and unused ticket generated by Ticketmaster in 1992. It was worn at all four corners and the print had faded. She could barely read the event announced in the middle. *San Diego Padres v. Los Angeles Dodgers*. "This was going to be a surprise for Richie. We were all going to L.A. for his birthday weekend in September. While you and your mom went sightseeing, Richie and I were going to the game."

CHAPTER SIXTEEN

Hubbard's "turf" was a home in Sun City Grand. Although he was employed by the city of Glendale, he didn't live within its boundaries. While the original Sun City was a modest, planned community of duplexes for seniors on fixed budgets, Sun City Grand was its upscale sister. Only the silver-haired with great pensions could afford to live by a lake—with their own pier.

Ari followed Jack's Subaru down wide streets that twisted and curved around a golf course and pulled up in front of a common beige stucco ranch house with a clay-tiled roof. It was spacious with a large bay window and a three-car garage. The third garage door opened as she and Jack met on the sidewalk. A golf cart, the usual and legal form of transportation around the community, putted down the driveway and stopped in front of them. Floyd Hubbard, dressed for golf and wearing a plaid cap, scowled when he saw Jack. "I should've known when your daughter visited me that you wouldn't be far behind."

"How ya doin', Floyd? It's been a long time," Jack said pleasantly. He reached into Hubbard's golf bag and fingered his expensive putter. "Practicing for retirement, huh?"

"I can't wait," he growled. "What do you want?"

Fearing the testosterone level was headed toward a physical confrontation, Ari pulled out Kelly Owens's picture and shoved it in Hubbard's red face. He took it from her and turned off the golf cart. It took a few seconds for him to place the face. "Why do you have this? What was his name?"

"Kelly Owens," Ari replied. "He was your informant, correct?"

"For a while. Then he disappeared. He was actually the first strike I got against me with the brass," he complained. "Surprised you had to remind me who he was."

"And he was the guy who killed my son," Jack retorted.

Hubbard paled as his gaze shifted from Jack to Ari. "Hold on. You said you had new evidence about your brother's case." He shook the paper. "*This* is the new evidence? What the hell?"

"A few days ago I came across a movie made by a friend on the day Richie died. Remember the autistic boy, Glenn Vershaw?"

"Yeah. So? We interviewed him."

Ari held back the urge to remind him that Glenn wouldn't have been interviewed had it not been for the persistence of Chris Taglio. Instead she let him grow uncomfortable while he waited for her to explain.

"What he didn't tell you and probably couldn't tell you, was that he recorded Richie that night at the 7-Eleven. Right before Richie was shot, Kelly Owens entered the store. This is a still photo from that movie."

"Kelly Owens murdered your brother?" he repeated.

"Yes. Elijah Cruz confirmed it."

Beads of sweat covered Hubbard's forehead, but Ari doubted it was from the eighty-degree temperature. He reached for the towel on the passenger seat and wiped his face. Then he said, "We never saw this. We had no idea…" He let the sentence die and handed the picture back to her.

It didn't surprise her that his instantaneous response would be to cover his ass. He was just a few weeks from spending his life zipping around on his golf cart, and the last thing he wanted was for anyone to jam up his pension. She guessed he'd already taken a demotion for the incident that landed him behind the front desk, and often such demotions came with a financial punishment.

"You need to tell us what you know about Kelly Owens," Ari said.

Hubbard turned to Jack. "Does the chief know about this?"

"Which chief? The Phoenix PD chief knows because I work for her. By tomorrow, when you return to work, I imagine your chief will know as well, and Richie's case will be re-examined. Instead of sitting in your golf cart talking with us, I imagine you'll be interviewed by whoever takes over the case, possibly IA if there's concern you obstructed justice and withheld information."

Hubbard seemed to rise out of the golf cart, his gaze flitting between the two of them, his mouth agape. He finally took a deep breath and shook his head. "Now wait. I did no such thing. These were completely separate investigations."

"But you knew the 7-Eleven was being used to traffic drugs," Ari said.

"Yeah, but that didn't have anything to do with a botched robbery. We interviewed the gang lords—George, Jesus, Damian. Totally stonewalled me. We got narcotics involved but they shoved it back to us. Said it was unrelated."

"But Kelly Owens was your informant," Jack said.

"Yeah, I got him to turn on the Homeboys. He was arrested with a group for selling pot at a track meet, and I knew he wasn't one of them. The Homeboys would never let a white kid into the inner circle. I gave Owens a choice, and since it was his second arrest, he was willing to make a deal. I gave his intel to narcotics, and once in a while they interviewed him." He rubbed the side of his head, as if a headache was forming. "God, this was so long ago. I don't remember the details, but this has nothing to do with your brother," he said emphatically.

"Did you know that Kelly was playing you?" Ari asked.

Hubbard looked at her suspiciously.

"The Homeboys knew he was a narc, but instead of killing him, they used him. He fed you the information the Homeboys wanted you to know and nothing else."

"He played you, Floyd," Jack repeated. "Did you have any idea it was happening?"

Hubbard shook his head. "It was all hopeless."

"What was hopeless?" Jack asked.

"Doing anything about drugs in that area. Like putting your finger in a hole in the Hoover Dam. Nothing worked. Still true today. People want drugs, they'll get them. A lot of wasted energy by good cops who could've been put to better use."

"Do you have any idea where Kelly Owens is now?"

He snorted. "No, do you?"

"Not a clue," Jack replied. "How did you discover he was missing?"

Hubbard leaned back and considered the question. "He was gonna meet me at the Glendale Eight Drive-In one night. That's how we did it. We'd meet at sundown. He'd pull up next to me in one of the last rows and we'd talk for twenty or thirty minutes. Then we'd leave once it got dark."

"How many times did you meet?" Jack asked.

"Ten? Twelve? Only a couple times a month and it wasn't for long, just six or seven months. He was always so skittish. I'd spend half the meeting talking him off the ledge. He was certain we'd get caught."

A thought occurred to Ari. "Who picked the meeting place?"

"He did. Why?"

She looked at Jack. "Wolf Martinez worked at the Glendale Eight Drive-In. I'm betting he's the one who told the Homeboys that Kelly was talking to the police."

"Could be," Jack said.

"I'm not surprised Owens played both sides," Hubbard said. "That boy didn't have much sense. Easily influenced by whoever was standing in front of him at the moment. I threatened him with prison, and I'm sure George or Damian threatened him with death. He was surviving."

"Don't defend him," Jack said coldly.

Hubbard raised his hands. "Didn't mean to." He coughed and said, "Jack, I'm sorry for how I treated you during the investigation. I wanted to solve your boy's murder. I really did."

Jack shifted his weight and glanced at the ground. Ari asked, "Do you remember talking to David Rubens? He was a teenager new to the area. He told a uniformed officer that the Homeboys were money lending."

Hubbard exhaled and looked away. "Yeah, I remember him. He'd overheard them talking at one of the MECHA meetings, you know, the Hispanic club?"

"Do you know where Rubens is now?"

"I think he went back to Mexico. He didn't stay in Arizona very long."

"Figures," Jack muttered.

Ari could tell her father's patience was waning. She looked at Hubbard and said, "What if we were to tell you there was a hole in Wolf Martinez's alibi?"

Hubbard's jaw dropped. "You're kidding."

"He left work at one point. Blythe Long, the young woman who sat in on Glenn Vershaw's interview, saw him that night."

Hubbard snapped his fingers. "That's it!" He pointed at Ari. "Remember when you asked me what made Glenn so crazy during the interview?" She nodded. "Blythe Long mentioned Wolf Martinez. That's what sent him twirling around the room."

Jack looked at Ari. "Maybe Wolf saw it happen?"

"Or maybe," Ari countered, "He was the doer."

"That wouldn't surprise me," Hubbard agreed. "That guy was one of the coolest customers I've ever seen, especially for a teenager. A born sociopath, through and through." He snorted and added, "Came by some of it honestly."

"What do you mean?" Jack asked.

"Father had a record. In addition to being arrested several times for inciting riots or disturbing the peace, Mr. Mario Martinez worked in one of the animal testing labs out in the west valley. He was a chemist who spent his days dropping sulfuric acid onto little bunnies, stuff like that."

"A chemist," Ari said. "Might he have been the meth maker?"

"That's what we wondered. But we couldn't get any proof."

Ari leaned against the golf cart. "What details do you remember from the night of the murder. Anything stand out to you?"

He winced, opened his mouth and closed it again. She thought he might have a stomach bug—or something was gnawing his gut.

"What?" Jack said.

"You know how you just know something is off? Something was wrong. Chris and I had a feeling, but we couldn't figure it out. It was like... We were certain we'd accepted something we should've looked at harder. But even after we checked and re-checked our thinking, it all added up, which meant we still didn't have a killer. The team interviewed at least two hundred people. We followed countless leads from the tip line."

He gripped the steering wheel tightly, and she could tell that despite all of the intervening years Richie's unsolved murder still bothered him, but she doubted he had the degree of interest to break into her house, which meant he was just another player in a very old story.

"What's your theory about Richie's murder, and what do you think happened to Kelly Owens?" she asked.

He sat up and leaned over the steering wheel, his massive frame swallowing it. "Well, from what you've told me, I think it's obvious even if we can't prove it. Like I said, Kelly Owens was a fraidy-cat. I'm guessing the whole thing got to be too much for him. He made a plan to run, but he needed cash. So he tries to rob the 7-Eleven, and Richie surprises him. He's so inept he shoots him—sorry to have to say that—and then he flees. The Homeboys find him and kill him. You need to lean on them."

"What if," Ari began, "and I'm just saying *what if*, Nora Martinez and that other witness were right, and Kelly Owens drove away in a car parked on the other side of the building." He opened his mouth to object, and she held up a finger. "Would that have changed your version of the story and satisfied your gut?"

He wiped his hand over his cheek and finally shook his head. "No, that wasn't what bothered us. I mean, it's important, and if Kelly had a car, that certainly gives merit to the idea that he's living it up in a South American country—"

"Or maybe he never left," Jack countered.

Hubbard shrugged his agreement. "And if there was a car, maybe there was a second person. A driver. Maybe Kelly Owens had help."

CHAPTER SEVENTEEN

"Floyd Hubbard's theory is plausible," Ari said to Molly. It was four-thirty a.m. and they were sitting in the airport terminal Starbucks, waiting for their early morning flight to Ontario, California. "Jesus couldn't remember how the Homeboys learned Kelly was the shooter."

"You're thinking Wolf Martinez told them," Molly said with a yawn.

"Exactly. He worked at the Super Eight Drive-In. Kelly picked the place to meet Hubbard. It would make sense he'd pick a place where he had a friend."

"So, he accidentally kills Richie and confides in Wolf."

"Who tells George or Damian," Ari concluded. "I'm thinking it was Damian. Manny, Damian's little brother, was friends with Richie."

"It was a revenge killing."

Ari nodded. Then she shook her head. "But that doesn't jive with Kacy's version of the story. She said her brother was looking for something big. And Mrs. Fairchild, the librarian, also believed Kelly would never shoot someone and run away."

Molly shrugged. "Sometimes not all of the pieces fit, babe. Human nature is only predictable to a point. In the end we're all capable of doing just about anything. Perhaps Wolf was in on it with Kelly. Maybe he was the driver."

"Well, to get him downtown for an interview we'll need probable cause. That conversation should occur in a Glendale interview room."

"Unfortunately, there's not enough evidence—yet."

"And maybe Wolf's the one who broke into the house and your office." Molly rubbed her chin. "What if Hubbard's version of the story is the truth? What if the Homeboys killed Kelly? How would you feel, knowing your brother's killer has been dead all these years?"

"I'd feel..." She stopped. She'd already thought of that possibility, but now, trying to vocalize it to Molly... She felt the tears coming.

Molly reached for her hand. "You don't have to answer that question. I can guess."

When they arrived in Ontario, they found their rental car and headed for Riverside. Their appointment was scheduled for eleven a.m., ensuring they would be back in Phoenix before late afternoon rush hour started. They agreed Ari would meet with Glenn alone. According to Moreno, he had few visitors and little interaction with other residents, so socialization was not an area of strength. Inserting Molly into the equation could jeopardize their one chance of obtaining vital information.

The facility was a Victorian home, painted a deep green with blue trim. A nondescript wooden sign spelled out COMPASS in bright yellow letters and sat alongside the curb, in front of a white picket fence. Well-tended flowerbeds lined the front, and it seemed the owners were doing everything possible to fit into the neighborhood. Communities often rallied against group homes, and it was clear COMPASS was doing whatever it could to be accepted by its neighbors.

Two men sat on the porch, hunkered over as if they were working on something. They looked up as the rental car pulled into a small parking lot on the west side.

"This is quite the place," Molly commented.

Molly and Ari followed the cobblestone path to the front steps. As they climbed up to the porch, Ari smiled at the two men, who were busy shelling peas. One of the men smiled back, but the other remained glued to his work.

"Can I help you?" the smiling man asked.

"Hi," Ari said. "We're looking for Moreno."

"He's inside. Try the kitchen."

"Thanks."

They opened the expansive front door, noting the detailed scrollwork on the fine oak surface. They entered a small parlor and found a middle-aged woman dusting a standing lamp with a feather duster. The sound of clanking pans and many voices carried through the swinging door just off the parlor, and the woman didn't notice they had entered. Dressed in jeans and a T-shirt, she pivoted to reach the top of the light and jumped.

"Oh, my, you scared me!"

Ari rushed toward her with her hand extended. "I'm so sorry. I'm Ari Adams. I'm looking for Moreno."

"I'm Mary," the woman replied, meeting Ari's handshake.

Ari introduced Molly and said, "We're here to meet with Glenn Vershaw."

Mary offered a sad smile. "Glenn. He's very special. And actually, it's just Moreno, not Mr. Moreno. I think he's in the kitchen, finishing KP duty with some of the residents. Just give me a moment to find him."

She hurried through the swinging door, while Molly and Ari studied the old house. Two enormous windows were the eyes of the place, looking out onto the wrap-around porch where the pea-shelling men sat. Curtains of yesteryear had been replaced with white wooden blinds, offering a stark contrast to the yellowed wallpaper. Just enough work had been done to keep the place nice, but it certainly wouldn't be featured on a home tour.

The swoosh of the door drew their attention to a tall, muscular Hispanic man with a pencil-thin mustache who called, "Ms. Adams?" Ari nodded and he said, "I'm Moreno." He was dressed in a blue Oxford-cloth shirt, chinos, and brown loafers.

"I'll wait here," Molly said, taking a seat on the brown leather sofa.

Moreno motioned for Ari to follow him up the winding staircase. She glanced at a series of framed photos that depicted various groups of people standing in front of the house. As they climbed to the second floor, the pictures turned back in time. At the second-floor landing, Ari paused and studied a very old black and white picture of a farmer and his family, she guessed the original owners.

"This house is on the historic register," Moreno said. "Its official name is the Quimby-Paternost House. It was built in 1909."

"How did it come to be a group home?"

Moreno sighed. "Long story. It was about to be demolished when the city stepped in and declared it historic. The COMPASS company worked with the city to keep it viable. Much of the superficial upkeep done on the house was performed by volunteers."

"It's quite impressive."

Moreno smiled his agreement and started down the long hall with brightly painted wooden doors. A nameplate in the center announced the occupant in formal language, such as Mrs. Klein or Mr. Wetherby. Ari wondered if Mr. Wetherby had chosen the peach color himself.

"Do you have any high-profile residents?" she asked.

Moreno nodded. "Yes, several have siblings or children whose names you would recognize from the music or entertainment industries."

She wondered how Glenn's mother had afforded such a place. While she'd only seen the woman once at the funeral for Scott's mother—her sister—Glenn's mother hadn't struck Ari as rich. If memory served, she'd driven an old '66 Mustang and carried a worn suitcase.

Moreno made a sweeping gesture. "This corridor is for our permanent residents, all of whom have been here many years."

Ari guessed which door belonged to Glenn before they reached it, and a lump formed in her throat. The background was blue—Dodger blue—and baseballs had been hand-painted all over it, somewhat obscuring his dark nameplate that read, *Mr. Vershaw*. She wiped a tear away and Moreno waited patiently for her to compose herself.

"Can I assume your brother was a Dodger fan?"

"Oh, yes. Back in the early nineties Phoenix didn't have a professional baseball franchise, so Richie picked the closest team. During the summer Glenn visited, Richie converted him. They bought and traded baseball cards the entire time until..." She let the rest of the sentence fade away.

"That explains what you're about to see."

She offered a puzzled look as he opened the door. Her gaze immediately locked on the adjacent wall, which was completely covered in baseball trading cards—as were the other three walls. They snaked around the windows and doorways, and there wasn't a free spot of wall anywhere. She gazed up and saw the ceiling was bare, but still painted Dodger blue.

"The fire marshal said no cards on the ceiling," Moreno said.

"No cards on the ceiling," a baritone voice repeated.

They stepped further into the room, toward an alcove where Glenn sat behind a card table. He was as skinny as she remembered, and he wore a Dodger baseball jersey. His Dodger baseball cap hid his face, his gaze fixed on the stacks of baseball cards on the table, and the three in his hand. Sitting on the corner of the table was an old, worn baseball glove, a ball in its pocket. She knew that glove. If she examined it, she'd find *Richie* written in block letters along the side of the index finger. She closed her eyes, remembering something she'd long ago forgotten: her parents had given her brother's glove to Glenn after the funeral.

The tableau of Glenn at the card table was one she remembered from nearly every day of her childhood, Richie sitting at the dining room table, organizing his cards and memorizing his baseball stats. She drew in a breath and willed herself not to cry.

"Glenn, you have a visitor, someone you knew a long time ago."

As he slowly lifted his gaze, his hands followed suit until the cards he held covered most of his face. But she recognized his dark brown eyes, the same ones that peered over the movie camera for an entire summer. She smiled and his eyes grew wider. He slowly lowered the cards away from his face.

"Well, that's a first," Moreno said.

He looked the same as she remembered, only small lines had formed around his mouth. She could make out the muscles in his forearms, and she imagined he'd grown strong. Moreno also seemed quite fit, and she guessed their pairing wasn't by accident.

"Hi, Glenn. Do you remember me? Ari?" He didn't reply but continued to stare, and made no effort to retreat into his own world. She took that as a good sign. "Are those your Dodger cards?"

He held them out to her so she could see that they were, but she was surprised to see a Darryl Strawberry card. She glanced at Moreno who said, "These are Glenn's favorite cards, the 1992 Dodger team. That was the year your brother passed, correct?"

"Yes." She glanced around his room and then said to Glenn, "I love all the baseball cards, Glenn. You've collected a lot of them."

"Like Richie," he replied, clearly pleased by her compliment. Then he frowned. "Richie dead."

She could only nod. She turned away, commanding her emotions to obey. She hadn't realized that visiting Glenn would catapult her back to 1992. She chastised herself for not asking Moreno more questions when she'd initially called. Time had stood still in Glenn's world.

Moreno pulled up two folding chairs and they settled across from Glenn. Ari pulled out her phone and activated the voice utility to record the conversation. Moreno gently took the cards from Glenn's hands and placed them in front of him. "I need you to focus, okay?"

"Okay," he said seriously. "Focus."

"Great. Ari needs to ask you some questions about Richie."

He immediately smiled. "Richie's here!"

Moreno shook his head. "No, Glenn, Richie's dead. You know that, right?"

His face fell and he looked to Ari for confirmation. She frowned and nodded. He slumped into the chair, as if he were withdrawing.

"These are important questions, Glenn. Ari needs your help."

When he lifted his chin and nodded, Ari pulled out the iPad from her purse. She avoided Moreno's stare, certain he would protest if she made eye contact. "Glenn, I need to show you one of your movies. Do you remember making all those movies that summer?"

He didn't reply, as he seemed fascinated by the iPad, as if he'd never seen one.

She tapped the screen twice and the movie started. Glenn's entire body seemed to absorb the film. He leaned closer, his mouth open, and he gasped when Richie rode up and showed him the baseball cards.

"Darryl!" Glenn exclaimed, noticing the Darryl Strawberry card on the top of Richie's stack.

When Richie waved goodbye, Glenn waved goodbye to his two-dimensional friend. Ari immediately tapped the screen to stop the film. She'd rehearsed this interview with Molly a dozen times, and they'd debated how to present the film to Glenn. They finally agreed that putting him back into the scene in chronological order would probably help him the most.

"Glenn," she said, waiting until he looked up from the frozen screen, "do you remember what happened next? Richie rode his bike to the front door and went inside. You were still under the light pole. Did you follow him into the store?"

He didn't seem to absorb the question, and he couldn't stop staring at the iPad. His face contorted into a look of agony and he started to cry. "No!" he wailed.

She reached for the iPad, prepared to close it and shut down the interview. Moreno gently touched her arm and shook his head. "Glenn," he said soothingly, "take a deep breath. C'mon, just one. Like we've practiced." Despite the tears dripping from his face, he followed Moreno's direction. His chest rose and his shoulders flew back as he filled his lungs to capacity. "Now, slowly release," Moreno whispered. As he exhaled, his eyes closed. "Glenn, I know it's painful to remember sad things, and there's nothing sadder than a friend who died."

"Richie. My friend," Glenn confirmed, his eyes still closed.

Moreno gently pushed the iPad away and leaned closer to Glenn. "I want you to answer Ari's question. After Richie left and went into the store, did you follow him inside?"

"Yeah. Not supposed to. Got kicked out. But he didn't see me."

"Do you mean the sales clerk didn't see you?" Moreno clarified.

"Uh-huh. Didn't see me. Not at first."

Ari quickly tapped on the iPad and opened a different app, one that allowed her to write on its surface. It was obvious Moreno was the link to Glenn's world, and he needed to ask the questions. She quickly scribbled, *Did he kick you out again?*

Moreno asked the question, and Glenn shifted uncomfortably in his chair, shaking his head. "If he didn't kick you out, why did you leave?" Moreno asked, looking at Ari for confirmation.

She nodded and they watched Glenn closely. He scratched his head and scrunched his face, as if it could help him remember. "Got scared."

Ari scrawled, *Were you looking at the trading cards with Richie?*

Glenn nodded. "He showed me. I showed him. No money. He buy one. For me."

Ari bit her lip. It was so like Richie to share with his friends.

"So, Richie was going to buy a pack of cards for you, and you went back outside to wait?"

"Uh-huh. Didn't want trouble. Get Richie in trouble. Went outside."

Ari wrote, *Did the clerk say anything to you?* Glenn shook his head when Moreno asked the question. She followed up with, *Are you sure he saw you?*

"No," came Glenn's reply.

Moreno looked at her for direction and she wrote, *What did you do when you went back outside?*

"Camera. Lightpole."

Did you turn on your camera?

Glenn exhaled, and Ari sensed he was tired. "Yes."

Ari withdrew the printout of Kelly Owens and wrote, *Did you see this man go in the store?*

Glenn took the picture and held it close to his face. She wondered if he would tear it up, but his brow furrowed, and then he set the picture down. "Yes."

Ari felt a chill down her back. She wrote, *What happened next?*

"Nothing. Then bang!"

He momentarily popped out of his chair. Ari and Moreno jumped. When Glenn dropped onto the seat, the chair slid away from the card table, but neither Ari or Moreno pulled him back. Ari scribbled, *Did you ride up to the front of the store to see what happened?*

"Yes."

Moreno automatically asked, *What did you see?*

"Gun. Rain. Yelling. So loud." He covered his ears and lowered his head to his knees.

Ari looked at Moreno, bewildered. She had no idea why Glenn was talking about rain. It had been a hot, sticky August day with zero chance of a monsoon.

"Richie, dead. Dead. Dead." He smacked his hands against his head, and his sobs turned to wails.

She whispered to Moreno, "Can he handle one or two more questions?"

Moreno winced, clearly torn between revealing Glenn's memories and sending him toward an emotional meltdown. "One more," he mouthed, holding up his index finger.

She leaned closer to Moreno's ear and whispered, "Did you see the man run out of the store after he shot Richie?"

Moreno asked the question, but it didn't seem to register with Glenn. He shook his head violently, and Ari couldn't tell if he was answering the question or reacting to the idea of his friend lying in a pool of blood. Moreno slid his chair beside Glenn and whispered to him while Ari packed up her things.

As she left, she heard Glenn say, "Guy killed him. Died! Died!"

She flew down the corridor, and when she barreled down the stairs, Molly stood and pulled her into a hug. "Are you okay? Was it that bad?"

"Awful," Ari mumbled. "I'm an awful person."

"No, you're not. You needed his information. It had to be done. Was it helpful?"

She sighed into Molly's chest. "I don't really know."

"Let's get out of here," Molly said, escorting her out the front door.

Ari couldn't wait to play the recording for Molly. If she was honest with herself, she'd lost all objectivity. Her interview with Glenn had torn her heart in half. At least she and her parents had possessed the capacity to compartmentalize Richie's death and move forward with life. She worried Glenn had no such capacity and would be imprisoned by those horrible memories forever.

They were practically to the parking lot when they heard, "Ms. Adams!" They turned to see Mary hurrying toward them, carrying a small plastic baggie. "Here," he said. "Glenn wanted you to have this. He said it's for Richie."

From her bland expression, Ari realized she had no context for the delivery and was repeating what Moreno had told her. Ari stared at what she held—an Eric Karros trading card. The card Richie had wanted the night he went to the store.

She burst into tears.

CHAPTER EIGHTEEN

Once Molly had tucked her inside the rental car, Ari regained her composure. She was as floored by Glenn's generosity and love for Richie as she was upset and enraged by the thought that her brother had died over a stupid baseball card, a fact that had upset her for the last quarter of a century. Molly made no effort to leave the COMPASS parking lot, but she rolled down the windows and the cool California breeze offered comfort. It was already pushing a hundred degrees in Phoenix, so they might as well take advantage of the gorgeous Pacific Coast weather for a little longer.

"We've got an hour before we need to return the car," Molly said. "Do you want to debrief now, or do you need some time?"

Ari gazed at her with a weak smile. "How did I get so lucky to find you?"

"You might recall our initial meeting was rather rocky," she snorted, referencing the murder investigation that had thrown them together a few years prior. Molly stroked the side of her cheek, and Ari relished the simple touch. "I can't imagine anything we've ever faced together being as difficult as this case. We've both been shot, threatened, held at gunpoint... But for you, I think this is the topper."

Ari nodded and took a deep breath. Without introduction, she cued up the interview and handed the phone to Molly. She leaned back in the seat, knowing Molly would listen without interruption or question. It was her way. She might replay sections of the recording, but she wouldn't comment. She would let the experience wash over her before she ever analyzed or judged. It was a strategy Ari had learned from her. In fact, she realized she'd learned so much from Molly, who was one of the most intelligent and admirable women she'd ever met. *God, I love her.*

Ari focused on the interview, thinking about Glenn's mood and body language, which could often be as telling as the words he'd chosen. Molly replayed the part where Glenn described what he saw after the shot when he returned to the window. She finished listening and handed the phone back to Ari. "I can't imagine how difficult that was for you."

"It was."

"Weapon was a Colt .45, right?"

"Yes."

"Those Peacemakers were so common back in the nineties," she murmured. "It was never found?"

"No."

"Easy to carry and hide in the waistband. Why was he talking about rain? Was there a monsoon?"

"I wish. If there had been a monsoon, I don't think Richie would've snuck out. I don't know why Glenn was stuck on the weather or why he thought it was raining."

"Cops checked all the receipts, right?"

"Yeah, but they were all cash."

"Walk me through it," Molly asked. "Put it together for me and tell me where there are questions or conflicting information."

"We know the store was heavy into drug trafficking, and at the center was Mellow, the day clerk. He had a relationship with the Westside Homeboys. We'll never know the particulars of that arrangement since he was killed in prison, coincidentally at the same time my dad got a lead."

"Has your dad mentioned what that lead was?"

"It was information about the shooter's identity. He'd learned there was a link between the Homeboys and the shooter."

"And thanks to Glenn's movie, you've already confirmed that the shooter was Kelly Owens and he somehow became involved with the Homeboys," Molly added.

"Correct. We know the Homeboys employed Kelly and Mellow for distribution. Out on the periphery were Elijah Cruz, Isolde Tovar-Cruz, and Wolf Martinez. I'm guessing Wolf is the link between the Homeboys and Kelly. I think he brought Kelly into the group. They all went to Glendale High together and were involved in MECHA, a club that celebrates Mexican heritage. They held a car wash for Elijah's dying sister, CeCe. Wolf apparently sent George Delgado, the leader of the Homeboys, on a terrible drug trip. My guess is Wolf was dealing meth. Maybe there was a conflict or competition for business between Wolf and the Homeboys."

"Could be. I know the Homeboys were into pot, cocaine, and pills, but I never heard they peddled meth."

"Maybe that became Wolf's market," Ari suggested. "We know Kelly and Wolf knew each other, and I've seen a picture of Elijah and Wolf having a meeting. And we know Kelly was playing both sides with the Homeboys and the cops."

"What if Elijah and Wolf started their own meth business out of the store?"

"That wouldn't have sat well with the Homeboys, would it?" Ari asked.

"I doubt it, even if they were dealing different products. Maybe Kelly was the center of the circle? They all knew each other socially, and then Kelly and Elijah decide to go into business together. Not much later, Kelly gets tapped by Hubbard to be an informant. If that were the case, I can't imagine how much pressure Kelly faced."

Ari shook her head. "I just don't see Elijah dealing meth. He was caught up in his sister's illness and Isolde. The women were running his world."

Molly raised her hand. "I get that you and your dad believe in Elijah. I'm just asking you to leave the door open slightly for the possibility that Elijah is involved."

She started the car and they headed to the airport. Ari leaned against the passenger window and closed her eyes. She much preferred to think of Glenn when he was little—with Richie. When they were all so much younger, before death corrupted their innocence.

Her mind settled on the day the soccer ball landed in Scott's mother's rosebush. Of course, it was Glenn who'd kicked the ball in the wrong direction, unwilling to remove the movie camera from his eye to improve his aim. A large thorn pierced the skin and deflated the ball instantly. Scott had been heartbroken but did his best to hide his anger at Glenn. Richie, always the optimist, proclaimed he could fix the ball with some duct tape. A sullen Scott led them to his father's tool shed and pointed to a high shelf. Richie climbed onto the rickety workbench and walked to the edge. He could reach the shelf if he stood on tiptoe and stretched. He was still a hair's distance away, so he jumped. His hand grabbed the tape, but it swung forward into a large tin can. The can fell onto its side and a few hundred rusty nails fell to the floor. Glenn covered his ears, the movie camera flying away from his face. He screamed to drown out the high-pitched, tinny wail of the falling nails. Nails that fell like rain.

She sat up and Molly turned toward her. "What? Are you okay?"

"The change. That's what Glenn heard that night."

"Explain, babe. Still not with you."

"Chris Taglio told me there was change all over the store's floor when he arrived. Some of it had even rolled down one of the aisles. Somehow it got knocked over during the robbery. Glenn said he heard rain. It wasn't raining outside. It was the change. He saw the change jug go over."

"Why is that important?" Molly asked gently.

"I'm not sure," Ari admitted. She sighed. "But it was important to him if he remembered it."

She pulled out her iPad and clicked on her photos. She'd taken digital pictures of the crime scene photos, and she swiped through them until she found one of the counter. It looked like any other convenience store counter, crowded with impulse purchase items placed near the register—beef jerky, aspirin, mints, lip balm. There was just enough room to slide a drink or some candy toward the cashier.

She scrolled to a picture that showed the plastic change jug. Somehow it had landed on the floor amid the change. It was plastic, wide-mouthed and large. A black and white photo of CeCe along with a plea for help was taped to the side.

She found another photo of the front of the counter. A small pile of money sat to the right on the floor. She returned to the close-up photo of the counter. She magnified it and studied the placement of the counter items, which sat on the right side, leaving enough room for the large jug on the left. She guessed customers couldn't help but notice CeCe's bright smile, and if Elijah somehow mentioned she was his sister, anyone with a heart would feel obliged to drop their change in the jug. And judging from the amount of change on the floor, Ari guessed it had been very full.

She turned to Molly. "Did you ever save change as a kid?"

"Oh, yeah. My family had a swear jar. Anytime any one of us swore, we had to put twenty-five cents in the jar. At the end of a year, the person who had sworn the least got all the money."

Ari cracked a grin. "I'm doubting you ever won."

They both laughed. "Nope. It was almost always my mom."

"What did it look like?"

"Actually I think it was a metal coffee can, not a jar. My parents were diehard coffee drinkers and went through a lot of those. And here's something else. My mom won most years since she hardly swore, but because she was so busy, she never had time to do anything with the can of money. Back then there weren't those automatic coin machines. So all the cans she collected over the years sat in her closet behind her shoes. When my parents finally remodeled, I lugged all of them to the bank. It about broke my back carrying them from the car to the lobby."

"Change is really heavy, isn't it?"

"Yeah."

"Then how in the hell did someone accidentally knock over this? Excuse my swearing," she added.

She held up the picture of the jug lying on its side. Molly stole a quick glance and shook her head. "No idea. Maybe was already sitting close to the edge of the counter? The manager wouldn't have wanted it crowding the front of the register. Maybe it was too close and got knocked over in the confusion."

"I suppose," Ari admitted.

But she didn't like that answer. It was definitely suspicious, and it was a question she would ask Elijah Cruz when she saw him again. She'd called him and asked if he would answer some more questions, and he readily obliged. She told him she'd call once she returned from Riverside. He mentioned he hoped the visit was for a short vacation, but when she mentioned she was visiting Glenn Vershaw, the autistic moviemaker from that summer, he grew quiet. He asked about Glenn's health and seemed pleased to hear he was in a good environment. He asked three or four more questions, and because Ari was naturally suspicious, she wondered if his inquiry was rooted in general care for the well-being of another, or if he was asking because he had something to hide and wanted to know about Glenn's mental capacity to remember.

Molly's belief that Elijah might know more than he was saying nagged at her. She trusted Molly's gut and Jack's gut equally, and she'd initially thought of bringing them both along to meet with Elijah, but she worried three visitors might seem confrontational. She had collected more pieces of the puzzle, and she was starting to doubt the star witness.

By the time they arrived home, Ari was physically and mentally drained. Molly ushered her into the bathroom and drew her a hot bubble bath. While Ari relaxed, desperately trying to turn off her brain, Molly made dinner, and soon the spicy smells of chili con carne wafted upstairs. The promise of food pulled Ari out of the tub. Donning only her robe, she joined Molly at the dining table. They basked in a rare evening together, one that included Mexican food, cold beer, and the definite possibility of sex.

Molly had muted the local news, but when Ari saw Richie's face fill the screen, she reached for the remote and clicked on the sound. The newscaster provided few details of the twenty-five-year-old case before the Glendale Chief of Police introduced Blake Fishburn, the detective who would lead the re-opened case.

"Fishburn's a great guy," Molly commented. "Worked with him once or twice when he was in narcotics. Good choice."

Fishburn appeared to be in his mid-forties, with graying hair, a round face, and intelligent green eyes. He looked directly into the camera and said, "We have new information regarding the death of Richie Adams, and we now consider Kelly Owens to be a person of interest. If you have any information regarding the current whereabouts of Mr. Owens, please call the number listed on your screen. If you have had any kind of a previous relationship with him—girlfriend, employer, co-worker—since nineteen ninety-two, please call us as well."

Side-by-side photos of Kelly Owens appeared, the still-frame lifted from Glenn's movie and a candid photo Ari imagined the police obtained from Kacy. He was standing outside a house in front of a VW Bug. His left arm was up, motioning to the car, as if he was proud of it. From the length of his hair and the maturity of his face, Ari guessed the photo was taken after he'd left Glendale High School.

Molly exhaled. "Let the circus begin. They'll get hundreds of ridiculous calls."

"Yeah, but there's no other way, not after twenty-five years. I'm guessing Kacy still believes he's alive, and if that's true and the letter she's got is legit, then somebody has to know something."

Molly poured a sparkling water and snorted, "Not if he's holed up in South America."

"True," Ari admitted.

Molly asked Alexa to turn off the TV and turn on their favorite Pandora jazz station as they enjoyed the rest of their meal. When Molly narrowed her eyes, Ari knew she was caught. "You're still thinking about the case."

"Yeah. I just can't believe Kelly Owens could vanish without some help. He was a kid. He wasn't adept and didn't have a lot of social skills."

Molly shook her head. "You're forgetting that he practically raised his sister. He knew how to survive."

"Do you think he's still alive?"

Molly shrugged. "I really don't know, babe. We could argue this all night." She stood and picked up their plates. "But there's no way in hell we're doing that. I'll clean up and you go find us a movie to watch on the couch."

"The couch," Ari repeated in her sexy voice.

Ari chose an old comedy, but despite the terrific physical gags, Molly's hands and lips continuously roamed between the folds of Ari's robe.

"I love you so much," Molly murmured between kisses.

"I love you," Ari replied, wiggling free of the robe. "Alexa, turn off the movie and turn on Pandora." Ari giggled once a John Coltrane tune filled the room. "The joys of technology."

Molly groaned and climbed on top of her, quickly shedding her own clothes. They laughed when her arms got tangled between her sweater and her shirt, but Ari's breath caught at the sight of Molly half-naked—her sculpted arms, erect nipples, and gorgeous smile. Ari cupped Molly's breasts lovingly and her thumbs caressed the tender skin as she slowly rocked her hips. Molly joined her, lolling her head back, exposing the fine arch of her neck.

Molly worked the button on her jeans and guided Ari's hand between her legs—as she entered Ari at the exact same moment. Ari craved each soft moan and tender whisper, sounds without sharp edges, that pushed away the pain, the blood, and Richie's brown eyes. And then...

They moved to the bedroom, Molly swatting Ari's buttocks, eliciting gasps of pleasure. They fell onto the bed in a tangle. While their mouths enjoyed rough kisses, Molly retrieved two silk scarves from the nightstand. Ari sighed as her hands floated to the headboard. She needed to be taken. Over and over. They lingered in ecstasy until Molly released her from the silk bonds and wrapped her in a comforting embrace.

CHAPTER NINETEEN

Ari awoke the next morning with a clear head. A sliver of pragmatism had cut through her emotions, balancing her feelings. She was coming to terms with the possible outcomes of the investigation, recognizing she would land in a place with more knowledge than when she started, even if she hadn't correctly pieced together the timeline of Richie's murder, nor confronted his killer.

The timeline. She leaned back in her patio chair and sipped her coffee. Chris Taglio had mentioned the timeline bothered him, but he hadn't yet called back. Ari thought about the confrontation with Nora and Wolf. Nora had turned into a "tiger mom," nearly wounding Molly's right-hand man Buster. Nora Martinez seemed almost psychopathic.

Molly had grudgingly left for the morning after Buster pleaded with her to attend a strategy session with Phoenix's Gay Pride Coalition. Ari completely understood since Buster's skill set was not public relations. But Molly was disappointed, as she'd wanted to meet Elijah, who was preparing for a camping trip with his family. They couldn't postpone the interview and Buster needed Molly.

She glanced over her shoulder at the large pieces of plywood covering the hole in the solarium. The replacement glass had to be special ordered and wouldn't arrive for another two weeks. She tried to picture different players hurling the decorative boulder through the wall. Her curiosity piqued, she set down her coffee to retrieve the rock. Molly had returned it to its spot along the garden, and Ari was amazed that it wasn't heavy. Kelly Owens, Floyd Hubbard, or Wolf Martinez could easily raise it above their respective heads, as well as Elijah Cruz. She doubted Chris Taglio would have the ability, but she couldn't see him or Grady Quigley having a motive to steal the case file since they'd been instrumental in obtaining the information for Jack.

She doubted Nora Martinez would have the strength, but Kacy Owens could certainly heft the boulder a short distance— although she'd not yet met Ari when it happened. But if Kelly were still around… Ari pondered the idea of Kelly reappearing and collaborating with his sister. Jack had run a check on her cell phone records with indifferent results. There were no calls or texts outside the Phoenix area, and the recipients of those calls all checked out.

More interesting were Kacy's financials. The Corvette had no lien, which meant Kacy had purchased it outright. Her bank accounts were modest, three hundred in checking and about a thousand in savings. The only deposits she made were her measly salary checks from the strip joint. Ari guessed most of her money was made in tips, but there was no record of their existence. Kacy lived on cash, which made it nearly impossible to find any clues that might point to Kelly Owens's current whereabouts. If he was hiding in plain sight, his success was commendable.

"We probably need to talk with her again," Ari mumbled.

Also interesting was the occupation of Nora Martinez's husband, Mario. A chemist. "Maybe he was the original Walter White," Jack mused, a reference to the popular TV series, *Breaking Bad*, and its main character, the mild-mannered chemistry teacher who becomes a meth maker. If Wolf and his father had been in business together, then Nora Martinez probably was involved somehow.

Ari's doorbell chimed and she glanced at her watch. It was still an hour before Jack would arrive. Glancing through her peephole, she found a stranger in a gray suit at her door. He was Hispanic, of medium height and build, and mustached. His thick hair was slicked back, revealing a high forehead. She guessed he was in his mid-thirties. Behind him was a Lincoln Town Car with tinted windows. A younger, taller Hispanic man waited alongside the front fender. She opened the front door, leaving the security screen door in place, and heard the hum of the running engine.

"May I help you?"

The gentleman smiled pleasantly. "Ms. Adams?"

"Yes?"

"My name is Manny Cortez."

She smiled and unlocked the security screen. "It's a pleasure to see you again, Manny."

He gently took her hand in his own. "I'm a lot taller and older now," he said.

"Would you like to come in?"

He nodded. "For a few minutes, yes." He gestured to his driver, who nodded but didn't move.

She led him through the house and he commented, "I love these historic homes. They have so much character."

"I agree. Can I offer you something to drink?"

He held up a hand as they reached the solarium and sat on the couch. "No, thank you." He pointed at the plywood and furrowed his brow. "May I ask what happened?"

"Unfortunately, we had a burglary."

When she offered nothing else, he looked at her intensely and said only, "I see. I hope no one was harmed."

"No, thank goodness. How can I help you?"

"I won't waste your time or jam you up with a fake story. I know you're investigating your brother's murder, and I know you've determined that Kelly Owens was the shooter. I wanted to offer my assistance, if it would be helpful."

"I see."

"Richie was my only childhood friend. When he died, it was a long time until I found a friend as loyal." His voice cracked as he finished the sentence, and he looked away, as if not to cry. "I can't imagine how hard it was for your family to lose someone so young. It was hard enough on my family when Damian was killed in prison."

"I'm sorry too, for you. I don't think age matters. Losing a brother or sister is devastating. I hope you have some wonderful memories to cherish."

He had tears in his eyes as he said, "I do." He sat up straighter and adjusted his tie. "I didn't come here to get sentimental or make either of us sad. I recently had a conversation with Jesus Santiago. He shared that he'd met with you and your business partner over breakfast."

"Yes, the conversation was helpful. I'm grateful Lorraine found him."

He chuckled at the mention of Lorraine's name. "Lorraine Gonzalez. She is quite a character. A wonderful woman who has done much for the Hispanic community."

"Agreed."

"Anyway, Jesus suggested I share with you some information that was shared with me by my brother Damian. Jesus didn't believe it was his place to tell this story, which is why I'm here. Of course, this is all secondhand. Still, I believe it is the truth."

She nodded and he pursed his lips. She suspected he knew details about the involvement of the Westside Homeboys in the drug trade, but he needed to carefully edit his comments since Jack Adams sat at the heart of the investigation. While there was a statute of limitations that would allow him to talk freely about drug crimes from the nineties, if it were tangled in current illegal activity, Manny could be prosecuted.

"I know Jesus discussed George's unfortunate experience with meth and El Lobo, and he said you correctly identified El Lobo as Wolf Martinez."

"Yes."

"But I imagine he didn't discuss the terms of the loan and why the loan was made in the first place."

Ari leaned forward. "No, he didn't. I thought it...a bit unusual...that a loan would be given to a rival business, assuming there were drugs being sold at the store," she added quickly.

Manny smiled mischievously. "I appreciate your diplomatic choice of words. Of course, business is about supply and demand, and the targeted audiences were completely different, which is partially why George allowed it."

Ari raised an eyebrow. "You seem to have a solid grasp on business principles."

"Does that surprise you?"

"A little," she admitted.

"I have an M.B.A. from Arizona State."

"Uh, wow. I...apologize. I shouldn't jump to conclusions."

He held up a hand. "It's okay. I understand. My family and my connections have an unsavory past. I'm working to change that. I know there are rumors, but I'm a legitimate businessman involved in community projects, supporting schools and families...anything positive."

Her eyes filled with tears, and Manny reached inside his jacket for a handkerchief. "I'm sorry if I upset you."

She shook her head. "Oh, you didn't." She wiped her eyes and returned the handkerchief. "Thank you." She looked at him and smiled. "If Richie were alive, I'm sure the two of you would still be friends."

He started to cry and held up the damp handkerchief. "It looks like I'll be needing this, too." He dabbed his eyes. "We have veered off topic." He cleared his throat and said, "Damian told me a story when I was a teenager. It was about El Lobo. I can't remember why it came up, but I'd guess it had something to do with teaching me a lesson. My father died in a shootout with police not long after I was born. As the oldest, Damian felt it was his responsibility to look after me and my four siblings. He was always telling us stories to make his point. Perhaps he told me this to teach me about recognizing a wolf in sheep's clothing."

"And that wolf would be Wolf Martinez?"

"Exactly. George made the deal with Wolf for one specific reason: he was afraid of him. I know the story about Wolf sending George on a bad meth trip, but Damian maintained that wasn't the reason. Damian was like a brother, and George told him Wolf gave him the creeps. He had no moral code." Manny put up his hands and admitted, "I know it seems hypocritical for a gangbanger to talk about morals, but back then, there was respect for turf, for someone's girlfriend, and of course, *la familia*." He paused and looked away. "Wolf didn't respect any of it." He leaned closer as if he were sharing a secret. "George told Damian a really sick story. There was a feral cat problem in downtown Glendale during the late eighties. They were everywhere."

"I remember that," Ari said, thinking of an orange tabby who sat outside their back door and meowed incessantly. "My mother couldn't help but feed them."

"Mine too. But think back to the early nineties, right around the time Richie died. Was your mother still feeding cats then?"

Richie had named the cat Dodger. One morning he and Lucia had gone looking for him. "No," she said. "There was one in particular but he disappeared."

"They all did."

Manny offered a hard stare and she guessed the cats' fate. "Wolf Martinez is a psychopath. He's also clever, which is why he's never been caught. And he can't hold a job. He gets angry very easily."

Ari remembered Wolf's McDonald's uniform. She couldn't imagine too many men in their forties worked at McDonald's.

"While Damian and George wouldn't get involved with Wolf, there was one person who did."

"Who?"

"Kelly Owens."

Ari nodded. "I suspected they were friends back when they went to Glendale High."

"Wolf was the leader and Kelly was the follower. But here's the part no one knows. Kelly had it bad for Elijah Cruz's sister, CeCe."

"The girl who was sick?"

"Yeah. She was in his year in school. They'd had classes together. She got sick and he dropped out. He was donating money to her and supporting his own sister. You know Kelly's mom was a druggie, right?" Ari nodded. "Kelly was working for George, but he was also working for Wolf. Pushing pot didn't net you a lot of money, but meth did. A lot of highly respected white-collar types got addicted to meth."

"Did George and Wolf know Kelly was working for both of them?"

"Yes, but what Wolf didn't know was that Kelly had turned informant." He paused and added, "at least not for a while. The rumor I've heard is that Wolf found out. I'm not sure what happened in the 7-Eleven that night, but you're never going to find Kelly Owens. Wolf Martinez killed him."

Ari gaped at him. "Are you sure about that? Did someone tell Damian, or did Wolf admit it to Damian?"

"No, but it makes sense. Very few people have the ability to keep a secret forever. It takes incredible restraint to hold something like that inside of you. Most people can't do it. They slip up. Not Wolf Martinez. And that makes him the most dangerous person I've ever met."

CHAPTER TWENTY

Jack drove toward Elijah's house, while Ari shared the details of her visit with Manny. "Some of it makes sense. Assuming Blythe Long's story is true, and she saw Wolf that night, then he probably met up with Kelly."

"Could be," Jack agreed.

"But if Kelly was in love with CeCe, how is it that Elijah doesn't know him? Wouldn't he have recognized him when he came into the 7-Eleven that night?"

"Not necessarily. Maybe Kelly was just a voyeur. Maybe he never really got close to her and donated the money anonymously. A lot of high school guys are like that, especially the shy ones. They might strike up a conversation before a class or say hello in the lunch line, but that's as far as it goes. Take it from me, I know."

"You were shy? I can't believe it."

Jack grinned and took the SR 303 exit. "Yeah, it's true. When I was a teenager, I could hardly string five words together in front of a girl I liked. I didn't gain any sophistication until I went to college and left puberty. That was awful. You've seen pictures, haven't you?"

"Yeah, I guess," she mused, "but I don't remember you being awkward."

"I was."

"That could also explain why, if Elijah had met Kelly in passing at the car wash fundraiser for CeCe, he wouldn't remember him over a year and a half later. He looked completely different."

"That's my point," Jack said.

They snaked through the winding roads of Elijah's subdivision until they came to the familiar cul-de-sac. Today Elijah's garage door was up and they found him bent over an upside-down canoe, running a belt sander across the rich cedar wood. He wore goggles, earplugs, and a face mask, so he didn't notice their arrival until they stepped in front of him. He nodded and turned off the sander. When he removed the face mask, he wore a pleasant smile.

"Jack," he said, offering a wave instead of his hand. "I'm completely covered in sawdust, otherwise I'd shake your hand."

"It's fine, Elijah." Jack slowly walked around the canoe, stopping at the bow. "Looks like you're undertaking quite a project."

He nodded proudly. "Got it at a neighbor's garage sale for practically nothing. My boys and I are working on it together. By summer it'll be ready for its maiden voyage. We're planning a family fishing trip, just us guys."

"Sounds fun." Jack crouched and studied the hull. "It appears to be in great shape."

"It is. Quite the find." Elijah grabbed a nearby rag and wiped the sawdust from his face and arms. "I know you both didn't come out here to admire my canoe."

Jack glanced at Ari. He expected her to take the lead. She said, "Elijah, we've done some more digging and we've got some more questions."

He gazed at her seriously. "Of course. How can I help?"

She opened the yearbook to the page with the car wash photo. "I'm hoping you can identify someone."

It took a few seconds for Elijah to recall the event, but then he offered a sad smile. "I remember that day. CeCe was still hanging on. We were so young."

Ari pointed at the long-haired version of Kelly Owens, standing in the back next to Wolf Martinez. "Do you recognize him?"

"The guy next to Wolf?"

"Yes."

Elijah squinted and brought the book closer. "I can't make out his face." He looked up at her curiously. "Is he a witness?"

"That's Kelly Owens, the guy who shot Richie and robbed you."

"It is?"

Ari and Jack nodded, as Elijah processed. He shook his head and stared at the picture. "Do you have the other picture you showed me?"

"Yes," Ari said, reaching into her bag.

She held it beside the yearbook photo while Elijah's gaze moved between the two photos. "It's hard to tell. Are you sure?"

"Yes," she said. "Do you remember seeing him during the car wash?"

He groaned and closed the yearbook. "Oh, no. That was forever ago. There was so much happening in my life back then. CeCe was so sick and my father was going through a terrible depression."

"Speaking of CeCe, we've heard that Kelly had a crush on her."

"What? When?" His surprised tone was laced with protective hostility.

"I'm guessing this was during their time together at Glendale High. We think CeCe and Kelly had classes together."

"Well, they never dated," Elijah retorted. "No stoner was getting near *mi hija*. Believe me, if I'd known that, I'd have popped him into next Sunday."

"It could've been a crush from afar," Jack suggested. "If you never saw Kelly hanging around your house, or if your sister never said anything about him, then I'd guess there wasn't anything going on. But it might explain why he came to help at the car wash. He probably cared about her."

Elijah nodded, accepting the explanation. "That makes sense."

"What *do* you remember about the day of the car wash?" Jack prompted.

Elijah settled against his workbench and looked down at the garage's cement floor. When he looked up, his eyes were closed. "I remember it was really hot. Everyone was in a good mood, though, because George kept spraying us with the hose. Of course, he didn't get wet, but in between hosing down the cars, he'd give us all a shower. It was funny, and all the girls were in tank tops, so you know…" He cracked a grin and looked away. "There were a lot of people there. Even a reporter and a photographer came by and interviewed us. They took some pictures. Actually, the one you just showed me was in the newspaper with the story."

"Do you have a copy?" Ari asked.

"Sure. Do you want to see it?"

"If it's not too much trouble."

"No, I'll be right back."

Elijah went inside and Jack turned to Ari. "Do you believe he doesn't remember Kelly?"

"I do," she admitted. "He looked genuinely surprised to learn Kelly had a thing for CeCe and worked the car wash."

"I agree. And he wouldn't have recognized him a year later when he shows up at the 7-Eleven. He looked completely different."

Elijah returned with a large frame. The story and photo had been custom-fit inside a white matte. Both had yellowed with age. Ari noticed the byline—Ryland Norris. She'd seen her name many times, as she was now the editor of the *Arizona Republic*'s editorial section. Ari guessed working the city beat for Glendale was one of her first assignments.

The story was a tear-jerking bio of CeCe, the promising volleyball player who was diagnosed with cancer in her junior year. The bills for her treatment were staggering, and her friends and family held the car wash as a benefit. The story tugged at the heartstrings and ended with an address where readers could send donations.

"Did the article help raise money for your family?"

"Yeah, I think so," Elijah said. He shuffled his feet and put his hands in his pockets. "I didn't have anything to do with that. My parents took care of everything when it came to CeCe and her care."

"When did she die?" Jack asked gently.

"About four months after your son." He took back the frame and asked, "Did you have any other questions?"

"I did," Ari replied. "What was your relationship with Wolf Martinez? Were you friends? Acquaintances?"

"Just acquaintances. I didn't have friends like other high school kids. My sister was sick. I was working or going to school, and I had Iso. We met at the end of freshman year and have been together ever since." When Ari looked at him skeptically, he added, "Here's what you need to understand about that time. There weren't a lot of options for Latino men in Glendale during the eighties and nineties. Most wound up in gangs or dead-end jobs. Some went to vocational schools, but there weren't a lot of those available. Very few Latinos went to college. My parents convinced me I could get there. And I almost did," he said quietly.

"Except Isolde got pregnant?" Ari asked.

"Yeah, so my dream changed. I still think it turned out pretty good." He forced a smile and she answered with one of her own. "Anything else?"

She could tell he was weary of her questions and wanted to get back to his canoe. "Just one more thing, Elijah, and we'll get out of your hair."

"It's no problem," he interjected. "It's never a problem." He looked from Ari to Jack with a serious gaze.

"Thank you," she said. "You mentioned CeCe's illness was long. I wanted to ask about the jug of change that was sitting by the register."

He nodded. "The money we were collecting for her."

"Yes. Somehow that jug got overturned during the robbery and that's why there were coins all over the floor in the crime scene photos. What do you remember about that?"

He opened his mouth and then closed it. He looked away and shifted his feet. After he'd scratched his head, he said, "I really don't remember. Maybe it got tipped over when Kelly pulled out the gun?"

Ari pulled out the crime scene photo that showed the jug lying on the cement floor. "That's what I thought at first. Here's what I'm struggling with, Elijah. There was a lot of money in that jug. I don't think it was possible for it to be accidentally knocked over. It would've needed an intentional push to be shoved off the counter. Do you see what I mean? Change is really heavy."

He stared at the photo, a blank expression on his face. Ari wasn't sure if he was trying to manufacture a lie or remember the event itself. His hands shook as he handed the photo back. "I really don't know. There are parts I don't remember. Like Detective Hubbard told me I fell in a mudhole racing outside to meet the first officers and that's why I had mud on my shirt. I have no recollection of the change jug tipping over. It must've happened after he fired the shot. Everything that happened after the shot is a blur or a blank. Maybe he got so mad after he killed your brother that he knocked it over in anger? I really can't remember. I'm so sorry I can't help you." He looked genuinely distraught, and she nodded her understanding.

"You look upset," Ari commented to Jack.

They were on their way back to Central Phoenix to meet with Ryland Norris, the reporter who'd written the article about CeCe Cruz. Jack knew Ryland, and she agreed to meet them at Lux, one of Ari's favorite coffee bar hangouts.

"I'm mad at myself," Jack said. "But I'm proud of you," he quickly added.

"Why?"

"I'd always assumed the killer knocked the change jug over when he whirled around and fired at Richie. You've proven that couldn't have happened the way we all thought it did. I dismissed what potentially could be an important clue. I'm mad at myself."

"Don't be."

"Can't help it."

He turned onto Central Avenue and pulled up to a red light. She stared at him and said, "There's a reason detectives aren't allowed to investigate crimes involving family. You know that. Dad, you had a very skewed perspective on this case. Not only were you dealing with Richie's death, you were shouldering Mom's and my grief. You were always the strong one."

"I disagree with that. Your mother was the strong one."

"Not when it came to Richie," she said, her voice barely a whisper.

"What do you mean?"

She gazed out the passenger window.

"Ari, what do you mean?"

She felt his stare. He wouldn't let it go. "It was apparent to me—and Richie—that he was Momma's boy and I was Daddy's girl." She checked his expression—a grimace.

"We always thought we were fair with both of you."

"You were," she conceded, "but Richie was more like Mom and I was more like you. So, like any kids, we played to our advantage. If you weren't home, and Richie and I wanted to go somewhere, he asked Mom. If you were home, I'd ask you."

He didn't reply, and when she glanced at him at the next red light, she could tell he was sorting through various memories. As they pulled into the Lux parking lot, he said, "That doesn't mean we loved either of you any less."

Once he parked the car, she took his hand. "I know. I really do. And so did Richie. We saw both of you as our protectors, our role models...our favorite people." He closed his eyes and she realized he was starting to cry. "Hey, it's okay."

He squeezed his eyes to cut off the tears. After he took a deep breath and composed himself he said, "If that's how you and Rich perceived us, and if that's how we behaved—perhaps unwittingly—then it must have destroyed you when I turned my back on you."

Her breath caught. She'd vowed never to discuss the depth of her pain with him since it was the past. He'd known, she'd forgiven, and they had moved on. Dr. Yee's words played through her mind. *You thought this was over. You'd placed your pain on a high shelf and locked it away.* She knew if she replied, they would both turn into puddles of sorrow and would need to cancel their meeting with Ryland Norris.

"That's a conversation for another day," she said, her voice wavering slightly. "Let's focus on Richie now. He needs us. You and I will have many more tomorrows to discuss our relationship, but today is about Richie."

He nodded, squeezed her hand, and they headed for the entrance. "Do we look okay?" he asked. "Or do we look like we just finished watching *Old Yeller*?"

The comment had the desired effect and they laughed. By the time they followed the queue to the cash register and claimed their respective lattes, their tears had dried. They wormed their way through several doorways as Lux was a series of interesting chambers fashioned with artwork for sale and a mishmash of eclectic tables, chairs, and loungers scattered throughout. They scanned the faces of businessmen and women conducting casual meetings, people staring at their laptops with their earphones plugged in to silence the café's noise, and friends chatting over a pastry and coffee.

A woman wearing a purple beret waved at Jack. As they approached, Ari realized she was sitting in a motorized wheelchair.

Ryland Norris was probably in her mid-sixties but looked much younger. She was well-dressed in black slacks and a white dress shirt. Her makeup was sparingly applied, and her sharp green eyes sat behind thick, black glasses. Jack leaned over and offered her a kiss on the cheek before he introduced Ari. As she leaned forward to shake Ryland's hand, Ari got a whiff of Ryland's perfume, a subtle fragrance that completed her classy presentation.

"Long time no see, Jack," she said with a smile Ari thought could be suggestive.

"It has been a long time, Ryland. But I'm still a faithful reader of the editorial section."

"Did you like my recent commentary on State Senator Dovorack and the Me Too movement?"

"I did," Ari interjected. "I think your editorial was one of the reasons the Arizona Senate voted to remove him after the sexual harassment allegations came to light."

Ryland looked pleased. "They were more than allegations. I speak from personal experience. I'll give Senator Dovorack credit for one thing: he saw past the wheelchair. Treated me like all the other women."

"I'm not surprised," Jack said.

Ryland blushed. "Flatterer." She reached down and picked up a manila folder from a large bag. "Enough small talk. You want to know about CeCe Cruz. Terrible tragedy." She adjusted her glasses and opened the folder. Inside were three reporter's notebooks and several sheets of paper with handwritten notes. She flipped through the first book until she came to what she wanted. She skimmed her notes and said, "I interviewed her three times in early nineteen-ninety. She'd been diagnosed with pancreatic cancer. Died in October of ninety-two. But that's not the story you're looking for."

"It isn't?" Ari asked.

"No, you want the story behind the story."

Jack and Ari exchanged a glance before Jack said, "Honestly, we were hoping you could shed some light on CeCe as a person. Did she have a boyfriend? What was her relationship with her brother Elijah? Who were her friends?"

"Those are easy questions. Nice, quiet girl. Very unassuming. No boyfriend. Worshipped her brother, and frankly, everybody was her friend because she was so nice. And I don't mean *nice* like we all say nice. I mean nice like couldn't kill a fly. That's why the community support was overwhelming."

"So what's the backstory?" Jack asked.

"The article did exactly what it was supposed to do, thank you very much. TV stations jumped on the bandwagon and ran the story. Several thousand dollars poured into the bank account the family had set up for CeCe's medical treatment." She paused and rubbed her chin. "In hindsight, I probably should've followed up with them, but that piece got the attention of the *Arizona Republic*'s publisher, who wanted me to come on board. I was busy gaining my own notoriety. So, like all the other people who'd heard about CeCe and given money, I just forgot about her. That's how these pop-up charity things work. You give the money and you walk away, assuming somebody else is handling the business aspect of it. You also assume it's on the up and up and everyone is honest."

"And somebody wasn't," Ari said.

"Exactly. I heard from Mrs. Cruz about a month after the story was published that the family had raised over fifteen thousand dollars, and she said the funds collected would bring the family's debt back to zero. The thought was that any additional monies they collected would be put away for further treatment, hospital visits, whatever might happen. She wanted to thank me again. I felt terrific. But instead, and unbeknownst to Mrs. Cruz, her husband Florio had been making withdrawals from the account and going to the track. He thought he could win big for them, but that was just a rationalization. He was a gambling addict."

"How much did he lose?" Ari asked.

Ryland flipped through a few more pages. "About half before Mrs. Cruz realized what was happening."

Jack finished his latte and set down his cup. "How did she find out?"

"The bills kept coming and were marked overdue. She confronted him, and he admitted what he'd done. He'd taken about eight thousand of the fifteen and bet on the ponies—and lost. At that point, she and Elijah became the owners of the account, Florio took a second job, and they did their best to keep the theft a secret. But secrets have a way of getting out. I got to work one day and had a voice mail telling me Florio Cruz had stolen CeCe's money. Proof would follow shortly. And it did. Later that morning a courier delivered a copy of a hospital bill marked overdue and dated a week before."

"Who sent it?" Ari asked.

"I never knew for sure, but my bet was on Isolde."

"Isolde?" Jack asked skeptically.

Ryland nodded. "She worked for Good Samaritan Hospital at the time. It was just a part-time gig because she was in school, but I'm guessing she got on their database and found it."

"What did you do with the information?"

"Exactly what I had to do as a journalist. I wrote a piece that alerted law enforcement. It all came out and the whole thing became a scandal for two news cycles. The family lost their friends, all the while wondering who'd told. Florio Cruz was sentenced to two years in prison, but the sentence was suspended so he could continue working the *three* jobs he'd taken to pay for CeCe's care."

"Why would Isolde do that to her father-in-law?"

Ryland looked away thoughtfully. "I'm not sure. There must have been some sort of bad blood between her and Florio. The family struggled financially until CeCe's eventual death."

"When Richie died, Elijah had a change jug by the register of the 7-Eleven where he worked. The money was for CeCe's care," Ari said.

"Hell of a way to pay astronomical hospital bills." She sat up straighter and said, "Don't get me started on health care." She glanced at her watch. "I've got to scoot, literally."

They all laughed, bussed their table and headed into the sunshine. Once Ryland was situated behind the steering wheel of her tricked-out van that allowed her to drive solely with her hands, she said, "What do you think this has to do with Richie's death?"

Jack shrugged. "We're not sure. But it's obvious a lot of people were trying to hide a lot of stuff."

Ryland bit her lip and Ari asked, "Is there something else you'd like to share?"

"Well, since I'm a real journalist and not a tabloid reporter, I don't like to gossip. With that said, I'll share one more fact: Florio Cruz attempted suicide shortly after his trial. He tried to hang himself in the garage. His wife found him in time."

Ari sensed she knew where the story was headed. "Did he try again?"

Ryland frowned and exhaled. "It wasn't just an attempt the next time. About a month after CeCe died, Florio Cruz rented a seedy hotel room on Van Buren and put a shotgun in his mouth. He wanted to make sure he did it right the second time."

CHAPTER TWENTY-ONE

"There is nothing more boring than a stakeout," Molly announced before she took a bite of her turkey sandwich.

"Agreed," Ari said, nibbling on the carrot sticks she'd brought. "But at least we're prepared." She reached behind Molly's seat and pulled out a sparkling water from the well-packed ice chest they'd assembled that morning. As two former cops, they knew stakeouts were about patience and preparedness.

They were sitting in Molly's truck, parked at a bar next to the McDonald's where Wolf Martinez worked. Molly had sent one of her female employees into the McD's that morning looking for Wolf. A chatty high school student said he worked that afternoon until closing at eleven. For fifty bucks the student was willing to forget the conversation.

Molly and Ari had decided the only way they would learn about Wolf Martinez's life was to follow him. Molly had spent the morning with her IT guy, delving into Wolf's financials with the help of Grady Quigley. Now that Richie's death was officially on the front burner again, Glendale PD was happy to have help.

On paper, Wolf Martinez had no life. He'd never owned a home, had no investments, and had one credit card with a thousand-dollar balance, most of the charges to a gaming store. He had a checking account that received his anemic McDonald's paycheck, and most of his debits were to a local grocery store, a hardware store, and Costco.

As they followed the money trail back to the early nineties, the time when Wolf supposedly peddled meth, there weren't any red flags. They imagined he'd hid his money quite well. He'd always lived in his parents' house, and he'd never bought a car through a dealership—only through private parties. His tricked-out '82 Trans Am sat in a parking space close to the front window, no doubt so Wolf could keep an eye on his prized possession.

"He's the scariest kind of criminal," Molly said when she shared the info with Ari. "He doesn't make mistakes, and whenever he senses danger, like the drug business at the 7-Eleven drying up after Richie's death, he pulls out. Great instincts."

"Like a real wolf."

"What about the parents' financials?"

"Nothing unusual."

"Wow," Ari said unenthusiastically.

So there was no other way to know Wolf's life than to watch him live it. She checked her watch. Ten fifty-eight.

"You know," Molly started, "I've been thinking about your conversation with Ryland Norris. Isolde has got some balls to turn in her own father-in-law."

"I've been trying to understand why she did that. She had to know it would tear the family apart and put even more stress on Elijah."

"True. But if she's got a streak of self-righteous indignation, the fallout wouldn't matter to her. Some people can't stomach wrongdoing of any kind. They're so filled with duty that they always do what they perceive is the right thing."

For a split-second, Ari thought of Richie. Molly could've been talking about him. "I don't know if that describes Isolde or not," she replied.

Molly finished her seltzer water and dropped the can into their recycle bag. "Well, if it's true, then I think that removes all suspicion from Elijah. I know you, Jack, and Hubbard were convinced of his innocence, but I wasn't."

"And you are now?"

"If Isolde is the type of person I described, and if Elijah was the killer, she wouldn't have allowed him to remain free. She couldn't have. It would've ruined her moral code."

"I see what you mean." She turned in her seat. "I'm thinking Kelly Owens is still alive and Wolf is helping him. What do you make of that theory?"

Molly leaned back and considered the question. "From what we've learned of Wolf, I think he's one of the few people I've ever met who's cautious enough to keep a secret for a lifetime, like Manny Cortez described. So, yes, I think that theory is possible." She pointed to the McDonald's. "Here he comes."

As the lights went out in the McDonald's and employees dispersed to the parking lot, Wolf ducked into his Trans Am and headed for the exit.

"That's interesting," Molly said. "He's not going home. His house is in the opposite direction."

As Molly stealthily followed Wolf, Ari dug out the binoculars and camera. He turned south onto the 101 and immediately hit the gas. In a half-mile he was going ninety.

"Do you think he made us?" Ari asked.

"No, I think he's a middle-aged idiot, trying to relive his teenage years with his hot car," Molly growled. "It's a good thing we put that tracker on."

While they'd staked out the McDonald's, another of Molly's associates had played a klutzy customer who spilled her purse next to Wolf's car. While she collected her things, she slapped a tracking device on the underside of his car. Molly had guessed Wolf liked to drive fast—and she was right.

The 101 was still relatively crowded. They were going eighty and weaving in and out of traffic carefully. Ari couldn't see Wolf, but the screen on Molly's phone indicated he was only a mile ahead.

"I think he slowed down," Ari commented.

"Probably an accident."

"No, he's getting on I-10, heading for Phoenix. Maybe there's a lot of traffic on the ramp."

"That's interesting. We'll get off a mile before the ramp and I'll take the surface streets. Then we'll catch up to him."

Three miles later Wolf exited the freeway and went south into Laveen, one of Phoenix's poorer suburbs. Two more turns into a sleepy, dark industrial area and they spotted him as he pulled up to a chain link fence with a rolling gate. Next to the well-protected parking area sat a single-story stucco building, the nondescript type found on thousands of corners in Phoenix and its suburbs. Behind the fenced area sat a Lexus, a BMW, and a yellow Corvette.

"That Corvette looks familiar," Molly said.

She killed her lights and parked across the street while Ari pulled out the binoculars. "The building may be nothing to look at, but it has a solid steel door and a keypad entrance."

Wolf rolled through the open gate which slowly closed behind him. He pulled into the space closest to a back door, also fitted with a keypad entry. Another minute passed but he remained in the car. "Why isn't he getting out?" Molly asked.

"Don't know. Maybe he's on the phone."

Just then the back door opened and a buxom woman wearing only a leopard-printed silk robe bounded down the short staircase, her enormous breasts jiggling from the effort. Despite the high blond wig she wore, Ari recognized Kacy Owens.

"And there she is," Molly said, leaning closer to the windshield. "That's Kacy, right?"

"Yup."

Wolf emerged from the car and Kacy flew into his arms. They exchanged a long kiss, one that gave Wolf enough time to grab her ass and pull her as close to him as possible. When the kiss ended, his hand moved to her right breast. They exchanged a few words while he blatantly fondled her beneath the folds of the robe.

"I don't even need the binoculars for this show," Molly deadpanned.

Ari focused on Kacy's face, which was caked in makeup, more than she wore at the strip club. Dramatic makeup. Wig. Robe. "I think we've found Wolf Martinez's real career. He makes porn. And Kacy's one of his stars."

They remained parked across from the building for nearly an hour—until a Phoenix black and white unit pulled up behind them. Molly identified herself as a P.I., and once Ari explained who she was, and more importantly, who her *father* was and why they were there, the officers were more than happy to answer some questions about the building on their beat. They had never had any complaints or reasons to knock on the front door. Some of the street people said it was a porn business, but the cops had no indication of illegal activity like drugs or prostitution. They had never seen anything but high-end cars in the lot and people came and went at all hours. The officers left, and Ari and Molly decided to leave as well, before someone came out of the building wielding something like a bat.

Ari called Jack on their way home and gave him the particulars, including the address of the building. When he appeared the next morning on her doorstep, he had more information about their visit with the cops. "A concerned neighbor called in to report a suspicious vehicle. I ran the phone number, but it was a burner phone. The location of the call, however, was from inside the building."

"So they have cameras," Molly said as she poured her first cup of coffee. "Then they're trying to protect whatever it is they're doing inside. Probably something illegal, even if the cops don't know about it."

"It could be they're trying to keep their adult porn studio under wraps," Ari suggested. "That building borders a residential neighborhood. If the neighbors got wind of what sat across the street, they'd probably show up at the city council chambers or the local police precinct."

"True," Molly conceded.

"Well, I ran a check on the building," Jack said. "It's owned by El Lobo Productions, aka The Wolf Productions, but Wolf Martinez's name is nowhere to be found. There are papers of incorporation and the officers are mostly people I've never heard of, and, according to our records, they don't exist. Except one. Kelly Owens."

Ari looked up from her bagel. "Seriously?"

He dropped a stack of papers on the counter, and she and Molly scanned them. The Articles of Incorporation listed five unknowns and Kelly Owens. Jack had also included a shot from the El Lobo Productions website, specifically its catalog page. Such titles as, *Wet and Steamy vol. 1*, *Beach Blanket Bang-O*, and *Filthy Friends* could be purchased for the low price of $19.99 each.

She rubbed her forehead and willed away the forming headache. "How did we get so far away from Richie's murder?"

Jack wrapped a comforting arm around her shoulder. "Because he walked in on some bad stuff with bad dudes."

She heard Jack sniffle and knew what would come next. She held up her index finger. "Don't. Don't blame yourself and don't start to cry. I'm tired of being sorry and feeling guilty. Neither of us killed Richie. We will always miss him, but we're going to figure out who pulled that trigger."

CHAPTER TWENTY-TWO

Ari and Molly spent the morning poring over the case file, the witness statements, and Ari's notes. Jack went downtown and spoke to various contacts about El Lobo Productions. The three of them believed Wolf was the key, but they had no leverage to make him talk. It infuriated Ari to think that he might have information about Richie's killer—might even know the killer's identity—but wouldn't assist them.

Molly looked up suddenly. "What about Jesus Santiago? Didn't you say that Westside Homeboys learned Kelly was the shooter? Who told them?"

Ari flipped through her notes. "You're right. Jesus was going to think about that some more. Let me text Lorraine and have her call him." Molly picked up the witness statements and headed for the living room. She dropped the statements on the floor.

"What are you doing?" Ari asked.

"I'm trying to see this from a different lens. I'm putting them in order based on geography, how near or far they were from the convenience store."

"Good idea, but you know, most of those statements weren't from witnesses. Nora Martinez told me and the statements confirm that most of the nearby neighbors were out of town on summer vacation."

Molly sighed. "I know, but I can't help thinking there's a keyclue here somewhere."

While she reviewed those statements, Ari pulled Hubbard, Quigley, and Taglio's notes, as well as Elijah's statements. Her father had brought over his whiteboard from the storage shed, and she grabbed a marker and drew three lines vertically, dividing the board into fourths. She wrote *Quigley*, *Hubbard*, *Taglio*, and *Elijah* at the top of each respective column.

"Now it's my turn to ask," Molly said. "What are you doing?"

"Chris Taglio said the timeline bothered him. Hubbard mentioned there was something sticking in his craw that he couldn't shake. Maybe if we look at their versions of the murder side-by-side we'll see what they missed."

"It's worth a try." Molly rose from the floor with a groan. "Let me help you. I got nothing from these statements."

"Above Elijah's column, I'll write the time Richie left the house. That was about nine-o-five, according to my dad. It's about eight minutes to cover the ten blocks, because Richie would've taken a longer route that was well lit. He didn't like riding in the dark alone. If he stopped to talk to people, it might've taken him twenty or twenty-five minutes."

"Okay, so if he didn't stop, he arrived at the store around nine-thirteen," Molly concluded. "He probably spent a minute with Glenn, but let's say he entered the store at nine-fifteen for good measure. Now, what time did Grady Quigley arrive on the scene?"

Ari grabbed a folder. "9-1-1 got Elijah's call at ten-o-eight. Officers Quigley and Prayman arrived at ten-thirteen."

"Man, that's a long time to look at baseball cards. Are you sure about the time he left the house?"

"Well, not exactly. He asked me to go with him a little before nine. I'm guessing that after I said no, he didn't wait much longer before he snuck out. He might've checked to see that our parents were busy before he crawled out his bedroom window."

"Okay. And what time did Elijah say he arrived?"

"He didn't offer an exact time. He said it was after nine." Ari made a bullet point under Elijah's name and added the note.

Molly picked up Elijah's file. "And he said other people came in, but he didn't count or know how many."

"Right. I'll add that."

"We also know from Elijah and Glenn's movie, that when Kelly Owens walked in, Elijah thought the store was empty, correct?"

"Yes," Ari replied.

Molly stroked her chin, deep in thought. "How long are people in convenience stores?"

"Under five minutes?"

"Max," Molly said. "You get in and get out, especially late at night."

"True."

"Sometimes you went with Richie when he bought cards, so how long did he usually take to pick out the packs he wanted?"

"It could take a while," Ari admitted. "He'd pick a pack out and tap it in his hand, and sometimes he'd put it back and sometimes he'd keep it to buy."

"Did you ever get annoyed with him for taking too long?"

Ari laughed. "Sometimes. I'd go get what I wanted, usually some animal crackers, and then I'd go find him still standing in front of the trading cards. He never came looking for me."

"What was the longest you ever had to wait for him?"

Ari settled on the edge of the dining room table and closed her eyes. One particular moment from that summer stood out. She'd wanted to hurry to Scott's and say hi to Blythe before Blythe left for her job at the mall. It seemed so important then. Ari agreed to go to the 7-Eleven with Richie before they rode over to Scott's, but she needed to arrive by ten-fifty to catch Blythe. But Richie had taken twenty minutes in the trading card aisle before he was ready to make his purchase. She'd been furious—and she'd missed seeing Blythe that day.

"Twenty minutes," she whispered.

"I get why the timeline bothers Taglio. Let's say Richie headed right over to the 7-Eleven. You said he was itching to get there. He was certain this purchase would net him the Eric Karros baseball card. If he was that determined, then he probably didn't stop to chat. Maybe he waved at people, but when a kid's impatient, he's focused on what he wants."

"I agree with that," Ari said. "Richie had tunnel vision sometimes."

"So he arrives at nine-fifteen. Even if he broke his own record for choosing trading cards and spent twenty-five minutes staring at the display, it's still only nine-forty."

"Yes, but the timeline still works under that theory. Nora Martinez says she heard the shot sometime around nine-forty and then saw the car just a few minutes later. Elijah admits he struggled to keep it together after Kelly ran out. He even threw up. He may have waited ten or fifteen minutes before he called the police. He might've been in shock. Grady Quigley told me that when he arrived, he found Elijah sitting on the floor in front of the cash register, surrounded by all the change from the jug."

She closed her eyes. The answer was close, but she couldn't see it. Then mariachi music from her phone filled the room. "Hey, Lorraine, you're on speaker. Molly's here."

"Hola, chicas. I called Jesus and he pinged me back in five minutes. We got lucky. He couldn't remember who told the Homeboys about Kelly, but his wife had been standing nearby when he played my message. *She* remembered. She said it was Wolf Martinez."

"Wolf Martinez told George and Damian that Kelly Owens shot Richie," Molly repeated.

"That's what she said. She recalled George showing up at their door at one in the morning, about two days after Richie's death. George was hyped up. She didn't hear what was said since she stayed in the bedroom, but she jarred Jesus's memory. Wolf Martinez had gone to George and Damian, saying he knew the identity of the shooter. He said he'd tell them, but he wanted a favor."

"Of course," Ari said. "What did he want?"

"He wanted another loan for twenty thousand. George and Damian hesitated because that was serious money, but Damian pleaded with George to give it to Wolf, because he wanted justice for Richie's killer, since Richie had been such a good friend to Manny."

"Did he say what he wanted the money for?" Molly asked.

"No."

Ari stared at the whiteboard, trying to plug Wolf Martinez into the timeline. She turned toward the phone. "Did he say how he knew Kelly was the shooter?"

"He told the Homeboys he saw it."

They were certain Wolf Martinez had refused to step forward in order to protect his own interests.

"Think about it," Molly said. "This guy is incredibly cautious. He halts his meth business after Richie's death. No way was he going to put himself in the middle of a homicide investigation. But he uses his leverage to get the capital for another business— maybe his adult film business. He gave the information to George, who he assumed would probably kill Kelly Owens and save the taxpayers a ton of money on an expensive trial."

"It's almost like he was trying to do my family a favor," Ari said and winced. "So we're back to thinking maybe the Homeboys took out Kelly?"

"Could be," Molly said. "But we definitely have a reason now to pick up Wolf Martinez for questioning. If he witnessed a homicide and didn't come forward, he could be arrested for obstructing justice."

CHAPTER TWENTY-THREE

"We're not picking up Wolf yet," Jack disagreed after Ari and Molly shared Jesus's information over the phone. Jack was still downtown and involved with his own case.

"What the hell are you saying, Dad? He's the key!"

"I've done some digging and I've called in a few favors with some old friends. Talking about El Lobo Productions is a different conversation than talking about Richie's homicide."

"Such as?" Molly asked.

"Over the years there's been a buzz that El Lobo Productions has a side business of human trafficking. Have you heard of it?"

Ari snorted. "You mean where teenage kids, usually runaway girls, are sold into slavery? Yeah, I've heard of it. Wolf Martinez is involved in trafficking?" She gritted her teeth. "I swear to God. If I get a chance to kill that sick son of a bitch, I'll do it."

"And I'll help," Molly said.

"You'd have to get in line behind all the police officers who've watched his operation for years and not been able to make a strong enough connection for an arrest. His studio's been raided half a dozen times, but everyone has I.D., the appropriate paperwork to be in the industry, an industry I might add that is more lucrative than anything else on the face of the earth."

"How come the local cops don't know about it?" Molly asked. "They told us El Lobo is a quiet neighbor."

"This is federal," Jack said. "They don't always communicate." Molly nodded.

"If they can't catch him for trafficking, why can't we go get him and threaten obstruction? I'm sure Jesus would testify to the conversation he had with George," Ari said.

"There's the issue of hearsay," Molly replied. "We need to get something on Wolf Martinez so he'll tell us what happened that night. He'll just deny everything, babe, and then we've shown our hand."

The conversation stopped as they each thought about a path forward. "What about Kacy?" Ari suggested. "Could we use her as leverage?"

"I don't see how, honey," Jack said. "You said she was close to Wolf, and she's certainly not going to implicate her brother as Richie's shooter."

"Even if she learns Wolf had him assassinated by the Homeboys? If she knows anything the cops could use as leverage, I think she'd do it to vindicate Kelly."

Jack said his goodbyes—he'd been summoned by the chief. Molly and Ari continued the discussion.

"There's no proof Kelly is dead," Molly argued. "And she's holding a letter that suggests he's alive and living...somewhere."

"I think it's worth a try. Let's go talk to her," Ari said, grabbing her purse, Kacy's address, and Chris Taglio's missing person's report. "Are you coming?"

Kacy lived in an old ranch house subdivision in Central Phoenix. Ari had sold many of these modest homes with their red brick exteriors and two-car carports. These post-WWII suburbs had grown the Baby Boomers, strongholds of community, family, and the American Dream. Many were now rentals owned by the Boomers who'd grown up in them, and the neighborhoods teetered between sketchy and respectable, depending on the rigorousness of the background checks done on the renters. Still, the houses commanded a hefty price tag because of their proximity to downtown.

Kacy's front yard was well-tended with freshly cut grass and spring flowers in the pots that lined the small porch. Hers was one of the few houses that possessed a garage. Ari imagined that with the flashy car she owned she wouldn't want to keep it in a carport, a thief's favorite quick stop. As they approached the front door, they noticed a child's trike strategically hidden behind the largest pot.

Molly pointed at it. "Kids?"

"We didn't find anything in her background that suggested children," Ari replied. "Maybe it belongs to a friend."

The woman who answered the door bore only a slight resemblance to the showgirl they'd met outside the cabaret. Kacy's short dark hair was cut in a punk style, nothing like the flowing blond locks she wore at the club. Her face was softer and her eyes wide. She actually was rather pretty without all the makeup. She rubbed the side of her head and yawned. "What are you doing here?" she asked.

"I'm sorry to bother you now, Kacy," Ari said, "but we need to talk to you about a few things. Can we come in?"

Her tired gray eyes studied Ari, and then she nodded, holding the door open. They stepped a few feet over the threshold, and Kacy closed the door. She leaned against the wall and crossed her arms. There were no pleasantries as they all knew solving Ari's brother's murder meant implicating Kacy's brother. The only bond they shared was a curiosity about the truth.

"Here's the thing. We know you're involved with Wolf in the adult film business." Ari paused and Kacy winced. "We've discovered that Wolf is at the center of our problems, both yours and mine."

"What?"

"Wolf told George Delgado that he saw my brother's murder. Kacy, Wolf knows the truth, whatever it is."

When Kacy's face remained stony, Molly said, "Did you know this, Kacy? Has Wolf told you anything about that night?"

Kacy's face awakened with the news. "What? No, he's never mentioned anything. He's always said that Kelly ran away when he heard the Homeboys were after him."

"If Kelly ran, it's because Wolf told the Homeboys he was double-crossing them," Ari added.

She frowned, but the gears in her brain were turning.

"Remember we told you Kelly was a police informant? He used to meet a police detective out at the drive-in where Wolf worked," Molly said.

She scratched the side of her head. "No, that can't be true."

"Unfortunately, it is," Ari said gently, "Wolf isn't who you think he is."

"Oh, he's exactly who I think he is," Kacy retorted. She went to an end table and grabbed a pack of cigarettes. After she'd lit one with a nearby Zippo and took a long drag, she dropped onto the couch. She didn't speak, instead choosing to stare up at the ceiling. Eventually she said, "What you're telling me makes sense. It explains some conversations."

Molly shifted her stance, and Ari knew she was growing impatient. "Look, we know you're involved with him, but if your brother is dead, there's a good chance Wolf Martinez is the reason why."

Kacy looked from Molly to Ari. She made a sweeping motion with her free hand. "He's been good to me, you know?"

"Whose tricycle is outside?" Molly asked.

What was left of Kacy's bravado evaporated. She carefully wiped her eyes, as if she were actually wearing makeup. "I told him to bring that in," she mumbled. She absently glanced down the hallway before she said, "I have a son. He's five. His name is Isaac."

Ari slid onto the couch next to her. "Does he live here with you?"

"Sometimes. Mainly he's with my aunt. I haven't found a way out of my life, and I know it's not the life I want for him. So until I do, he mainly stays with her." She stared at Ari, her eyes steeled with resolve. "I'm going to make that happen soon."

"I doubt that will happen with Wolf in your life." Ari hoped she sounded gentle. "Is Wolf the father?"

Kacy nodded and wiped her eyes again. "He doesn't know Isaac is his, at least I don't think he knows."

They heard a thud and a deep voice said, "Shit!"

"Is someone here?" Ari asked, worriedly. "It isn't Wolf, is it?"

"No, it's not Wolf. It's my co-star, Mitch. We're kind of a thing. It happens sometimes when you spend a lot of hours in bed with someone."

"Does Wolf know?"

Kacy looked flabbergasted. "No. Wolf and I are strictly a meet-on-his-turf type of couple. He's never been to this house, and he knows nothing about my life outside of work. When I found out I was pregnant four years ago, I disappeared. He and I had broke up anyways, so it didn't matter. When I returned, all he cared about was me going back to work."

"How would he feel if he knew he was a dad?" Molly asked.

Kacy turned toward Molly slowly. "Are you blackmailing me?"

"No," Ari said. "We're trying to solve the murder of an innocent eight-year-old. My brother wasn't you, Kacy. He didn't grow up in your rough life. And I'm sorry. I'm sorry you had such a shitty parent and you and Kelly had it so hard. But I need your help. We need something on Wolf so we can use it as leverage and make him tell us what he knows."

"I'll tell you if she won't."

A shirtless, tall man, whose tanned muscles looked as if they were about to explode through his skin, sauntered into the room. He wore pajama bottoms and his chest was covered in blond hair that matched his Mohawk and mutton chops.

"Mitch," Kacy warned. "Don't."

Mitch shook his head. "I'm sick of sneaking around that no-good turd."

He fished a cigarette from the pack on the end table and lit it before he turned to Ari and Molly. "He's a bad dude into bad shit. From what I've heard him say, and what Kacy has said, everything you need is in that house."

"What house?" Molly asked.

"That house he shares with that psycho mother of his."

"Mitch," Kacy said in a harsh tone. "Don't go there."

Ari cocked her head skeptically. Mitch smirked at her. "Had you fooled, didn't she? The old hippie lady that wants to save the world? Wants to bust all the criminals and protect her neighborhood?"

"She doesn't?"

"Shit, no," Mitch snorted. He turned to Kacy. "Are you going to tell them, or should I?"

Kacy shook her head and fled the room.

As the bedroom door slammed shut he said, "The only person she wants to protect—and control—is her son. Seriously, there's evidence in that house. Everybody's afraid of Wolf, and they should be. But who's Wolf afraid of?" He looked at them as if they should ask him the question.

"Who is Wolf afraid of, Mitch?" Molly asked impatiently.

"His mother."

CHAPTER TWENTY-FOUR

"We don't have enough for a search warrant," Molly said as they drove home.

After Mitch's announcement about Nora, he elaborated that Wolf had once told Kacy his mother kept him in line with a secret file. She claimed to have evidence that would send Wolf away for a long time. Wolf also mentioned that his mother might have murdered his father, but he'd never be able to prove it. Consequently, he did whatever Nora said—got out of the meth business, continued to live at home, and took a crappy job to conceal his true wealth. Molly and Ari had attempted to talk with Kacy through the locked bedroom door and confirm Mitch's statements, but she just kept shouting, "Go away!"

"How much do you think Nora knows?" Ari mused.

"A lot, I'd guess. She might even know who killed your brother, and if Wolf was the doer, and she knows it, I'd guess that picture of the fender and the story about the killer driving away is a ruse. She was casting suspicion on someone else since Wolf could've strolled across the parking lot and through his back gate in ten seconds. Maybe Nora's story of tripping over some toys before she got to the fence is a lie."

Nora could easily be a conspirator. If she had a secret file, it probably was filled with pictures and notes. *Pictures.* Ari thought of the stacks and stacks of craft boxes filled with horrible photos. Maybe that was the point. Maybe Nora was deliberately taking poor photos in case somebody ever came looking for her secret file. It would take days to properly peruse all of those boxes. It all seemed farfetched, but sometimes people were just that crazy.

She thought back to the box of photos Nora had shared with her. It was filled with nothing usable—except the two photos that had slipped to the bottom: the one with Wolf and Elijah, and the other of Wolf and an unknown female. And since Ari had been smart enough to keep them with her, they were the only two photos that hadn't been stolen.

She jumped out of the truck as soon as Molly stopped.

"Hey, what's on fire?" Molly called.

"I've got an idea," Ari said, racing through the house to the dining room. She rifled through the various piles of notes and files until she found the picture of Wolf with the young girl. She hadn't studied it carefully, nor had she investigated the girl's identity. It hadn't seemed important.

While Wolf only offered his profile, the girl had unwittingly faced Nora's camera. She was a teenager, with a round face and dark, feathered shoulder-length hair. She had on a T-shirt, jeans, and a jean jacket with a variety of buttons on the front, and she wore a backpack.

"Who's that?" Molly asked over her shoulder.

"I don't know, but I'm thinking it's important we find out."

Four hours later they had an answer from Molly's former police partner, Andre. They had emailed the picture to Jack, who was involved in the arrest of the man allegedly killing homeless people, so Jack had forwarded the photo to Andre.

"This is Emily MacMillan," Andre explained over the phone. "She's a runaway, or rather, she *was* a runaway fourteen years ago from Provo, Utah. Left a note for her Mormon parents saying she was suffocating. Told them she was gay, and she thought her choices were to run away or kill herself. She begged them not to look for her. Of course they launched a manhunt, but it turned up nothing."

"When was that exactly?" Molly asked.

"She left on June 23, 2004. A week after high school graduation."

Molly groaned. "I don't think that helps us. We can question Wolf, but he could just say they randomly met."

"Ah, but then the story gets interesting. There was a police report filed on March 28, 2007. Emily's mom says Emily called. She was whispering. Said she was being held against her will. She had no idea where she was. She managed to say, 'Help me,' before the phone was yanked away and she screamed. Then the line went dead."

"She was kidnapped," Ari concluded. "Maybe sold into slavery. This picture could be Wolf's initial meeting with her."

"Any idea how old this picture is?"

"No, not at all. I'm thinking it accidentally got shoved into the box Nora let me borrow. The night she gave me the box she mentioned an incident caused by her nephew where most of the boxes toppled to the floor. He helped her pick them up, so he may have unwittingly shoved this photo in that box."

"Lucky for us," Andre said. "Emily MacMillan's disappearance is still an open case. This photo, along with the circumstantial evidence the vice squad has put together, is enough for a warrant. I'm working on it now with Jessie Gunter, one of the Glendale detectives assigned to Richie's case. And we're formally bringing in Kacy to discuss whatever Wolf might have said to her about his mother or her house. And Ari, since you've already spoken with Nora Martinez and been in the house, Detective Gunter wants you present when we go knock on the old lady's door."

Detective Jessie Gunter was a pint-sized firecracker who didn't reach five feet, but her serious expression and firm handshake told Ari and Molly she was all about business.

"Call me Jessie," she said to both of them. "And please accept my condolences on the passing of your brother. I lost my little brother to leukemia in two thousand eight."

Ari nodded, grateful for a kindred spirit.

Just then the front door swung open and Nora charged down the path to greet them. Her expression telegraphed her displeasure. "What ya doin' here, fuzz?"

Andre laughed. "Haven't heard that one in a few decades."

Jessie introduced herself and presented Nora with the search warrant and told her the particulars. Nora took her time reading it while Andre and the officers went inside.

Her eyes narrowed and she turned to Ari. "Are you responsible for this, Ms. Adams?"

"No, this is on you and Wolf."

Nora folded the warrant until it was only a small square, a symbol of what she thought of it. Ari saw the cruelty in her eyes and pictured a domineering, hard, and unforgiving mother. For a brief moment, she felt sorry for Wolf.

"C'mon, babe," Molly said, as she took Ari's arm and led her away. "That woman is a viper. Probably drove her husband to an early grave. Or, she might have put him in it."

They stayed out of the way as the officers searched. Ari's gaze frequently traveled to the front window and Nora Martinez, who sat ramrod-straight on her porch rocker. She seemed to have no interest in the hubbub transpiring inside her home. Maybe she was confident they would find nothing, or she'd accepted her fate and had known this day would eventually come. She couldn't protect Wolf forever.

All of the craft boxes filled with photos were confiscated and loaded onto dollies. Ari pitied the poor officers stuck with the tedious task of combing through the thousands of photos.

"Got something!"

A diminutive female officer rushed into the living room holding an envelope in one hand and what looked like a safety deposit box key. She handed the find to Jessie, who confirmed it was a key to a box at a nearby bank. "I guess we'll be taking a field trip," she said to Ari and Molly. "Any idea what might be inside?"

"The truth," Ari replied.

"Got something!" another officer called before Andre could finish verifying the location of the bank.

A tall Hispanic officer appeared with a rustic wooden box, the lid of which opened like a book. Inside was a stenographer's notepad and dozens of photos. Jessie, Andre, Ari, and Molly migrated to the couch and the officer placed the box on the table. They all donned gloves, and Ari immediately gravitated to the notepad, while Andre and Molly rifled through the pictures.

"Wolf is in every single one," Molly said.

Ari scanned the dozens of entries on several pages of the notepad. A date was listed followed by a hashtag and a number. "Do the photos have a number on the back?" she asked. Molly and Andre nodded. On the sixth page of the notepad the entries abruptly stopped, the last one dated being August 10, 2010.

Ari grabbed some photos and after thumbing through them, made two stacks: one held pictures of Wolf talking to young women, the other of Wolf talking to young men. She returned to the stack of young women, and based on the body language in the picture, put a few of those photos in the other stack.

"What are you seeing?" Molly asked.

"In this stack, Wolf is making an exchange, sometimes to women, but mainly to men. In the other stack, he's talking to women and he's much more animated. He really seems to be enjoying himself."

"You're right," Andre observed. "His facial expressions are clearly different."

"And he's not making any furtive gestures, and they don't seem to be exchanging anything," Molly added.

"Exactly," Ari said, glad that these two formerly combative friends seemed to be communicating. "He's also much younger in this first stack. I'm thinking that stack with men and women are drug deals, and the other stack… Well, maybe those pictures show a wolf hunting his prey."

Nora Martinez requested they chat in her backyard. Her back was killing her from sitting on the hard porch swing too long, and after presenting her medical marijuana card to Andre, she pulled out her vape pen for a smoke. She didn't seem nervous, and after a few hits, she settled on a cushioned rattan chair that was part of a larger patio set. She offered a weak smile to Ari.

She looks relieved.

They had found nothing that directly implicated her in anything illegal, and the idea of her being a co-conspirator was only a theory. She'd taken pictures. That was all. They had no tangible proof and she knew it. Jessie and Andre had asked to chat, and after assurances that she wasn't under arrest, she agreed to speak with them.

Jessie motioned toward Nora's wooden box, which she'd placed on the patio table. "Tell us about these photos."

She slowly met her gaze. Even stoned, she was cagey and careful. "What do you want to know?"

"Why are these photos in this special box we found in your bedroom and not with all the other photos in the cardboard boxes?"

"They're pictures of my son. I'm his mother. I take his picture. It's what mothers do. Doesn't your mother take your picture, detective?"

She offered a pleasant smile. "Of course." She reached into her jacket pocket and withdrew the photo of Wolf with Emily MacMillan. "I think this might be a photo that belonged in your box."

Nora studied the photo and took a deep inhale from her pen. Despite her relaxed state, she tensed. Nora realized the implications of a police detective possessing one of her confidential pictures. She held up the photo and looked at Ari quizzically, as if to say, "Did I really give this to you?"

"It was stuffed underneath the stack in the box you gave me," Ari explained. "I'm guessing your nephew tossed it in there when he helped you pick up the dropped boxes."

Nora closed her eyes momentarily and shook her head. She glanced at the photo once more, and then her gaze wandered amidst the three of them. "So, who is she?"

"You don't know?" Andre asked skeptically.

"Haven't the foggiest."

Andre reached into the box and withdrew five more pictures of Wolf talking to different young women. "What about these girls?"

She shrugged. "Not a clue." They eyed her suspiciously and she added, "Seriously. I have no idea who *any* of these people are in these pictures. I don't know what their relationship is with my son. I mean, yes, in some of those pictures, it looks like Wolfie is exchanging something with the other subject in the photo. But I don't know what it was. Didn't want to know. Didn't need to know."

The pieces were coming together. Ari set a hand on the box. "You've got another set of these photos, don't you? In the safety deposit box."

"I do. So what?"

"Why?" Andre asked.

Nora remained silent.

"In case Wolf ever decided to destroy this set," Molly concluded. She glanced at Ari, who nodded. Nora shrugged.

"You really don't know what Wolf is involved in, do you?" Ari pressed. "Like you said, you didn't need to know so long as you had something to hold over him. As long as you had leverage."

Nora's shoulders drooped and she clicked off the pen. "Do any of you have children?" They all shook their heads and she smirked. "Didn't think so. You have no idea what it's like to lose control of your child, your baby. I've known Wolfie wasn't right in the head since he was eight. I wanted to take him to a counselor, but my dumb macho Latino husband wouldn't hear of it. First time Wolfie killed one of the neighborhood feral cats, he brought it home to show me. He couldn't understand why I was horrified. My husband shared my revulsion but not enough to get Wolfie some help. And then it just got worse.

He was into the drug scene before his thirteenth birthday. One day I happened to be taking out the trash. I saw him behind the 7-Eleven, talking to an older guy. They both looked suspicious and nervous. That was when I started taking pictures of *him*." She paused and took a deep breath. "I'd been trying to help the community for decades. I took pictures of anything suspicious, not just Wolf. I tried to convince the police about Mellow, the day clerk. I kept my eyes on the Homeboys, especially George and Damian." She turned and pointed her finger at Ari. "And I'm telling you, whether you believe me or not, a car drove away after your brother's murder."

"When did you share this with Wolf?" Andre asked.

She pointed at the box. "I shared what I had with him soon after your brother died. Whenever the date of the last entry is in the book, I shared it the next day. I gave him an ultimatum. I told him he *had* to get out of the drug business…"

"Did you ask him about the drugs he was selling? Which, by the way, was methamphetamine, one of the worst street drugs ever designed." Andre's voice rose with his anger. "Did you ask him?"

"No." She lowered her head and wiped the tears from her face.

"Was your husband involved?" Ari asked.

The look Nora Martinez gave Ari was deadly. It said *Don't go there*. "No," she whispered.

"What about the photos of Wolf with the teenage girls?" Ari asked. She picked up the picture of Emily MacMillan. "This girl was a runaway who's never been found. Did you know that?"

"No, I didn't, and I don't know her," Nora whispered, clearly ashamed. "But one night I was watching the TV news, and the newscaster said something about a missing girl and showed a photo. She looked familiar so I scrounged around my box. I found a blurry picture of a girl who sort of looked like the one on TV, but the image was distorted and the hair color was different. I told myself there was no way Wolfie could be involved in something that horrible. He just couldn't," she said adamantly, her voice quaking. "What would it say about *me*?"

"So when you confronted Wolf the second time," Andre said, "you didn't mention your suspicions. You didn't ask him directly about the girl on the TV?"

"No, I told Wolfie that I didn't know what he was doing, and I didn't care, but it was going to stop." She raised her tear-stained face and met Ari's gaze. "I told him if he didn't quit whatever he was doing, I'd just take the photos to the police and let them sort it all out. And if it meant I went to jail, then maybe I deserved it. I couldn't bear what he'd done."

A sick feeling wrenched Ari's gut. "Are you talking about the drugs or the missing girls? Or are you talking about… something else?"

Nora didn't answer Ari. She turned and looked at Jessie. "I know Wolf was at work the night Richie Adams was killed. I know people vouched for him, but he came home a little before ten. He stormed through the house looking for his gun, which I'd hidden. Once he found it, he left. I ran outside to my perch. I'm almost positive the fender I photographed was his." She wiped her hands and said, "There you have it. That's all I know."

CHAPTER TWENTY-FIVE

"It's completely out of our hands now," Molly said as they cruised back to Central Phoenix.

Andre had called Jack and they agreed to meet at the Glendale precinct. Jessie arranged for Jack and Andre to be present for the interrogation of Wolf Martinez. She and Andre had arrested Wolf as he arrived at McDonald's for his shift. The youthful manager seemed astounded as they led him away in handcuffs. She told Jessie she couldn't believe he was guilty of anything. He was the ideal employee and one of the few people she could count on to show up to work.

"I want to go to the park," Ari announced. "It's a beautiful day, and I want to rent a canoe."

Molly glanced at her. "Right now? You want to get a canoe? Are you okay? What if your dad and Andre need you to look up something from the case file? What if there's something important in your notes that they need to disprove Wolf's story?" Molly was hyped. It was her usual mode when she felt a case was about to break.

Ari wasn't so sure. There were too many players to think about, and she was now positive most of them had had nothing to do with her brother's murder. Wolf's meth business, Kacy's relationship with Wolf, the Homeboys, Kelly's disappearance—all of it—was just life. It was twenty-five years' worth of collective baggage that belonged to some sketchy people.

"I'm thinking. Can we just get a canoe and paddle while I think?" she pleaded.

"Absolutely," Molly said. She kept her eyes on the road and stopped asking questions. Ari knew Molly's habits and Molly knew hers, and with Dr. Yee's intervention, they were that much more aware of each other's needs.

Something about the case still didn't make sense. She thought back to the timeline. She knew approximately when Richie had snuck out of the house. He wouldn't have waited long after she'd said no. She saw Chris Taglio's face as he put the crime scene photos in chronological order. He'd never called her back, and she assumed it meant he hadn't thought of anything new to tell her.

They arrived at Encanto Park. She followed Molly to the boathouse and waited by the shore, lost in her thoughts, while Molly paid for the canoe rental. She had to focus to get into the canoe, and it was fortunate she did since Molly slipped on a patch of mud and nearly went overboard. They laughed and started to paddle. Her mind returning to that night, she replayed the facts—twice—by the time they circled the lagoon.

She groaned and Molly said, "Not coming yet, huh?"

"It's close."

Her phone rang and Molly pivoted so she could hear as Ari turned on the speaker. "Hi, Dad."

"Hey. So Wolf refused to say anything until his attorney arrived…except…"

"Are you okay, Dad?"

"Yeah. Not done with the emotions, I guess. We were getting out of the car, and Martinez says to me, and I quote, 'I'm going to tell you one thing about your son's murder. It's the only thing I know, but I'm telling you because you had a great kid.'"

Ari heard the quake in his voice. He coughed again. "Martinez said, 'One day I heard a kid yelling. I ran outside and your son had just pulled up on his bike. He was pointing and yelling at two bangers running away. They'd tried to steal my expensive hubcaps, and your son stood up to them. I wanted to give him a reward, but he wouldn't take it. Said he was just being a good citizen like his parents taught him.'"

She felt Molly squeeze her hand as she blinked away the tears. She gulped some air and asked, "What did Martinez tell you about that night?"

"According to him, he left work to confront Kelly Owens. He didn't say anything about going home for his gun, not surprising, but when he stopped at the 7-Eleven to ask Elijah if he'd seen Kelly, the doors were locked. The lights were off and the front door was locked."

Molly and Ari exchanged quizzical looks. "What?"

"That's what he said."

"Do you believe him?" Molly asked incredulously.

"At this point, I don't know why he'd lie. I asked him why he didn't come forward with the information sooner, and he shrugged. Then he mumbled something about Detective Hubbard being a dick."

"That's not surprising," Ari said.

"I'm going to hang around until his attorney arrives. I'd like to hear what he says then. Might be helpful. You think about that piece of information and how we should proceed."

"Will do."

They hung up and Ari stared at the water. She wasn't sure if she agreed with her father. She could think of all sorts of reasons why Wolf Martinez would lie. He was a master of manipulation, and when it came to Richie's murder, Jack Adams had little objectivity. *But do I?*

"Son of a bitch!" Molly yelled, pulling off her leather boot. "That wasn't mud I slipped in. It was dog poop. Shit!"

"Literally," Ari said.

They both laughed and Ari retrieved some tissues from her purse. They did what they could to remove the poop and the smell from the inside of the canoe before they paddled to shore and a restroom.

"At least I didn't get it all over myself," Molly mumbled.

"Right."

And then the pieces fell into place.

CHAPTER TWENTY-SIX

Ari and Jack found Elijah out in the garage again, sanding his canoe. She hadn't yet shared her epiphany with her father, worried that if she did, he would come unglued.

"Hola," Elijah offered before he shook Jack's hand. "Sorry if I transferred some dust onto you."

"No worries," Jack said with a wave.

"Elijah, we need to talk."

Ari tried to keep her tone even, but she could tell Elijah knew something was different. He set his sander on the workbench and backed onto a nearby stool. Then the back door opened and Isolde appeared.

"Oh, hello. I didn't realize we had company. Could I offer you some lemonade or water?"

"We're fine," Jack said.

"They say they need to talk to me."

Isolde wiped her hands on the dishtowel she held but made no effort to go inside. "What about?" she asked, moving next to her husband.

Ari nodded at Jack. They'd already decided in the car that he would share the information provided by Wolf Martinez. "We found a witness, Elijah," Jack began.

"What? You mean, in addition to Glenn's film?"

"Yes."

They watched Elijah's blank stare. He looked at Ari and then settled his gaze on Jack. "And?"

"He came to the 7-Eleven a little before ten. He said the front door was locked and it looked like no one was there. The lights were off."

Elijah licked his lips. He shook his head and crossed his arms. Eventually, he looked up at both of them. "I don't know what to tell you."

"Yes, you do," Isolde scolded. He looked at her and she turned to Jack. "I am sorry, Jack. There's a piece of the story Elijah hasn't shared because he never thought it was important." She glanced at her husband and continued. "After Kelly Owens left the store, Elijah ran to the front and locked the door. Then he threw up and fell to his knees." She squeezed his shoulder. "He wasn't proud of his actions. Some would call it cowardice, but I think he was just responding to his fear. You understand that, yes?" She glanced at them before she added, "I'm guessing whoever came to the door couldn't see around the counter. He didn't see Elijah sitting in front of the counter, sobbing, while your poor son lay just a few more feet away."

Elijah reached up and clasped his wife's hand. "Thank you, mi amor." He turned to them. "I never mentioned that part because, well, I'm not proud."

"When did you call the authorities?" Jack asked.

"Um, after I locked the door, I guess. That's always been fuzzy."

Ari stared at Elijah. "And when did you turn off the lights?"

Elijah nodded, acknowledging he'd forgotten that part. "Sorry. I turned out the lights after I locked the door."

Jack shuffled his feet. "And when did you *unlock* the door?"

"When I heard the sirens. I got up, unlocked the door, and ran to meet the first responders. I slipped in a mudhole. That's how I got mud on my shirt. The stupid parking lot was littered with potholes. I told that to Detective Hubbard," he added.

"I remember those potholes," Ari said and Elijah nodded. "And that's in your initial statement to Detective Hubbard. But here's the other problem, Elijah. Detective Hubbard wasn't the first responder. Officer Grady Quigley and his partner, Officer Forrest Prayman were first on the scene. Grady's statement is different. He says they ran inside and found you sitting on the floor, surrounded by all of the change from the overturned jug. When I checked with him a little while ago, he says he's absolutely positive the front door was open."

"He's incorrect," Isolde spat. "My husband knows what he did or didn't do."

Elijah held up a hand. "Iso, don't lose your temper." He looked at Ari, and she saw his fatigue. He slumped on the stool, and he was starting to sweat. "I don't remember. I won't call anyone a liar." He sighed. "It was so long ago."

"Yes, but there's one other problem, Elijah." When he looked up at her, Ari knew the truth. "There hadn't been a rainstorm in a week. There were no mudholes. How did you get the mud on your shirt?"

He opened his mouth, but his wife interjected. "He probably got it from that filthy storeroom! That day clerk Mellow was a pig. I lost track of how often Elijah came home with a rip in his shirt. Sometimes his pants were covered in dirt and mud from that filthy storeroom. And those Slurpee machines leaked constantly."

As Isolde ranted, Elijah's gaze never left Ari. She saw the tortured man he was and had been for a quarter of a century. She was about to cry, so she simply said, "Please."

"Elijah, tell them about those working conditions. You—"

He put his index finger over her mouth. "Iso, mi amor, *silencio*. I can't carry this anymore."

He covered his face with his hands and Isolde wrapped herself around him, as if she could cocoon him from the truth. Perhaps that was what she'd been doing all along.

"Isolde, I'd like to know why you broke into my house," Ari said suddenly.

Isolde pulled away from her husband and crossed her arms. Gone was the caring wife. It was as if she'd lowered a shield around her. Elijah might be willing to talk, but Ari doubted Isolde would say another word.

Elijah looked at Ari curiously. "Are you insane?" Ari stared at Isolde, and he finally realized his wife had offered no protest. "Iso? What's going on?"

"I'd like to speak with an attorney," she said. "I understand neither of you is police, but you're only a step away." She turned to Elijah with a sad smile. "You were always too good for me. Do what you will." She kissed him on the forehead and disappeared into the house.

Elijah shook his head. "You deserve the truth. So long ago," he said wistfully.

"Try," Jack growled.

"You know about the drugs and the Homeboys. I wanted no part of that and for the most part they left me alone. George, the leader, had a crush on my sister CeCe and he always felt sorry for me. He knew a part of my life was focused on her care. So I was never pressured to join their gang, and I looked the other way when buyers came to the store asking for Mellow. It was sort of a gentleman's agreement."

He reached into his pocket for a handkerchief and blew his nose. "I didn't know Kelly Owens very well. He was a gringo wannabe-gangbanger, I guess. He ran some stuff for Mellow." He looked at Ari and said, "I had no idea he was ever interested in CeCe until you told me." He sighed. "CeCe got worse. My parents were about to lose their home. The bills were killing them. My father had misappropriated some of the donations." He bit his lip, took a deep breath. "I came home one day and found him hanging from a rafter in the garage. I cut him down and managed to save him, but he was never the same after that. He'd given up hope and was convinced he was a failure. That same night my mother gave me his gun, a Colt .45. She told me she never wanted to see it again. I knew she was afraid he'd use it on himself. Little did she know, he had a shotgun.

"Something had to be done. I needed cash, so I went to Wolf Martinez. I'd heard from Mellow that he was selling meth, and a lot of it. The Homeboys left him alone, partly because he was scary and partly because meth was so crazy scary. But he was making a lot of money, a lot more than the Homeboys. He never flaunted his money and left them with their pride. I think that's how they coexisted. Wolf was excited that I'd help him. He knew the store would be a lucrative location." Elijah gazed at Ari. "I'd only been selling for two weeks when your brother died. And I hated it. I vowed I'd get out as soon as I could."

He rubbed his hand along the side of the canoe and continued. "People on meth are dangerous when they need a fix and can't afford it. I'd almost been attacked, so I started bringing my father's .45 along with me to work. Then…"

He stopped talking and swallowed. "That day was an awful day that turned into the worst day of my life. Wolf called me in the morning and told me to be very cautious. He'd heard the police were cracking down on the Homeboys and their turf. He was worried his business would get caught up in the investigation. I started my shift completely shook up. And it was horribly hot. That rotten owner was dragging his heels about fixing the swamp cooler, and when I got there, Mellow looked like he was ready to pass out. He also told me Isolde had come by, and she was upset. She came in twenty minutes later and I could tell she'd been crying. It was busy so we couldn't be alone. When there was a break at the register, she pulled me to the side and told me she was pregnant.

"It wasn't joyous news. I was just putting my life on track with a degree. This money from Wolf would save my parents and pay for college. I saw her pain. Her fear. But there was no way I'd abort my child. I hugged her and told her everything would be all right. Then she left."

He looked up at Ari. "At some point your friend Glenn came in by himself. I was horrible to him. He got on my last nerve. I yelled and he left. I spent most of the day in a fog. There were a few transactions for Wolf, but I don't remember them. I was totally lost in the problems of my own life. I thought of the gun right under the counter. I thought about putting it against my head and ending my problems. I wasn't in a place to see anything good."

He stopped speaking and closed his eyes. She knew what was coming next and wondered if the lump in his throat was as large as the lump in hers. She started to cry before he uttered a word. "Around nine-fifteen, your brother came in. He waved and said hello. I didn't really notice him. I had two hours left in my shift, and I was counting the minutes. I needed to get home to Iso and talk about the baby. Others came in. A movie must've let out or something. That's how it sometimes goes at convenience stores. If Glenn snuck back in, I didn't notice. If he left because he thought I saw him, well, I didn't.

"Then Kelly Owens came in. I'm guessing he'd waited around the corner of the store until he thought it was empty. He was desperate, maybe as desperate as me. He was ranting about the cops being after him. How George and Wolf were going to kill him when they found out he'd really given the police valuable information about George's loan sharking deals. He wanted me to talk to them because they treated me differently. We had a level of respect. He was going to leave town for a while. I said I wouldn't get in the middle, and he just got louder. He got in my face and told me if I didn't help him, he'd tell the cops about me. Then he mocked me. How everybody thought I was a good guy, how I had them all fooled. I was just a drug dealer and no better than anyone else.

"I don't remember pulling out the .45, but I guess I did. I told him he needed to shut his mouth."

Elijah paused and clasped his hands. "I was pointing the gun at Kelly when your brother came around the corner. He'd heard everything. He'd actually been listening." Elijah looked up at Ari with pleading eyes. "He was so righteous. He didn't sound like a little boy at all. He sounded like a cop. He pointed at us and said we were bad men, and he was going to tell his father, the police detective, all about us. The last thing he said was that we were going to jail. I must have lowered the gun and set it on the counter. I felt so horrible. And I could never point a gun at a child. I don't remember Kelly picking it up, but he did."

Elijah tried to form words but he couldn't. He couldn't say it. Ari's tears bled upon other tears and she made no motion to stop them. She'd waited twenty-five years for this story, and now all she wanted was for it to be over. *Why did I ever want to know?*

"I screamed, 'Jesus Christ, you shot a kid!' I don't think he heard me. He dropped the gun and grabbed the counter. He was doubled over, wailing. I threw up in the garbage can. I looked at your brother, at Kelly. I saw my life ending. I saw Iso, alone and raising my child.

"My instincts took over. I opened the register and took all the cash. I ran to the front door and locked it. I grabbed the gun and helped Kelly up. I told him he had to get out of there, and I'd help him. He started to protest, said he wouldn't go. I got so mad I pushed over the huge change jug. All the coins went clattering out." He glanced at Ari. "Like rain. That got him moving. We ran out the back and I flipped off the lights. If anyone came by, they'd think the place was closed. I guess that's when your witness came by.

"Kelly got in my car and we headed north on Grand. He was freaked out, screaming, crying, all at the same time. He didn't ask me where we were going, and at first I didn't know. But I kept seeing Iso's face, and then I decided. I turned north and then west. We only drove about ten minutes. Nothing was developed out there. That was still a few years away. We went off the road into the desert. By then he knew something was up. We stopped and I pointed the gun and told him to get out. He was crying by then, begging me not to shoot him. I screamed something about both of our lives being ruined and shot him. It was very fast. I'd wrapped my hand in a rag to prevent gun residue, and I threw the gun, the money and the rag nearby and went back to the store as fast as I could. I must've tripped while I was out there and got mud on my shirt. There was always pockets of water from the monsoons. I was probably gone thirty minutes at the most. Then I called the cops. I never told a soul."

"Not even Isolde?" Ari whispered.

"No," Elijah said emphatically, but Ari knew he was lying.

He started to sob and they waited patiently for the horrible ending. Through the tears he said, "Believe me, when I turned those lights back on and saw your brother lying there, I wished I'd killed myself after I shot Kelly."

"You should have!" Jack screamed, as he lunged for Elijah.

Ari attempted to intercede but Jack got in three good punches before Elijah's cries were answered by two men who emerged from the house with Isolde. They pulled them apart and were about to mete out their own justice, when Elijah yelled, "No! Don't hurt him! I deserve it!"

The two men, who Ari guessed were Elijah's sons, let go of Jack and looked at their father with puzzled expressions. Isolde ran to Elijah and cradled him in her arms. They sobbed together, and in that moment Ari was certain Isolde had been his confidant and his co-conspirator, but she knew Elijah would never allow her to shoulder any of the blame. Just as she would never admit to breaking into Ari's house to save her husband, she would never admit to knowing he murdered Kelly Owens. Ari imagined Elijah and Isolde had practiced the "what if" conversation dozens of times over the last twenty-five years.

While the Cruz family huddled together on the lawn, Ari turned to Jack. He was bent over the canoe, but he'd stopped crying. Unlike the Cruzes, who were experiencing that first gut-wrenching horror that would forever change the rest of their lives, the Adams family had already been there. *And back.* She put a hand on her father's shoulder, and he pulled her into a hug.

"At least now we know," he whispered. "He died trying to do the right thing. Like always."

CHAPTER TWENTY-SEVEN

While Ari had visualized solving Richie's murder numerous times, she'd never created a narrative for the fallout that would inevitably occur afterward. Her life—and her father's—had turned into a media circus with the arrest of Elijah Cruz. Richie became famous again, the same cute picture of him splashed over the various front pages of several valley newspapers. It was always big news when a child's murder was solved. As part of a plea for leniency, Elijah had led officers to Kelly Owens's grave, now a field just past an abandoned warehouse. The day after he killed Kelly, Elijah had returned to bury him, along with the gun. He'd also thrown the wad of cash from the register on top of the body.

Amid the brouhaha about Richie, Wolf Martinez disappeared. Federal authorities had plucked him out of jail. No doubt they had much to discuss with him. Ari hoped they had the goods on him and that he paid dearly for all of his crimes, especially the alleged imprisonment and death of so many women.

One bright light was the renewed friendship of Molly and Andre. They'd already met for a long lunch, and Andre had agreed to come to dinner next week.

Learning the facts surrounding Richie's death overwhelmed Jack. While there was closure, there was also the knowledge that Elijah Cruz had lied to his face for the past quarter of a century. Jack couldn't forgive himself for missing any tell-tale body language or verbal slip-ups he was certain had occurred and should have signaled to him that the conscience-stricken Elijah was a guilty party in Richie's death.

Ari reminded him that George and Damian lived by a code of honor, and as much as they wanted to bring Richie's killer to justice, they never would've allowed their gang or their families to suffer. And that meant no one would talk to Jack.

"He needs time," Molly said to her a week later at breakfast. They were sitting on the patio, enjoying the hour before the sun blistered everything in its path. "You need to leave him alone for now," she continued. "He carried the weight of Richie's death, but also he carried your grief and your mother's grief as well."

"I never asked him to do that," Ari said quickly.

"No, I know you didn't, but as the parent, as the husband, *and* as a police detective, he felt he had to." She got up, kissed Ari goodbye and headed to work. Ari felt no need to jump into the Monday grind. Lorraine had forbidden her from entering the office for at least two weeks, and she'd complied. There was no way she could face the Carpenters and handle their petty issues without exploding.

She knew Molly was right about giving her father space, and Dr. Yee had said the same thing. Dr. Yee had also encouraged her to attend Kelly Owens's memorial service. At the suggestion, Ari had stormed out of her office—a first. Ten minutes later, she'd called her from the parking lot. "Attending the service would mean I forgive him! I don't. Not at all."

At first she thought Dr. Yee had hung up on her, but after a long pause Dr. Yee said, "I will acknowledge that this is by far one of the most difficult situations I've ever encountered with a client, but do you remember what you told me your mother had instructed you to do with Richie when he got on his self-righteous high horse?"

She thought of the day on the street with the police officer. "She said it was my responsibility to teach him to use compassion. It was his weak point. She couldn't always be there when he'd need reminding, and I needed to do it for her."

"If your mother were alive, what would she do?"

And so Ari had gone to the service, Molly at her side. They had come upon Mrs. Fairchild, the caring librarian, who seemed nearly unable to walk, and Molly offered her other arm. When Kacy Owens had seen Ari, she'd rushed to her and thrown her arms around her—another photo op for the papers. Kacy had apologized profusely and cried. Using her finely tuned compassion, Ari thought about how it would have felt to believe your brother had abandoned you, only to find out he was dead and a murderer. Elijah had admitted he found the letter in Kelly's pocket before he buried him. He couldn't explain why he'd mailed it to Kacy years later, and Ari suspected Isolde had done so, most likely to prevent Kacy from urging the police to take another look at her brother's disappearance when the ten-year anniversary loomed.

While Isolde stayed away from Kelly's memorial service, Elijah's sons, the ones who had pulled Jack off their father, attended and offered their condolences. The minister, a woman Kacy's family had known since childhood, spoke of redemption, choices and compassion. Ari knew her mother would have been nodding in agreement.

Ari's backyard gate squeaked, jolting her to the present. "I have a surprise!" Jane called.

Ari laughed. Thoughts of Richie, her mother, death, the past, loss, and compassion slipped from her mind. She yearned for whatever her best friend wanted her to see. She didn't know anyone with as much zeal for living as Jane.

Yet the first person who strolled through the back gate wasn't Jane, but her lover, Rory. Her graying hair was longer, but she still looked buff in walking shorts and a tank top.

"Hiya, sugar!" Rory cried, swooping Ari into a hug.

"You're a terrific surprise," Ari said.

Rory gazed into her eyes. "I've been thinking of you."

"Thanks."

"Ahem," Jane interrupted, waving her manicured hand in front of Ari's face. While Rory was dressed for a picnic, Jane wore linen pants and a silk blouse. She'd pulled her blond locks away from her face with a barrette, displaying a hickey on her neck.

Ari grabbed her fingers and gasped at the diamond ring. "What?"

"We're engaged!"

Ari pulled her and Rory into a group hug. "I want to hear all the details. Did this happen on the cruise ship?"

"It did," Rory replied. "I'm not sure you could picture Jane speechless, but she was."

"I'm so happy for you both," she said. She squeezed Rory's arm. "What brings you to Phoenix?"

"Telling you, of course!" Rory replied. "I wasn't about to let Jane spill the big news all by herself, not to the woman I consider responsible for our union. Oh, no. I wanted to be here."

Ari shook her head. "I have no responsibility."

"Wrong," Jane said. "You told me Rory was the one. The fact that I disagreed with you for so long was my own shortsightedness." Her joyous face morphed to a sad smile. "Besides, I thought you could use some good news. While I know it's a relief to finally know the truth…" She didn't finish the sentence, but instead started a new one. "I've never been to Richie's grave. Could we go there today so I can pay my respects?"

Despite her infrequent visits to Greenlawn Cemetery, Ari knew the marker location by heart. She knew where to stop her SUV and how far up the hill to walk. She'd invited her father to join them, but he'd not returned her call—until they started the ascent. Seeing his name appear, she gave quick directions and encouraged Jane and Rory to proceed without her.

"Hi. We're at the cemetery. I invited you—"

"I know," he interrupted. "I'm downtown. There's been a development in the case."

"Your homeless killer case?"

"No, the Kelly Owens murder case." He took a deep breath. "Elijah Cruz is dead."

"What? How?" She knew Elijah was out on bail because after twenty-five years, the prosecutor couldn't argue he was a flight risk.

"We're still trying to sort that out. It was a drive-by. He was sitting in his dining room reading the paper. A bullet came through the front window. Right into his skull. He was dead before he hit the table."

"Professional hit?"

"Yes, it seems that way."

She flipped through the cast of characters and could only think of one person who might harbor a grudge against Elijah and who had the resources to hire someone. "Manny Cortez."

"Yes, we think so, but we couldn't find anything to link him to it. We questioned and released him an hour ago."

"I can't say I'm unhappy."

"Me neither, but I wanted you to know in case reporters start calling you for a comment. They've gotten wind that Richie and Manny were friends."

"Thanks."

They said their goodbyes and Ari gazed up the hill at Jane and Rory, who were bending over Richie's marker. They were pointing at something. Ari groaned. Most likely the crazies were out. All the media hoopla and the retelling of Richie's story—how he was going to the store for a baseball card—surfaced the vultures who reveled and sought profit from someone else's pain.

She walked faster and soon saw dozens of flowers, so many that they stretched past Richie and Lucia's graves to the neighboring plots surrounding her mother and brother. Jane took her arm and said, "Can you believe this?"

Ari plucked a card protruding from three dozen white and red roses arranged to look like a baseball. The card said in Spanish, *Eres la luz del mundo.* Her Spanish was rusty but she thought it meant, "You are the light of the world." The card was signed, "Your friend, Manny."

There were many other notes, candles, and Dodger memorabilia. And baseball cards. Richie's marker was framed by baseball cards, all of the same player, Eric Karros, the card he'd longed to have. She succumbed—again—to the tears that lately seemed to live just behind her eyes, waiting to burst forth. Jane and Rory wrapped their arms around her, their strength and joyous news a shield against the pain. Her gaze wandered through the tributes laid on the grass, and she was touched to think so many would care about her brother, a stranger.

But then she realized he really wasn't a stranger. Richie didn't believe in strangers, just potential friends. She stepped back and took out her phone, opening the camera feature. Her father and Molly would want to see this.

"We're going to give you a few minutes," Jane whispered before she and Rory started back down the hill.

Her phone rang. An unknown caller. "Hello?"

"Ari, it's Manny Cortez."

She went suddenly still. She hoped he didn't confess to killing Elijah Cruz. "Hello, Manny. I'm at the cemetery. The flowers you sent are beautiful."

"I'm glad you think so. Richie was a beautiful person."

"I agree."

"You probably don't know this, but my family has sent Richie flowers every year on the day of his death."

She blinked, remembering that each year she'd found white roses on his grave. "I always wondered."

"Ever since we met again, I've been thinking a lot about Richie. I've also been following your progress, and I'm glad you exposed his killer. I only wish Elijah Cruz had allowed Kelly Owens to be brought to justice, but justice…it finds a way."

Before he could say anything else, Ari said, "I understand how you feel."

"Thank you. I called because I wanted your opinion about something."

"Oh?"

"As I said, I've been thinking a lot about Richie, and I want to honor his memory. When we met and talked about the old 7-Eleven, I realized something else needs to go there. I've talked to the family who own the land, the Krists. They agreed with me and are allowing me to demolish the structure and build a community garden, The Richard Adams Community Garden. I called the president of the historic society who was absolutely thrilled. I hope you will be too."

As quickly as she wiped the tears away, more came. She couldn't speak.

"Ari, are you there?"

"I... I'm... I think it's a wonderful idea," she managed to whisper.

"Good. It will help the community and maybe it will give some of those Homeboys something else to do." He laughed and added, "Once I find an architect, I'll call you. I want your ideas included."

"Yes, please," she whispered.

"Take care, Ari."

He was gone before she could say goodbye or thank you. She stood there, stunned. And then she remembered she had something to leave on Richie's grave.

She found Glenn's Eric Karros card. She set it in the center of the headstone and took a photo for Glenn. She walked back down the hill, and just as it plateaued, the sun broke free of the tree line and shone squarely on her face. It was blinding and rejuvenating. And it triggered one of her favorite memories...

She and Richie were riding bikes around noontime, the sun beating on the tops of their heads. She complained about being hot and glanced over at her brother, whose face was turned upward, his eyes closed, a smile on his face.

"Open your eyes, ding dong!" she yelled as they approached a four-way stop.

When he didn't comply, she yelled again. Fortunately, there were no cars around, so she didn't feel compelled to reach for his handlebars. She watched as he glided to a stop—right next to the sign.

"How did you do that?"

"I counted the wheel revolutions between the last couple of stop signs."

She looked at him, dumbfounded. "Why?"

"There's a blind kid at school who said he wants to learn to ride a bike. His parents think it's impossible, so I said I'd help him figure out a way. I'm practicing being a blind bicycle rider." He grinned. "Did I scare ya?"

She'd rolled her eyes. Only Richie.

Yes. Only Richie.

Bella Books, Inc.

Women. Books. Even Better Together.

P.O. Box 10543
Tallahassee, FL 32302

Phone: 800-729-4992
www.bellabooks.com